Praise for the novels of

carly phillips

"Fast-paced and fabulously fun, Carly Phillips entertains
with witty dialogue and delightful characters."
—Bestselling author Rachel Gibson

"Popular Phillips' first attempt at romantic suspense should
be eagerly received by her loyal readership, and the
denouement hints at a future romance for Hunter as well."
—*Booklist* on *Cross My Heart*

"Who doesn't love a reunion of long-lost loves?
Add a diabolical villain as Carly Phillips does and
you have everything you need for a beach read."
—*Columbus Dispatch* on *Cross My Heart*

"Contemporary pizzazz with a good
old-fashioned happily ever after."
—Michelle Buonfiglio,
Romance: B(u)y the Book, WNBC.com/romance

"*Cross My Heart* engages readers with a light and perky story
that will absorb you from start to finish.... You'll be smiling
while you read the book, and grinning when you finish."
—Lezlie Patterson, MCT News Service

"Phillips has penned a charming,
fast-paced contemporary romp."
—*Booklist* on *Hot Item*

"A great summer read that should not be missed."
—*BookReporter.com* on *Hot Item*

"A sassy treat full of titillating twists
sure to ring your (wedding) bell."
—*Playgirl* on *The Bachelor*

"A titillating read...on a scale of one to five:
a high five for fun, ease of reading and sex—actually
I would've given it a six for sex if I could have."
—Kelly Ripa on *The Bachelor*

carly phillips

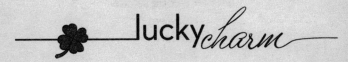

lucky *charm*

HQN™

ISBN-13: 978-0-373-77331-2
ISBN-10:   0-373-77331-5

LUCKY CHARM

This edition published by arrangement with Harlequin Books S.A.

® and TM are trademarks of the publisher. Trademarks indicated with ® are registered in the United States Patent and Trademark Office, the Canadian Trade Marks Office and in other countries.

www.HQNBooks.com

Printed in U.S.A.

Dear Reader,

I am so excited to bring you a brand-new series starring three sexy men dogged by a centuries-old family curse. It's common knowledge in the small town of Stewart, Massachusetts, that any Corwin man who falls in love is destined to lose his love and his fortune. After all, every male in the family line has fallen victim.

Lucky Charm introduces Derek Corwin, the first of three cousins to tackle his unwanted birthright.

Derek has never gotten over his first love, Gabrielle Donovan. When they were young, he'd broken up with her rather than lose her to the curse. But a decade later—with a failed marriage to a woman he didn't love and a child he adores behind him—she still haunts his dreams.

Now Gabrielle is back in town. She's become a successful author who, not so coincidentally, debunks myths and curses for a living. And she's determined to put the Corwin curse to rest once and for all and reclaim her man. Only, it's soon clear someone doesn't want her disturbing old ghosts....

Don't miss the next two books in the series, *Lucky Streak* (6/09) and *Lucky Break* (10/09). And in between, enjoy a reissue of *Secret Fantasy* in January 2009.

Visit www.carlyphillips.com for release dates and more. You can write to me at P.O. Box 483, Purchase, NY 10577 or e-mail me at carly@carlyphillips.com.

As always, thank you for buying my books, and happy reading!

Best wishes,

Carly Phillips

12/08

To the professionals in my life who make all things possible:

To Dianne Moggy, Tracy Farrell, Brenda Chin and everyone at HQN Books—thank you for believing in me and allowing me to bring my characters to life.

To Robert Gottlieb, Kim Whalen and Jenny Bent for your guidance and support—you're all the best.

And to the people who make my everyday life special:

To Phil, Jackie and Jen—I love you always!

To Mom and Dad—thanks for setting the best example in life and in romance. I love you, too!

And last but not least, to the Plotmonkeys—Janelle Denison, Julie Leto and Leslie Kelly. As usual, I couldn't do it without you and I wouldn't want to try.
XXX OOO

lucky charm

INTRODUCTION

IN THE LATE NINETEENTH century, the small village of Stewart, Massachusetts, 1.5 miles west of Salem, site of the now-infamous witch trials, fear of curses and witchcraft ran rampant. During this time, William Corwin fell in love and eloped with a woman who was already betrothed to another. The man William wronged, Martin Perkins, was the oldest son of the wealthy Perkins family, from the neighboring village of the same name. To William Corwin's misfortune, Martin's mother, Mary Perkins, was a witch.

And she immediately sought revenge on her son's behalf with this curse: Any Corwin male who falls in love will be destined to lose his love and his fortune.

No male Corwin since has walked away unscathed....

CHAPTER ONE

THE SMALL TOWN OF STEWART, Massachusetts not so proudly boasted two claims to fame. Its proximity to Salem and the Corwin Curse.

Derek Corwin was well acquainted with *that damned curse,* as his family had come to refer to the albatross one of their ancestors had saddled them with. All because William Corwin couldn't keep *it* in his pants, what should have just been a scandal had turned into a centuries-long damnation.

So said town lore. So said history.

Every male Corwin since had suffered its wrath. Derek included.

A man with half a brain wouldn't return to the scene of the curse, but Derek had figured when the chips were down—or in his case, the Dow Jones—he might as well head home. That had been six months ago.

"Dad!" His eleven-year-old daughter's yell reminded him of why it was a good thing he'd come back.

After two long years of keeping his child from him, Derek's ex-wife had just remarried and decided she wanted a summer alone in Paris with her new husband. She'd sent his daughter, Holly, to live with him here in Stewart, in the renovated barn directly behind the house that had been in Derek's family for generations. All the girl had were males to guide her through this long, hot summer. Poor kid.

But Derek was happy to have her back, to get a second chance at being a father who was *there* instead of one focused on his career. He wanted to get to know his daughter. Unfortunately he didn't have a clue how to deal with her moods or her girlish tastes.

"What's wrong?" he asked, pausing at the landing of the stairs that led to the loft, which held two small bedrooms, his and hers.

After two years of living alone in an apartment that was huge by New York City standards, Derek actually enjoyed being among family in the small barn he was slowly but surely making his own.

"The dog chewed up my Abercrombie flip-flops!" Holly yelled downstairs.

He closed his eyes and groaned. The damn dog. "He chewed what?"

She came into view at the top of the loft and rested her elbows on the ledge. "My flip-flops. You know, sandals? Thongs? *Flip-flops?*" she asked, exasperated.

He nodded, finally understanding the problem. "Sorry. We'll pick up a new pair at Target."

"Target? But, Dad, then they won't have the moose on them," she said in a pleading yet sweet voice.

"In other words, you want to go to the mall near Salem?" he guessed.

"Yes!" She pumped her fist in the air and whirled away, disappearing from view.

He laughed, pleased he'd made her happy. Even if *happy* translated into him spending more money. He should be used to it.

His ex-wife didn't shop down, as she'd reminded him over the years. The harder and the more hours he'd worked, the more money his ex had spent to compensate for his absence.

Although they'd been divorced for more than two years, he didn't think she'd changed her habits. Certainly his monthly child support and alimony had guaranteed her the lifestyle she'd come to expect. At least it had, until he'd lost the bulk of his wealth in a huge investment gone bad and moved back home. He'd been about to petition the court to change the payments, since he now earned much less than he had in the past, when his ex let him know she was remarrying. That ended Derek's obligation to pay alimony, leaving him with child support only. That he could definitely afford without issue.

He glanced upstairs. "How about we get ice cream while we're at the mall?" he asked.

"I'm lactose intolerant!" came the reply.

He winced. Shouldn't he remember that? He consoled himself with the fact that by the time the summer ended, he'd know everything there was to know about his daughter.

"We'll get lunch instead!" he said.

"Okay! I'll be down in a sec. I have to change."

Another thing she'd learned from her mother… She was obsessed with fashion, even at her young age. He figured she'd be at least twenty minutes.

"I'm going to return Fred to your grand-father's." He patted his leg and whistled.

The basset hound came down the stairs slowly, sauntering toward him. Fred didn't look any more guilty for chewing Holly's sandals than he had after he'd peed in the shoes Derek had left at the foot of his bed this morning. Why should he? Fred pretty much did as he pleased, and nobody had said anything for the past ten years. If Holly didn't love the dog so much, Derek would move Fred to his father's place for good.

Derek snapped a leash onto Fred's collar, neither of which the dog had owned before Derek had come back home. Holly joined him just as he walked out the front door.

"I told you I'd be down in a sec!"

"I thought you'd take longer. Sorry."

"That's okay." They made their way over the grass that divided the yard. The barn was on the back acreage, the main house on the front. Suddenly, she said, "I'll meet you at Grandpa's!" She took off across the yard at a run.

He debated jogging over, too, but one look at Fred's sad face and he changed his mind. "You're going to make me fat, old man," Derek said to the dog, slowing his pace a little more.

"Dad!" Holly shrieked, shattering the silence of the quiet morning. "Grandpa has a gun!"

"Good Lord," Derek muttered, pulling Fred into a jog, whether he liked it or not. What was his ornery father up to now?

Holly ran back to him and he handed her the leash. "Stay here," he instructed his daughter. Then he headed over to where his father stood fooling with the old, pump-action shotgun that had been in his family for generations.

"Put that away before you shoot yourself!"

Hank Corwin lowered the gun to his side, glanced at Derek and frowned. "It's not loaded."

Derek breathed a sigh of relief. At least his father wouldn't blow a hole in his addled brain.

"Not yet, anyway." Hank chuckled.

Derek scowled at the older man. "What are you doing with that thing?" As far as Derek knew, the twelve gauge had never been removed from the cabinet where it was displayed.

"I'm polishing the hardware so I can make a point down at the library tonight." Hank ran a hand over the gleaming weapon, the pride in his movement unmistakable.

Derek glanced at his father. At fifty-seven years old, Hank was a handsome man, not that you'd know it by the company he kept—his brother and his long-eared dog, Fred. Appearance wasn't important to him. He rarely cut or styled his dark hair and never worried about what he wore. Why should he, considering the ladies in town were all well versed on the curse and stayed clear of all the living, breathing Corwin men? Hank's summer attire consisted of worn khakis, which he paired with a white T-shirt—for his job as an electrician and on days off.

His father's generation of Corwin men had all discounted the curse and lived to regret it. Hank and his brother Thomas now lived together in the main house. Their third brother, Edward, was a loner, a recluse of sorts, mainly because Thomas had married the woman Edward loved. Derek had two male cousins with whom he was close, one per uncle, and Thomas also had two daughters, both happily married. The Corwin women had prospered. The men had floundered.

Growing up, Derek wasn't sure he believed in curses, but after seeing his father's and uncles' lives shattered, Derek had lived his life very carefully. Not that it had helped him. Derek had even given up the woman he loved to protect them both from the curse. His life—and finances—had gone down the tube, anyway. He was finished taking chances.

"What's happening at the library that's got you packing heat?" Whatever it was, it couldn't be good, Derek thought, eyeing the weapon.

"This." Hank stalked over to the old wooden picnic table and picked up a flier. "Read it and weep. And not just because your high-school sweetheart's returning."

"Gabrielle's back?" Derek asked, certain he'd misunderstood.

Hank inclined his head. "Yep. And I'm not going to let that girl stir up trouble by getting people talking about that damn curse again."

That girl. Derek's high-school love and the woman he'd pushed away rather than subject to the despair that inevitably followed any woman who allowed herself to love a Corwin man.

His father had liked Gabrielle. She'd come to dinners at their house and he'd had many meals at hers. Her parents had treated him like a member of the family while Hank had welcomed her into theirs. For a gruff coot even back then, Hank had been fond of Gabrielle.

Derek sighed. "You aren't going to shoot Gabrielle just because you don't like her choice in subject matter."

Hank glanced at him, defiance in his stare. "I

don't like being talked about. It's been quiet around town for a long while. I'd like to keep it that way."

"Just because you don't hear people talking about the curse doesn't mean they aren't still whispering behind our backs. It's a fact of life." Derek grabbed the flier and scanned the page.

Apparently the Perkins-Stewart Public Library was hosting a lecture titled Curses: Irrational Psychological Suggestion, by onetime resident and bestselling author, Gabrielle Donovan.

Derek knew Gabrielle had written a number of books, debunking popular myths in print and then discussing those books on big-time talk shows. It was no coincidence that she'd chosen to study the occult and New Age, Derek thought. His past had defined both of their lives.

Although she hadn't been back to visit, the town claimed her as their own local celebrity. The diner on Main Street had a signed photograph on the wall, although Derek had seen the signature and doubted its validity. He wouldn't put it past Henry, the owner, to forge it instead of contacting Gabrielle and asking for one.

Even Derek's father was one of her fans— Derek had seen her books on Hank's shelves. In reality, Derek wasn't worried that his father would shoot her. But that didn't mean he couldn't cause trouble in other ways....

Derek placed the flier down on the picnic table

and looked Hank in the eye. "You aren't going anywhere near the library, Pop."

"Want to bet?" Hank asked.

"Well, you sure as hell aren't taking a shotgun." Though Derek spoke to his father, his thoughts were far away, already in turmoil over the chance of seeing Gabrielle again. He'd spent enough time avoiding watching her on TV. Seeing her in real life would be far more painful. He didn't need to worry about their reunion occurring over the barrel of his father's shotgun.

Derek grabbed the rifle, intending to lock it up tight at his place or in the trunk of his SUV. There was no telling how easily an old rifle like this one could go off if Hank started waving it around to make his point.

Hank stamped his foot and shook his finger in Derek's face. "You don't play fair."

"And you don't play rational. Want to go to the mall with me and Holly?" Derek waved his daughter over.

"No. I have to pick up some things in town. Then I'm going to prepare a rebuttal to that girl's speech tonight. No curse, my hiney," Hank said, stomping toward his house.

Derek laughed and let him go. Hank was all bluster. Derek couldn't imagine Hank showing up any place where the Corwin Curse was the subject of public discussion.

A discussion started by Gabrielle Donovan.

Damn. He couldn't believe she'd returned after all these years.

He'd broken up with her after the prom. Post graduation, her parents had moved away, and she'd gone with them. At least he hadn't had that summer to watch her, longing for something he could no longer have. But while they'd been together, his life had been spectacular. At eighteen she'd been the most beautiful, sensual woman on the planet. He could only imagine what the intervening years had done to her already lush body and china-doll-like face. With her mother's French genes, she hadn't been afraid of passion or sex, and they'd indulged in both often, until Derek realized it was no longer just physical attraction that kept him coming back for more.

She'd been smart, too, the only daughter of parents who were both professors. She had a sharp wit and had been insightful, understanding Derek's love of high-stakes finances even before he had the money to indulge his passion. She probably wouldn't be surprised to learn he'd gone to Columbia undergrad and directly on to Wall Street as a trader until he was hired by an investment-banking company and made himself rich from lucky, huge deals.

He'd made himself poor the same way, investing

too much in a company that went south instead of north. These days Derek was a financial planner, getting his thrills by building other people's incomes more slowly and sensibly, not toying with his own.

He shook off the memories and headed to where his daughter was trying to play fetch with Fred. The dog was lying on his fat stomach without moving, staring at the stick she'd tossed.

"Ready?" Derek asked her.

Holly wiped her dusty hands on her jeans shorts. "I'm ready."

"Good." He ruffled her long hair. "Let's drop Fred off at the house before we go."

Holly nodded and pulled the reluctant dog's leash. Fred trotted along at her side.

"Daddy? What's wrong?"

"Why would you think anything's wrong?" Derek asked.

His daughter met his gaze, squinting as the glare of the sun hit her eyes. "Because you look sad."

"Hey, how could I be sad when I'm spending time with my favorite girl?" he asked, determined not to let anything dampen the time he had with his daughter.

She giggled. "I'll go give Fred to Grandpa." She walked to the house, leaving Derek alone with his thoughts. The most tempting woman in his past had shown up to wreak havoc with his future.

Maybe she wasn't here to stay.

Yeah, right. And maybe the Corwin Curse wasn't responsible for the breakup of every male's marriage down the family line.

GABRIELLE DONOVAN DROVE her black Lexus convertible down Main Street. She took in the stores and the colorful awnings and decided other than a few newer, more modern shops, nothing major had changed. She wondered if Derek Corwin had.

From her long-time friend, Sharon Merchant, Gabrielle knew that Derek had returned to their old hometown about six months ago. Gabrielle, herself, had moved from Florida to Boston about one month earlier, following her parents, who'd relocated from Florida six months before. She was used to being near her close-knit family. And as a writer, Gabrielle could work anywhere, so relocating wasn't a hardship.

Was it a coincidence that Derek had returned around the same time?

Gabrielle shook her head. There were no coincidences. She might not believe in curses, but she definitely believed in Fate and true love. Derek Corwin had been hers.

From the day they'd met in the cafeteria in sixth grade, there had been *something* between them. Over the years, a solid friendship had turned into a crush. A middle-school dance had led to a kiss and suddenly they were inseparable, hanging out after school, doing homework together and sharing secrets.

Derek and Gabby, Gabby and Derek. He'd been her other half from eighth grade through senior year. She knew about the curse. Everyone in town knew.

Derek feared the power of the curse, and though Gabrielle had never believed in such things, given his family history, she'd respected the threat it held over the Corwin men. Derek had never used the "*L*" word, not even the day after the prom when he'd ended things and broken her heart. She knew he'd loved her too much to take their relationship further, thereby setting the curse in motion, so he'd said goodbye. He hadn't even given her a choice in the matter.

But she had a choice now. And she chose to believe that she and Derek were in such close proximity after all this time for a reason. For Gabrielle, the reason came down to second chances. She needed to know if the flame between them still burned.

The memories she had of him were strong. She'd idealized him and their relationship to the point where no other man could live up to the standard he'd set. No man since had understood her or given enough of himself. No man had been Derek.

So after years of moving from relationship to relationship, always being the one to break up, always looking for more than whatever the man of the moment had to offer, Gabrielle saw this as her chance to revisit the past—and find out, once and for all, whether her future could include Derek. If it didn't, at least she'd *know*. Then she could move on.

It helped that her best friend was also the librarian of the Perkins-Stewart Public Library. By asking Gabrielle to speak, Sharon had given her a reason to come to town. Gabrielle was ready for her talk at the library, but she didn't expect to see Derek there tonight. She considered herself a pretty good judge of character, and given what she knew of Derek, he'd avoid her lecture on curses at all costs.

That was fine with her. Gabrielle preferred to set her own agenda where Derek was concerned.

Her first stop this morning was the Rhodes Inn, which consisted of a trio of rooms in an old boarding house. Though Boston was only an hour away, Gabrielle wanted to visit for a few days so she'd taken a room at the inn run by Adele Rhodes, Gabrielle's fifth-grade teacher, a nice woman who'd indulged Gabrielle's love of school and writing. When Gabrielle had called to rent a room, Mrs. Rhodes had been thrilled to hear from her now-famous student.

Gabrielle checked in and shared a warm reunion with her former teacher. She unpacked her suitcase and personal items, climbed back into her convertible and drove to Sharon's house on the outskirts of town.

Sharon and her fiancé, Richard Stern, had bought their own home in Perkins. But until they married after the election in the fall, Sharon still lived with her parents. Richard was running for mayor of Perkins against the previously uncontested Mary Perkins. He couldn't afford the scandal living in sin would cause. Once upon a time, Sharon would have had no problem flouting convention, but a painful episode in her past had changed that. These days, Sharon was happy but more subdued.

Gabrielle parked out front and rang the doorbell of the old Cape-style home. Sharon opened the door and greeted Gabrielle with a huge hug.

"I'm so glad you're back," Sharon said, releasing her.

Although they'd kept in touch by phone and e-mail and Sharon had visited Gabrielle in Florida, this reunion was different. Gabrielle hadn't been back in town for almost fourteen years. She'd avoided this place—and the memories of Derek—for way too long. But now that she was living within driving distance, she was finished staying away.

Gabrielle smiled. "I'm happy to be back, too. You look great," she said, taking in her friend's long blond hair and flowered sundress.

"Back at you!" Sharon gestured to Gabrielle's hair, cut in the latest style. "I'm dying for a good haircut, but I can't bring myself to trust anyone locally!"

"I found this great stylist in Boston. If you're serious, we can go next week and you can get it done."

Sharon nodded, her eyes filled with excitement. "I would love it. Maybe I'll even cut it above my shoulders, like yours."

"You'd look gorgeous with shorter hair." Their conversation reminded Gabrielle of an adventure they'd shared in high school, when they'd both dyed their hair with hydrogen peroxide, hoping to become shining blondes. Instead, they'd wound up living with green hair until their mothers agreed to pay for a professional fix.

"Let's shop Boylston Street and Copley while we're there," Sharon said, making a disgusted face as she pulled on the fabric of her dress. "I need some new clothes."

Gabrielle laughed. Some things never changed. They both loved shopping. She and Sharon were just like sisters—sisters who never fought and just enjoyed each other's company.

Sharon led her inside and they sat in the living room decorated by photographs of Sharon and her brother and eclectic other odds and ends favored by Sharon's mother.

"I'm so grateful you came to give that lecture for Richard. He's convinced that in order to beat Mary Perkins, he has to get rid of the towns-people's fear." Her friend was a huge supporter of Gabrielle's work and kept the library stocked with her books.

"My pleasure." Gabrielle reached out and squeezed her friend's hand. "I'm so excited to be living close by you again."

Sharon leaned forward. "Same here. But right now, I want to know about your newest project. What do you have planned for your next book?"

Gabrielle drew a deep breath. "I'm going to write about the Corwin Curse." And hopefully dispel it for good.

"Wow."

"Exactly. I'm going to do some research, as well as interview the Corwins and the Perkins. I'm determined to shed some light on this thing, once and for all," Gabrielle said, definitively.

For years, she had dispelled other paranormal rumors like ghost sightings or UFO reports, writing about everything but curses to try to heal her pain over losing Derek. But avoidance hadn't helped. The Corwin Curse had taken the man she loved away from her because Derek was a believer. If not for that curse, Gabrielle would probably have married Derek and been the mother of his children. She'd still be a writer because it was in her blood, but her personal life would have played out so differently. It was time for her to deal with that, Gabrielle thought. She planned to face her past, define her future and confront old ghosts.

"How do you think they'll react?" Sharon asked.

Gabrielle shrugged. "I can't worry about it. I need to do this for myself." From the day Derek had broken up with her, her life had been defined by that curse.

After moving to Florida after graduation, she'd gone to college there. She'd majored in psychology and minored in human behavioral science. Over time, she'd let her writing become a means of working out her feelings. She hadn't been able to fight Derek's beliefs when he'd broken up with her, nor had she understood how he could allow an old curse to destroy the future they could have shared.

Gabrielle needed to understand how human beings with free will could have their behavior swayed by things that didn't exist. She had to somehow comprehend how the man she loved and who she thought had loved her had dumped her because he believed he was cursed.

"I just can't get over the fact that Richard's future hinges on an old, ridiculous myth," Sharon said.

Gabrielle gave her friend a wry smile. "Why not? Mine did."

Sharon slapped her hand over her mouth, deliberately dramatic. "I'm sorry! What an awful thing for me to bring up. I just wasn't thinking!"

"It's fine. I was kidding. The problem is, when people believe in this kind of stuff, their beliefs are based on things that are just so hard to refute. For one thing, history has repeated itself over and over, making it appear as if the original curse on the Corwins has validity." That was why Gabrielle needed to research it in detail.

Sharon scrunched her nose, her disgust with the subject clear. "You mean, because all the Corwin men have been unlucky in love, people believe that a witch caused it to happen?"

"It's not just that they're unlucky in love. It's also because Mary Perkins's family, who've run the town for years, have used those failures to cement their position. By reminding everyone of the Corwin Curse, the Perkins are able to manipulate those around them, holding on to their power by playing on people's fears."

Sharon nodded. "She's as much as insinuated that, since she's the namesake of the original Mary Perkins, she has the power to brew up another curse. Just when Richard thinks he's making headway in reaching people, she'll bring up the past and remind people of her power."

"In what way?" Gabrielle asked, wondering how one woman could have so much sway.

"Well, a large development group came to town to buy property that they wanted to turn into an ocean-front resort. Mary doesn't want to chance anyone coming in and usurping her position, so she coerced the owners to sell their otherwise profitable land to her at a cheap price rather than to the developers."

Gabrielle rose and smoothed the wrinkles in her linen skirt. "How? And why in the world would anyone take a lesser price?"

Sharon got up, too. "Mary claimed the town owned the land through eminent domain. She threatened to take the individual landowners to court, informing them she'd win and they'd probably get much less than what she was graciously offering now. She also mentioned she was a direct descendant of *the* Mary Perkins, and not so subtly reminded those homeowners that she could bankrupt them with a few choice curse words. Darned if they didn't sell cheap. And of course, after the fact, nobody would admit they'd been threatened, either." Sharon shrugged.

Pausing by the window, Gabrielle glanced out at her convertible parked on the quiet street. "Well, I can see why Richard has his hands full." Gabrielle didn't want to tell her friend that a few lectures might not be enough. Old beliefs were powerful. Too often, not even persuasive reasoning or common sense could overcome them.

"So…we've talked about the curse long enough. When are we going to discuss the five-hundred-pound elephant in the room?" Sharon asked.

Gabrielle raised an eyebrow, pretty sure she knew what her friend was referring to but wanting to hear it before she jumped to the wrong conclusion. "Care to elaborate?"

"The man himself? Derek Corwin? I know that seeing him again won't be easy."

Gabrielle smirked. "Five hundred pounds? Guess I won't have to worry about that old attraction rearing its head again after all."

"Very funny."

"I thought so." She shrugged and remained quiet.

Sharon exhaled loudly, breaking the silence. "Okay fine, I get the message. We won't talk about Derek today. So here's the plan. I need to stop by the library and pick up my cell phone first, since I left it there last night. Afterward, I thought we'd go shopping. There's a new mall you'll love. What do you think?"

Gabrielle nodded. "Sounds good."

Anything that changed the subject, Gabrielle thought.

She'd become an expert at that. Whenever Sharon tried to impart gossip about Derek, Gabrielle deliberately asked about something else. But that hadn't stopped Sharon from letting some pertinent facts slip over the years, from Derek's early marriage to his more recent divorce. Hearing about him only reopened old wounds, but Gabrielle had recently been forced to accept that those wounds had never really healed.

She may have tried to move on with her life, but

even all these years later, she hadn't been successful. It was time she confronted the past. She had no choice. Derek had left her incapable of moving on.

CHAPTER TWO

DEREK AND HOLLY MADE A STOP at the library to return a few books and take out some new ones before hitting the mall. Derek dropped her off at the library while he went to get gas and pick up lightbulbs at the hardware store.

Half an hour later, they were on their way. Holly's mother had called her on her cell phone, and the two spoke for the duration of the ride to the mall. Marlene was loving her trip and had to buy an extra suitcase for all the goodies she'd bought for Holly. After twenty minutes of listening to Holly regale him with stories her mother had told her, getting to the mall almost seemed like a relief.

Which was ironic considering shopping was his least-favorite activity. Normally he preferred to get in and out of stores as quickly as possible. But today, he enjoyed his time with his daughter, hitting shops he'd never been in before, from Limited Too to Abercrombie, and now Bloomingdale's.

His daughter, he realized, had her mother's genes. She gravitated from store to store, "oohing" and "aahing" over each item, but unlike her mother, she didn't ask for everything she saw. Although she let him replace the Abercrombie flip-flops Fred had chewed up, she didn't request anything else.

That puzzled him.

They ended up in Bloomingdale's. The escalator down to the girls' department let them off in bedding, where a huge sign proclaimed Summer White Sale. He suddenly remembered what he was missing at home. "I need some new towels. Mind if we take a detour?"

She shook her head. "Nope."

They weaved through the displays of sheets and duvets toward the towels, when he realized Holly had stopped in front of a bed made up with a bold pink-purple-and-white pattern.

"What did you find?" he asked.

"Check these out!" Her blue eyes lit up as she pointed to the bed display and matching throw pillows. "My best friend, Robin, has something like this at home. It's so cool, don't you think?"

"I sure do. For a girl." He ruffled the top of her head.

As he spoke, Derek realized that from the day Holly had come to stay with him, she'd used old linen from his father's house without complaint. It had never dawned on Derek that she might like something new, or to make the room she was living in her own.

"Would you like these for your room here?" he asked.

She turned toward him, her eyes huge. "Really? I can have them?"

He nodded, wanting her to be happy. This bedding seemed to do the trick.

"You're sure? I mean, we don't know how long I'm going to be here. And Mom will never let me use them at home since they don't match my room." She wrinkled her nose. "It's probably a lot of money." She trailed off, obviously disappointed in the conclusion she'd reached.

She was probably right. He hadn't looked at the price, but whatever the cost, for Holly he'd suck it up. "What's that sign say?" He pointed to the billboard in the center of the department.

She tucked her long blond hair behind her ear, squinted and read the words. "Sale. But…"

"But nothing. If you're worried about me spending money, I can afford these. I promise." Derek wasn't broke.

He'd just lost a lot in the stock market and had given up most of his assets in the divorce, wanting to spare his daughter the pain of more fighting.

If he'd split his money with his ex, he might never have given the curse a second thought. But he'd willingly given her more than she deserved because he felt responsible for things not working out. Then he'd invested a chunk of his money in a company that was supposed to be a sure thing. Instead, he'd lost nearly everything, depleted the bulk of his assets and decided then and there that the curse was in full force. Even if he hadn't married Holly's mother for love.

He'd married Marlene for the little blond reason standing in front of him now. He'd gotten his ex-wife pregnant their second year in college. Like father, like son, Hank had told him, lecturing him over not learning from the past. His father had a point. He'd been careless. But Derek thought it would go differently. His father had been desperately in love with Derek's mother. Derek didn't feel that way about Marlene.

It hadn't mattered. Marlene didn't believe in abortion, not that he'd have asked it of her. So Derek had stepped up and done the right thing. His father had tried to do the same thing with Vivian, Derek's mother, but her family had intervened. They'd sent her to a home for unwed mothers, intending to make her give the baby up for adoption. Hank and his brothers had confronted them, paid them a hefty amount of money and taken Derek home. Vivian's family moved away and to this day, Derek's mother refused to acknowledge him as her son.

He could never do that to his child. So he'd

married Marlene. It made sense, he'd thought at the time. They had fun together and he cared for her. Once he realized she carried his child, he came to see logic in their union. In Marlene, he saw a way to circumvent the curse. They could share a life, a family and a future without risk, because he wasn't head over heels in love with her.

Their disaster of a marriage and wrenching divorce had proved Derek wrong. It seemed that just being a male Corwin was enough to set the curse in motion.

"Dad?" Holly tugged on his arm.

"Sorry, I was thinking about something." He cleared his throat. "Why don't you go find where they have these set up?"

She nodded and began to dart through the short stations and finally waved to him. "Found them!"

"Coming!" His life was different these days, he mused, watching his daughter practically hop up and down in excitement, waiting for him to join her.

He had less money but more time on his hands, which worked well since Holly would be staying with him for the summer.

He kept enough in savings to feel comfortable, but like the other men in his family, he now stopped short of building up wealth that could easily be lost. Life seemed simpler that way even if he did miss the adrenaline rush of taking risks and watching them pay off.

"Look for a package that says queen size," he told Holly. "And then the pillow cases will probably say king or regular. We want regular."

"I can't believe you're getting me these. I really can't," she said as she knelt down and began sorting through the sealed sheet sets.

A sharp pain sliced through his chest. "Hey, Holly? Why wouldn't I want to buy these for you?"

She glanced up at him. "Promise you won't be mad?"

He nodded. He couldn't remember ever being truly angry at her. Then again, he'd worked so many hours a week, he hadn't been home enough to get mad about anything. And during the past two years, he hadn't had Holly for more than a short weekend or two, if he was lucky. He'd threatened to fight his ex over custody, but she always had a *rational* reason why Holly couldn't come visit. A sleepover at a friend's, a birthday party she couldn't miss. It was as if Marlene was punishing him for not being there for her.

Only recently, after she'd gotten engaged to John Bartman, did she soften toward Derek. She'd fallen in love, and John treated her the way Derek should have. She'd finally declared a truce. That had given Derek more access to his daughter and he was grateful.

He smiled at Holly, who rose to face him.

"I promise I won't get angry."

Holly drew a deep breath. "Mom used to say that you hated giving her child support, that you considered spending your hard-earned money on me a waste." She bit her bottom lip with her teeth and her eyes filled with tears.

The knife in his chest twisted deeper. While he wasn't surprised Marlene had been so bitter, it infuriated him that she'd lie to his daughter about something so serious.

"Did Mom ever not buy you things you wanted or needed?" he asked.

She shook her head. "No! And she hasn't said that in a really long time. But she did once and I couldn't ever forget it." Holly sniffed.

"I don't have any tissues. Want to use this, instead?" Derek grinned and held out his sleeve.

She giggled. "Dad!"

He laughed. "Listen to me." He took her small hand in his, overwhelmed by the connection between them. "I promise you I'm not angry," he told her, squeezing her palm tighter in his. "I made a lot of mistakes with your mom. I'm upset that I made her so unhappy that she felt that way." He struggled for the right words so it didn't seem as if he was bashing her mother.

He and Marlene had come a long way.

"Let me make a few things clear to you right now. Number one, I love you. I didn't walk out on you. Your mother and I agreed that me leaving was for the best. Your mom was angry at me for a lot of grown-up reasons, but that's over now. I'm happy for her and John. Are you?"

Holly nodded. "He's not bad. And Mom seems a lot happier now so that's good."

Derek exhaled, relieved she understood. Divorce wasn't easy on kids. "So how about you and I start over? No assumptions, no misunderstandings. If you want something, ask. I reserve the right to say no if I think it's bad for you, but it'll always be out of love. Okay?"

His little girl, who at eleven looked much older, stood in front of him, merely staring.

"Do you understand what I said?" he asked, wanting to be clear.

She nodded and sniffed. "I think you said you want to buy me those sheets. You just used a long explanation to get there." She shuffled from foot to foot, her excitement tangible. "Can I pick them out now?"

He laughed, and despite knowing better, he pulled her into a hug.

She froze and his heart felt as if it had stopped. It had been too long since they'd been that comfortable around each other and he held his breath, waiting for her reaction. Inch by inch, she wrapped her arms around his waist and hugged him back. His heart began to beat again.

She bent back down and handed him the

items—sheets, pillow cases and, of course, the extra throw pillows and dust ruffle that added to the cost but increased her smile by a yard.

"You need pillows to fit inside the odd shaped shams," he told her. "I saw them over there by the sample bed." His arms were full with her choices.

"I'll get them." She ran back to the display and returned a minute later with three small pillows in her arms.

Once again, she began squirming, obviously excited about something new.

"What's up?" he asked.

"While I was there, I heard two women talking," she whispered. "One was Ms. Merchant, the librarian. The other was a lady I met while checking out my books at the library."

Derek wasn't sure where she was going with this. "Well, this is the only real mall in town. It isn't that odd she'd be here."

Holly nodded. "I know. I was going to tell you about her because she was really cool. I liked her clothes and all."

He grinned, not surprised his daughter had noticed that.

"But then Mom called and I forgot all about it until I saw her again just now. I didn't realize she was Ms. Merchant's friend because they weren't together at the library," Holly continued, rambling at ninety miles an hour. "Anyway, I heard her say your name! So you already know her. She's wearing *Manolos,* like Mom's."

"They aren't Manolos, they're Christian Louboutins," a hauntingly familiar voice said.

Derek drew a deep breath and lifted his gaze, meeting the eyes of the woman he'd reluctantly pushed out of his life years ago. And he'd regretted it ever since.

GABRIELLE AND SHARON HAD been taking the escalator down to cookware to find Sharon a new coffeemaker. They'd been discussing Gabrielle's purchase of chocolate truffle crème body wash, body crème and candle in contrast with Sharon's choice of French vanilla. In Gabrielle's opinion, there was no comparison. Chocolate was the most decadent thing in life next to sex, and she'd said so.

Then she'd caught sight of Derek.

Older and more mature, but no less handsome. His dark brown hair wasn't as long as she remembered, but the tousled locks were vintage Derek. Styled to look as if he had no set style. And those eyes, those deep-set hazel eyes looked at a woman as if she were the only person in the world that mattered. A pair of baggy khaki shorts hung to his knees and a white T-shirt accented his tanned skin. Razor stubble covered his rugged yet defined face.

God, the man was still sexy.

Unaware, Sharon walked beside Gabrielle into

the sheet department without questioning her motives. Gabrielle continued extolling the virtues of chocolate, something she could discuss easily while distracted.

She'd wanted to be in control when she ran into Derek again. She'd even thought about ambushing him, the way she used to after school, pulling him behind a tree for a surprise kiss, and see whether those old sparks still burned.

Then she heard him. And she'd been the one caught by surprise. Her toes curled in her pointy-toed shoes and her stomach did one of those sensual turns only he'd ever caused.

She pulled to a stop and placed her finger over her mouth, silently asking Sharon to keep quiet.

Gabrielle had tiptoed toward him and realized he was talking to the inquisitive young girl she'd met in the library. A child, she realized now that she saw the two side by side, who was clearly his. Her hair and eyes might be a different color, but her mouth, those white teeth and full lips were all her dad's.

Derek's daughter.

Gabrielle's stomach dropped as she faced the little girl who could have been theirs if…

She gave herself a mental shake. There were no ifs. Only the here and now. She had to face the fact that while her life had gone on, so had his. Until now she'd never let herself think about how. True,

Sharon had told her he had a child, but hearing about it and facing it were two different things. She knew now she'd pushed the child out of her mind, unwilling to deal with what the little girl meant— that he had fallen in love with another woman not long after saying goodbye to Gabrielle.

She placed her hand around her stomach. God, it hurt badly. And that's when she knew that the old feelings were still there, as strong as ever.

"Go get your coffee machine," Gabrielle whispered to Sharon.

"But—"

"I'll fill you in later. I don't want any witnesses," she said.

Sharon hesitated, so Gabrielle gave her a gentle shove. "I'll be fine. Go." She waited until her friend was on her way to the kitchen department before she walked over to where the father and daughter stood, in time to hear the preteen extol the virtues of Gabrielle's shoes.

She hadn't even seen the girl checking her out.

"They aren't Manolos, they're Christian Louboutins," Gabrielle heard herself say.

Two sets of eyes glanced up at her. One in awe. The other in recognition.

"Christian Louboutins," the young girl said, shaking her head. "My mom doesn't even own a pair of those."

"I'm sure that will change while she's in Paris

with her new husband," Derek said, his stunned gaze still firmly on Gabrielle's face.

He cleared his throat. "I heard you two met at the library," he said a little awkwardly.

"Not officially. Just long enough for me to tell her we had the same taste in books when I was her age." Gabrielle never tore her gaze from his.

"Hey! Aren't you going to introduce us?" Derek's daughter asked as she dropped her armful of pillows onto the nearest counter and tugged on her father's sleeve.

He unloaded the items in his arms, too. "Holly, this is an old high-school friend of mine, Gabrielle Donovan. Gabrielle, meet my daughter, Holly." He gestured between the two.

"You two knew each other in high school? Wow!"

Derek met Gabrielle's gaze.

And as his daughter spoke, about what Gabrielle couldn't focus on, Gabrielle's shallow breathing eased. The heat simmering between her and Derek did not.

"And you have the coolest clothes on the planet," Holly added.

"Or at least in Stewart." Derek laughed.

Gabrielle remembered that smile too well. She recalled what he could get her to do with that charm of his even better.

"How old did you say you were, Holly?" Gabrielle asked.

"I'm eleven and three-quarters," she said proudly.

"When is your birthday?"

"August 15," she said.

"I think that makes you more than eleven and three-quarters," she said to the bright-eyed girl.

Derek nodded. "Someone has a birthday coming up next month."

Holly grew more animated. "Ooh, I do. I need to think of a gift, don't I?"

He laughed. "Yes, you do."

"Clothes," she said, drawing out the word.

"That means more shopping?" Derek asked, a mock grimace on his face.

Gabrielle met his tortured expression with a grin of her own. "What's your favorite store?" she asked Holly.

"Different places. I got these flip-flops today at Abercrombie." She waved her foot in the air.

"Ever hear of Isaac Mizrahi?" Gabrielle wondered if she sounded as silly as she felt, talking to a child about fashion.

Holly shook her head. "Who is he?"

"He's a designer," Gabrielle said. "If you love these bright-colored things," she said, pointing to her choice in bedding, "I think you'd love the line he does for Target."

"Now I know why the name rings a bell," Derek said. "The guy began designing for Target around 2003. Their stock skyrocketed when he launched

his line of affordable clothes with designer flair."
Derek folded his arms across his chest, looking
like a man pleased to be finally participating in the
conversation.

Holly rolled her eyes. "Dad," she said with a
groan.

Gabrielle chuckled at both father and daughter,
but somehow kept her focus on Holly. "Maybe
your father would let me take you to Target one
afternoon and show you." As soon as she spoke,
Gabrielle couldn't believe the words that had
escaped her mouth.

She and Derek hadn't said more than hello. She
had barely gotten over meeting his daughter, yet
she'd already invited her shopping.

"Oh, wow, Dad. She's amazing!"

"Yes, yes, she is," Derek said, his gaze never
leaving Gabrielle's.

Her body warmed beneath his stare. The sexual
undercurrent between them was as strong as ever,
but thankfully his daughter didn't seem to notice.

"Can I, Dad? Please?" Holly tugged on his
sleeve, bouncing with the enthusiasm of a soon-to-
be teenager.

He smiled at her, the love and indulgence in his
eyes doing crazy things to Gabrielle's heart. He'd
once looked at her with that intensity and devotion.

"We'll see," Derek said, wanting to spare his
daughter any hurt. For all he knew, Gabrielle was

just being nice to Holly for the moment, having been caught off guard by their sudden meeting.

He was still trying to get over the shock. She'd changed. And she hadn't. Her chestnut-colored hair no longer hung long and straight down her back but instead brushed her shoulders in a sexy sweep. Long side-swept bangs dangled enticingly over one eye, and he'd noticed she often tucked her hair behind her ear as she spoke. Though her features were more defined, her makeup more seductive and professional, her beauty was still evident, inside and out.

"When did you get back to town?" Derek asked. He'd seen the flier, but there hadn't been any whispers of her return, at least none that he'd heard.

She inclined her head, and the ends of her hair brushed at her shoulders, reminding him of the times he'd kissed her bare skin. Their encounters had usually been rushed, due to their inexperience and the fear of getting caught. If Derek had his way with her now, two adults with plenty of time on their hands, he'd take things slowly, savoring every sensual touch and taste….

"Derek? Did you hear me?" Gabrielle's voice along with her hand on his shoulder brought him out of his daydream.

He shook his head. "Sorry," he muttered, embarrassed.

"That's okay. As I was saying, I drove in today

to visit with Sharon. I'm giving a lecture at the local library tonight as a favor."

"I heard about your talk."

"Really? People are discussing it?" she asked hopefully.

"You could say that," Derek said.

"My grandpa pulled out his old shotgun!" Holly joined in on the conversation again with exactly the point Derek had been hoping to avoid.

Gabrielle's cheeks flushed red. "He what?"

"He wouldn't really use it," Holly said. "At least, I don't think he would." She wrinkled her nose in thought. "Dad?"

Derek groaned. "Why don't you start moving all this stuff up to the register," he said, pointing to the far wall where there was a small line.

It would take Holly a couple of trips, giving him a few minutes to talk to Gabrielle alone.

"Okay. I can take a hint. Just don't do anything I wouldn't do." She winked at him.

It was his turn to flush. "Hey! Just how old are you, anyway?"

"I've been around Mom and John long enough to learn a few things"

He waved his hand toward the register. "Go! If you behave, I'll take you for lunch afterward."

"Okay. Can Gabrielle come with us? Please?"

His daughter's request took him off guard. It was one thing to see Gabrielle again, to realize she still had that punch-in-the-gut impact on him. It was another to get to know her. To let his daughter get to know her.

To hear Gabrielle laugh and let the old feelings and yearnings resurface…knowing he'd have to let her go again.

CHAPTER THREE

DEREK LOOKED AT HIS daughter's pleading expression and cleared his throat. "I'm sure Gabrielle has to get ready for her talk tonight," he said to Holly. "She probably doesn't have time for lunch."

Gabrielle met his gaze and folded her arms across her chest. "Actually I'm well prepared."

He shoved his hands into the front pocket of his jeans, hoping his discomfort wasn't obvious. "But you can't very well leave your friend stranded." He knew he was grasping at straws, but he really didn't want to navigate a three-way lunch that included his daughter. Holly was obviously smitten with Gabrielle.

Not that he blamed her. She'd been surrounded by men the past few weeks and Gabrielle's warmth was contagious.

Even Derek was finding Gabrielle hard to resist. Though he knew all the reasons he shouldn't get involved, he felt drawn to her. As if he were seventeen all over again.

"Right?" he asked, seeking confirmation that Gabrielle knew better than to accept the invitation.

But instead of agreeing, Gabrielle straightened her shoulders and frowned.

Uh-oh. Derek recognized that stubborn look and immediately realized his error. The girl he'd known didn't take well to being told what to do.

Gabrielle shook her hair, let it sway in defiance. "Actually, Sharon's having lunch with her fiancé. She won't mind if I don't join them. Besides, since I'll be around for a while, she and I can catch up anytime." Gabrielle's fiery gaze met his, as if daring him to come up with another reason she should opt out.

He swallowed hard. "Then I'm guessing you're free for lunch?"

"I'd love to join you," she said, speaking past him to his daughter.

"Excellent!" Now certain she wasn't going to lose out on time with her new idol, Holly turned her attention to the packages of sheets and pillows, grabbed as many as she could carry and headed for the register.

Derek turned to face Gabrielle, but before he could think of what to say now that they were alone, she spoke.

"You don't want me to come for lunch." Her glossed lips turned downward in a luscious pout.

"I'm not sure it's such a good idea," he admitted.

She stepped closer. A sensual whiff of what smelled like chocolate assaulted his senses, giving him a craving for so much more than food.

"Is there something wrong with two old friends catching up?" Her mouth hovered close to his cheek.

He clenched his hands into tight fists. "Is that all we are?" he asked her, his body stiff from her nearness, his defenses against her nonexistent.

"Isn't that what you told Holly?"

"What did you want me to tell her?" he asked, his jaw tight. "That we were lovers?" The word, the thought, the reminder set him on fire.

A slow smile spread across her face. "She's too young for the truth. I just wanted to see if *you* remembered," she said in a husky voice.

His heart slammed harder inside his chest. "I never forgot."

She inclined her head, a pleased expression on her face. "That's all I needed to know. I really should get back to Sharon and tell her about the change of plans. Where and when should I meet you for lunch?"

He felt as if he'd been sucker-punched by the past. By her. He needed time to regroup before seeing her again. He glanced at his watch. "There's a restaurant upstairs. How about we meet there at noon. Does that give you enough time?"

She nodded. "That's perfect. But I'm afraid I'll need a ride back. I left my car at Sharon's place."

"Not a problem. I'll drive you wherever you have to go when we're finished."

"Thank you."

Holly ran between them. "The lady started to ring up my things. I just have to grab these, too." She swept the rest of the pile into her arms. "Are you coming, Dad?"

"In two seconds."

"Okay. See you at lunch, right?" Holly asked Gabrielle.

"I wouldn't miss it," she assured his daughter, her gaze warm and friendly.

Holly darted back toward the cash register and Gabrielle laughed. "She's a whirlwind."

"That she is," he said proudly.

Derek had never envisioned these two females meeting face-to-face, but now that they had, he should be amazed at the instant connection between them. But Holly was his daughter and his connection with Gabrielle had also been instant and intense.

After their breakup, he'd moved on with his life, one day at a time. He'd had no choice. But now that he was with Gabrielle again, his throat grew full with emotions too complex to separate, though he recognized a mix of desire, regrets and hope.

He took the moment to study her. From the tips of those high-heeled shoes his daughter loved, up her long, lean legs, over her hips and waist, she was really something. His gaze lingered on the cleavage peaking above her lacey, sexy top. She was better than the chocolate she'd always loved, he thought.

He reached out and touched her cheek. "You look good, Gabby."

A visible tremor rippled through her at his touch. "You do, too," she said.

"Dad! I need money," Holly called to him.

"You should go to her. I need to tell Sharon about my lunch plans."

He nodded. "I'll see you in about an hour."

She inclined her head and turned to walk away, then pivoted back. "Derek?"

"Yes?"

"You owe me a proper hello," she said, then turned, her high heels clicking as she walked.

He closed his eyes and exhaled hard, trying to let himself think. But only short spurts of thought penetrated the haze of surprise and desire clouding his head.

Gabrielle was back.

And she definitely wasn't ready to leave the past where it belonged.

GABRIELLE CAUGHT UP WITH Sharon, who had cornered a salesman into demonstrating various coffeemakers. She found Gabrielle and quickly turned back to the salesman. "I'll take that one," she said.

"Are you sure?"

Sharon nodded.

"I'll go get it from the back," the man said.

"Thank you," she said, then whirled on Gabrielle. "Well?"

"Well." Usually not at a loss for words, Gabrielle splayed her hands in front of her, unable to express what had just occurred. She needed time to digest it herself.

"Are you okay?" Sharon asked, her voice filled with concern.

"He called me Gabby," she said, admitting what had sent her into an emotional tailspin.

Nobody but Derek had ever shortened her name. Hearing it again on his lips had brought back a flood of memories, some good, some bad. Like the late-night phone calls, whispering so she wouldn't wake her parents, and the long nights tossing and turning afterward, fighting the urge to call him just to hear his voice or the sound of his breathing while she fell asleep.

Whenever she had good news, Derek was the first person she'd tell. And when something went wrong in her life, he was the one she'd turn to for a shoulder to cry on. She didn't always do as he suggested, and she recalled his frequent frustration at her single-minded determination to do what she wanted. But he'd always supported her.

She'd loved him for that.

She'd loved him. Period.

Sharon placed a hand on her shoulder. "I'm here if you want to talk."

Gabrielle smiled. "And I appreciate that so much. Listen, they invited me to stay and have lunch with them. Derek said he'd drive me back later to pick up my car."

The salesman strode through a set of double doors with a large box in his hands.

"Did you pick that one in a rush? Because I don't want you to have to come back and return it later," Gabrielle said.

Sharon unzipped her purse and pulled out her wallet. "I was killing time waiting for you, so I made him earn his commission," she whispered.

Gabrielle laughed. "You are too much."

With a shrug, Sharon followed the salesman to the register nearby. While he rang up her sale, she focused on Gabrielle.

"Are you sure spending time with Derek and his daughter is a good idea?"

"I'm sure. Holly invited me and she seems like a great kid. One minute she's rambling like an eleven-year-old and the next we're talking about designers," she said, laughing. "Besides, Derek and I have a lot of catching up to do."

"Do I need to remind you how badly he hurt you? It might have happened a long time ago, but from the look in your eyes, it might just as well have been yesterday."

Gabrielle shook her head. "No, you don't need to remind me." She remembered it all too well.

The morning after their senior prom, he'd taken her off guard by announcing their relationship was over for good, breaking her heart. "A lot has happened since then. Maybe he's over the curse thing." She wondered who she was trying to convince, Sharon or herself.

"I'll take that to mean I'm right and you aren't over him."

"Exactly." Why argue the point? Her friend knew her too well.

Gabrielle came from a family of females who were academics on the surface but passionate romantics at heart. Even at seventeen, she'd had a deep appreciation for things that made her feel good. Sex and chocolate had been two of those things. Sex with Derek had been even better.

"Oh, sweetie, listen, you can't let yourself go back there. From what I've seen over the years, not much has changed with the Corwin men," Sharon said as she handed the salesman her charge card.

"Maybe not, but you haven't kept up with Derek personally, right? He could have decided the curse was nothing more than an old family story. I mean, he did get married." Much as she hated to think of him with another woman.

She'd been with other people, too, but she hadn't fallen in love with any of them. She hadn't had their child. She swallowed over the painful lump in her throat.

"A lot has gone on in his life," Sharon reminded her as if reading her mind.

"True." But he still looked at her with that intense expression that said he only had eyes for her. His feelings were still there. Whether he'd allow himself to act on them was the question.

Gabrielle was determined to push him hard enough to find out. "I have to get to know him again. I need to know if there's hope."

"Okay," Sharon said, but her tone implied she clearly didn't agree with her friend's choice. "You know where to find me." She signed the credit-card slip, accepted the receipt and put both it and her wallet back in her handbag.

Then she picked up the large box holding the coffee machine.

"Need help getting it to the car?" Gabrielle asked.

"I'll be fine. Will *you?*"

Gabrielle smiled. "Yes. I will. Because this time I know the worst-case scenario ahead of time. I dealt with it once and I survived. Besides, I'm older and wiser now."

Sharon frowned. "Then why are you going back to hit your head against the same brick wall?"

"Because some walls can be moved with the right kind of force. Quit worrying. I'll see you tonight." She turned and started to walk away. She'd just do some browsing before she had to meet up with Derek and Holly for lunch.

"Richard has some nice friends he can introduce you to," Sharon called out.

Gabrielle merely laughed and waved, ignoring the suggestion. She had spent the past dozen years trying to find a man who compared to Derek, one who could fill her emotionally and physically the way he had. None had even come close.

If she was being offered a second chance with Derek, she had to take it.

DEREK NEEDN'T HAVE WORRIED about lunch being awkward. Not when his daughter and his childhood sweetheart had bonded over hamburgers and french fries. How Holly had talked Gabrielle into trying her favorite food, he still couldn't figure out.

They had more in common than he'd ever have believed. From books Gabrielle had read as a child to current shows on TV, Gabrielle could relate to his daughter. Derek was so drawn by the animated way his daughter spoke to Gabrielle and fascinated by the serious way Gabrielle listened to Holly, he barely tasted his burger.

Holly, who'd been living with Derek for a few weeks without a female in sight, suddenly blossomed in front of him.

Although his father had introduced her to a few

kids in town, the one girl Holly had hit it off with had gone on vacation with her parents almost immediately. She'd be back soon and he hoped then Holly would have someone to hang out with. But until today he hadn't realized how starved his daughter must have been for female attention.

A short while later, Derek drove them back. Gabrielle's car was at Sharon's parents' house at the far end of town. He turned onto Main Street as he, Holly and Gabrielle talked about the newest hit song on the radio.

"Dad, that's Grandpa outside the hardware store. Look!" Holly pointed at the window where his father stood talking to a bunch of older men. "Can I go say hi?"

Derek slowed the truck down and pulled over. Rolling down the window, he called for his father's attention. Hank waved, then returned to his conversation with Burt, the owner.

"If he's going straight home, I'm going to get a ride with him, okay?"

"Sure. Just make sure you wave, so I know it's okay with Dad. And remember to look both ways before you cross the street." There weren't many cars, but he wanted to make sure she was safe. "In fact, let me help you—"

"Dad!" she said, horrified. "I live in Manhattan. I think I can handle Main Street."

Beside him, Gabrielle chuckled.

"Sorry. I'm a parent. What can I say?" he said, spreading his hands out in front of him.

"Actually, I think it's sweet," she said, her eyes drinking him in with a heat that hadn't been there while she'd been focused on his daughter.

But Holly was now leaving, and apparently, Gabrielle took that as a sign.

"I had such a good time. Can we take that trip to Target one day soon?" Holly asked Gabrielle.

She nodded. "You bet."

Holly's eyes lit up. "Bye!" She leaned into the front and hugged Derek, her earlier mortification over his protective comments forgotten.

Then she was gone. He watched her look both ways before running across the street and exhaled a sigh of relief.

"She's amazing, Derek," Gabrielle said, not letting an awkward silence take over.

"Thank you. I like to think so, but I can't take much credit for it." As he watched, Holly spoke to her grandfather, then turned and waved, indicating to Derek he could leave.

Suddenly eager to be alone with Gabrielle, at least for a short time, he put the truck in Drive and pulled back into traffic. Maybe it would be easier to tell her more about his daughter while he was occupied driving.

At least then he wouldn't have to look into her beautiful eyes and admit the truth—he'd been a bad parent. "I wasn't there for her much," he said, forcing the words out.

Gabrielle placed her hand on his shoulder. "I can't imagine that. Why don't you start at the beginning?"

He nodded. They both knew that their ending was his beginning and he drew a deep breath before diving in. "I was a mess after we broke up. I threw myself into partying at school, skipping classes…anything to forget."

She leaned closer, her hand remaining on his shoulder. As a distraction while driving, it was a potent one, and he forced his concentration on the road where it belonged.

"And were you able to forget me?" she asked, her fingers stroking the sensitive spot at the base of his neck.

He shivered. "No," he said, his voice hoarse. "But I wasn't functioning on all burners, either. I met Marlene, Holly's mother, at a party." He swallowed hard. "She was fun and we had enough in common to stay together for a while… I eventually got her pregnant."

"Turn left," Gabrielle whispered, her breath warm in his ear.

He remembered where Sharon's parents lived, but he wasn't about to remind her and change the subject. He needed to get this story out.

"I did the right thing," he continued. "I married her. Her mother was widowed and living in New

York City, so she helped with the baby, and somehow we both finished school."

"Turn right. Last house on the left," Gabrielle
said.

He flipped on his signal and turned. "I figured
since we weren't in love in the traditional sense, it
would work out. After all, the curse was supposed
to only affect Corwin men who fell in love. Only
it didn't turn out that way." He pulled into the last
driveway on the left and put the SUV in Park.

She hadn't spoken. "Are you still with me?" He
turned toward her.

She still leaned close, her lips hovering near
his. "Did you just say you weren't in love with
her?" Gabrielle asked.

"That's exactly what I said."

She unhooked her seat belt and it snapped back
into place. "Thank God." Her sigh of relief got
lost as she threw her arms around his neck and
kissed him.

He should have been surprised, but this was
Gabrielle. His body had been primed since laying
eyes on her, ready since she'd set her delicate fingers on the base of his neck. She'd always known
just how to touch him to set him aflame.

Time hadn't changed a thing.

Her lips were full, warm, lush and welcoming.
She kissed him as if she knew him inside and out,
yet still had more places to find and things to learn.

Her tongue slid back and forth inside his mouth, tasting and teasing. She nibbled his lower lip with her teeth, then soothed the sting with a silken slide of her tongue. And all the while, her fingers traced his face, as if relearning him all over again.

His body burned and he groaned aloud. Cupping his hand around the back of her neck, he tipped her head and took control. He'd never wanted a woman the way he did Gabrielle. He could make love to her once and want her again almost immediately. And if he thought their teenage passion had been something, the intensity of their adult need surprised even him.

His tongue tangled with hers and her body melted into him, as close as she could get with the center panel of the SUV lodged between them. She shifted and her elbow hit the horn, the loud noise jarring them both.

She jumped back into her seat, laughing. "Wow. I think I had more finesse when I was younger."

He drank in her flushed face and red lips as he tried to catch his breath. "Oh, I think you still have plenty of finesse."

She bit down on her lower lip. "You haven't lost your touch, either." She reached across the divider and clasped his hand inside hers.

Her touch warmed him inside and out, but it wasn't just the sexual chemistry that had his head spinning and his mind filled with regrets—

although that alone was enough to knock him on his ass. It was the woman herself that got to him.

She'd come back into his life after all these years and without any bitterness about the past, she'd accepted his daughter. Just like that. One quick meeting and she'd given Holly everything the girl was missing in her life without hesitation.

No man could walk away from a woman whose heart was that big.

He had no choice.

"Gabby…"

She tipped her head to the side. "Please don't tell me you still believe in curses."

"How can I not believe in something that keeps proving itself over and over." He reached out and stroked her hair. "How can I not want to protect you?"

"Derek, let me make something very clear. I didn't appreciate you making decisions for me when I was seventeen and I appreciate it even less now. Your kiss made it perfectly clear how you feel about me. Don't expect me to just walk away from you again."

Before he could reply, she opened the door and hopped out. "Thanks for the ride," she said, her voice cheerful.

Clearly she hadn't listened to a word he'd just said.

His body was glad.

His mind and heart told him she was better off without him.

He ran a hand over his eyes, then slammed his hand against the steering wheel. When in the hell would what *he* wanted count? Or was the fact that his last name was Corwin stronger than anything else in this world?

He put the SUV in Reverse and pulled out of the driveway, slowing to watch Gabrielle let herself into the car. She stopped to pull a flier from beneath the windshield, glanced at one side and then the other before she crumpled it in her hand and then opened the car door.

The cute convertible suited her personality, he thought as she waved, indicating he could leave.

He drove away, certain of one thing. No matter how difficult it would be, he had to keep his distance. He couldn't let the curse in his life destroy hers.

GABRIELLE TURNED ON THE ignition and hoped the air-conditioning kicked in fast. Her car, which had been sitting under the hot sun all afternoon, felt like an oven.

Her heart was racing a mile a minute, but it wasn't just due to Derek's kiss, nor was it the heat. The note on her car made her uneasy.

She pulled out the paper she'd crumpled so Derek wouldn't think anything was wrong. But something was *very* wrong. The flier had been a threat. One side announced her talk at the library. The other had a handwritten warning scrawled in red crayon that read, *"Go home or else."*

Gabrielle exhaled long and hard. While she disliked being told what was best for her, threats and ultimatums really ticked her off.

As if she didn't have enough on her mind… After that kiss, did Derek really think she'd let him walk away? As long as she knew he still cared, she wasn't going to allow his ridiculous beliefs to stop them from being together any more than she'd let some coward prevent her from speaking out tonight.

When Gabrielle was told no, her determination merely grew stronger. She recrumpled the paper and tossed it across the car.

Watch out, Derek Corwin. Gabrielle was back. And she was going to get what she wanted.

CHAPTER FOUR

DEREK HAD NO INTENTION of going to the library tonight. God knows, he didn't need to hear any more about a curse he was already intimately familiar with. Unfortunately, after dinner, which he and Holly had shared at his father and his uncle Thomas's house, Hank was still determined to go.

They were still sitting in the kitchen around the table. Derek rose to help his uncle clear the plates while his father began to rinse and place the rest of the dishes in the dishwasher. Holly had taken Fred for a walk, so when his father began discussing the library talk, Derek figured now was as good a time as any to get things out in the open. Derek didn't want Holly exposed to the details about the family curses at her young age.

"Do you really want Gabrielle going on about our family history in public? Dragging our dirty laundry through the mud?" Hank asked.

"Excuse me for stating the obvious, but would it change anything? Everyone already knows we're cursed," Uncle Thomas said as he finished loading the dishwasher. "There's no reason to go to the library and provide people with a sideshow."

When it came to the curse, Uncle Thomas had always been the more rational of the two men. Still, there was no question both brothers had suffered. Hank might have lost the woman he loved, but he'd been one helluva father. A little crazy on this one particular subject, but a solid man nonetheless.

Uncle Thomas had a more colorful personal history. He and Uncle Edward had both fallen in love with the same woman. But Sara Jean Wilder had been dating Uncle Thomas first and she'd stayed with him—out of obligation, Uncle Edward claimed. Uncle Thomas loved her, though. They had three children and remained in a marriage that even Derek knew had been strained until Sara's death from ovarian cancer two years ago.

Uncle Edward never forgave his brother. Surprisingly though, he'd moved on enough to fall in love with Derek's aunt Renee. But their marriage, too, which had started out with promise, had been tense. Renee hadn't been able to deal with Edward's gruff demeanor and unwillingness to forgive. Eventually, she began to believe rumors around town that she had been Edward's second choice. They'd had one son, but Aunt Renee had been miserable. They finally divorced. She'd moved on and remarried while Uncle Edward withdrew into himself and became the town loner.

The once-booming family construction business fell apart thanks to the rift between the brothers, resulting in bankruptcy. Afterward, the brothers earned a living by trade. Hank became an electrician, Thomas a handyman and Edward a plumber until he became such an oddity, people in town quit wanting him around. The Corwins had respectable jobs but no longer a thriving business.

Can anyone say *curse?*

Derek glanced around the small kitchen at his father and uncle. "I agree with Uncle Thomas," Derek said. "Come on, Dad. Let's stay home tonight. If none of us acknowledge the talk, maybe the gossip will die down sooner."

"There's no chance. Not as long as that Perkins family draws breath," Hank said.

"You're starting to sound like one of the Hatfields or the McCoys. Come to think of it, you're starting to look like one of them, too."

Tonight Hank's hair was messier than usual. With his shirt buttoned incorrectly and hanging longer on one side, he looked as if he didn't give a damn about anything. He liked it that way. But he wasn't the most wild-looking of the brothers. That distinction belonged to Uncle Ed.

Uncle Thomas, on the other hand, prided himself on always facing talk, scandal or just life in general, looking his finest. When not working with his hands, he dressed immaculately in a collared, button-down shirt and Dockers.

Uncle Thomas chuckled. "You do need a haircut," he said to his brother.

Hank scowled at him. "Why? Who's lookin' at me that I care about?"

"Your granddaughter," Derek reminded him. "If nothing else, how about cleaning yourself up for her benefit?"

As if on cue, Holly ran into the room, Fred at her heels. "Dad, it's almost time for Gabrielle's talk at the library. I don't want to miss it!"

Derek winced. He hadn't anticipated Holly having any interest in the talk, but given her new obsession with Gabrielle, he should have.

"Listen," he said, walking over to his daughter. "I don't think any of us are going to go tonight."

"Speak for yourself," Hank said.

"Can I go with you, Grandpa?" Holly asked, eyes wide and pleading.

Hank paused. "I don't know that the subject's one that you need to hear about," he said kindly. Hank might be opinionated and outspoken, but he respected Derek's role as Holly's parent. "Who cares about curses and the like, anyway? Fred loves having you around. Why don't you keep an eye on him while I'm gone?"

She frowned. "Do you think I don't know about

the family curse?" She propped her hands on her small hips.

"Just what do you know and how?" Derek asked.

"Just about everything!" She rolled her eyes in that adult way she had. "Mom told me that once a long time ago, a wicked witch named Mary cursed the Corwin men and ever since they can't fall in love or else they'll lose everything," she said matter-of-factly. "Just like you did."

"When did Mom tell you this?" he asked.

"While I was packing to come stay with you."

Apparently marriage had mellowed his ex even more than Derek had realized if she was willing to blame their divorce on the curse rather than on Derek's workaholic feet.

"So can I go with Grandpa? Please?"

Derek groaned. If she knew about the curse, that was one less thing he'd have to explain to her when she got older. As for tonight, he was still on the fence. "Do you believe in the curse?" he asked.

She pursed her lips in thought. "I don't know. It seems kinda silly, but Mom pointed out how Aunt Ruthie and Aunt Allison are still happily married. It's just the men in the family who can't get it right."

Derek exhaled a groan. "That's one way of putting it. But listen, you know how mean people can be? Talking and saying things they shouldn't?"

She nodded.

"Well, that's why I don't want you to go to the library tonight. If they're talking about our family, why should we go and listen?"

"Because it's about *us,* silly! We can go and either tell the true version or make sure they say nice things."

If only it were as simple as that, Derek mused.

"I think Little Missy has a point. We should show up and hold our heads high," Hank said. "Maybe that'll keep them from telling tales that aren't true, at least."

Derek rubbed his hands over his eyes.

"Please, Daddy?" Holly said, eyes wide, deliberately batting her lashes.

How could he argue with his daughter's sweet face, his father's obstinate insistence or his own desire to see Gabrielle again?

GABRIELLE ARRIVED EARLY at the library. She liked to see where she'd be speaking and get a feel for the place before she actually did her thing. It helped ease the jitters that went with public speaking. As her other writer friends liked to say, they preferred being behind the computer screen, not in front of a crowd. Gabrielle didn't mind the attention as much as some people, but she still appreciated time to warm up.

She stood at the small podium and was reading through her notes when the first guests arrived—an older woman accompanied by a younger one with a pad in her hand. Gabrielle didn't recognize either of them.

"Are you Gabrielle Donovan, the author?" the older woman asked.

Gabrielle put her papers in a neat pile and stepped down so she'd be on the same level as her visitor. "Yes. And you are?"

"Mary Perkins." She shook Gabrielle's hand. "And this is my granddaughter and indispensable assistant, Elizabeth."

Gabrielle shook Elizabeth's hand, too. "Nice to meet you both. It's Mayor Perkins, isn't it?"

The older woman nodded. "Of Perkins. My family founded the town," she said proudly.

"And will continue its legacy in the next election," Elizabeth said with certainty, her hand on her grandmother's shoulder.

Gabrielle smiled. "Nice to meet you," she said, sizing up Richard's opponent and the woman who apparently struck fear in many.

It was hard to believe.

She couldn't be more than five foot three inches to Gabrielle's five foot five. Her hair was gray and professionally styled. She wore a tailored suit and what Gabrielle's mother would call sensible heels. The outfit complemented her conservative style. Her granddaughter was a younger version of the mayor. Her brown bob wasn't as chic as it was conservative. Utilitarian, even, along with her clothes.

They'd both greeted Gabrielle with a welcoming smile—even though the subject of Gabrielle's speech tonight went against everything the Perkins family stood for.

"Congratulations on your success. I understand you're a fixture on the bestseller lists," Mary said.

"Thank you. I feel very fortunate." And at the moment, very off balance, Gabrielle thought. She wasn't sure what Mary wanted or what to make of her friendly overture.

"Nonsense. Never sell yourself short. Fortune occurs because of talent." Mary reached into her purse and pulled out a paperback copy of Gabrielle's latest book. "I was hoping you would sign this for me."

Gabrielle nodded. "Of course." She accepted the book, opened to the title page and signed it as generically as she could get away with. *Best wishes, Gabrielle Donovan.*

She placed the date below her signature and handed the book back to the mayor. "Thank you for asking."

The other woman smiled. "My pleasure. I think it's wonderful that you're returning to your hometown to speak. Some people become famous and forget where they came from."

Gabrielle forced a smile. She hadn't been back in years, and though she'd had her reasons, this woman's comment struck a nerve.

From behind Mary, Gabrielle noticed people were beginning to file into the room, filling the seats. "It was nice to meet you," Gabrielle said, hoping Mary would take the hint and leave.

"You, too." Elizabeth stepped out from her grandmother's shadow. "I'm looking forward to hearing you speak. It's fascinating how you debunk popular myths." Her inflection never changed nor did her expression.

"I just write the facts as I see them, based on research, psychological evaluation. The theories, however, are my own."

"Yes. We all have our own ways of viewing the same phenomenon, don't we? That's why so many people from both my town and Stewart are showing up to hear you."

Gabrielle glanced toward the rapidly filling room where people—neighbors, friends—congregated. "I suppose you're right."

Mary straightened her shoulders and Elizabeth followed suit. "Yes, we usually are. Well, best of luck." She lifted the signed book in the air. "Thank you again." They turned and walked away to find a seat.

Gabrielle shivered. "That was the strangest thing," she said aloud.

"What did the wicked witch and her mini me want?" Sharon asked as she joined her.

Gabrielle hadn't seen her friend come in. "To say hello and have me sign a book for her."

"That's odd."

So was the way everyone in the room gave the older woman a wide berth. "For a woman who's been the uncontested mayor of Perkins for years, she doesn't have many people wanting to talk to her," Gabrielle mused.

"There's a reason for that. She's not likable," Sharon said.

Yet she had been very pleasant to Gabrielle. "I need to get ready."

Sharon nodded. "You'll be great. And I'm here for support. So is Richard." She pointed to her fiancé, who was meeting and greeting people in the audience. Since the towns of Stewart and Perkins were so close, their pasts so intertwined, people from both places wanted to hear what Gabrielle had to say.

All under the watchful eye of Mary Perkins, who was obviously staying for the talk. She and her granddaughter had taken seats in the back.

By themselves.

By the time Gabrielle walked up to the podium, the small library was filled to capacity. Chairs had been set out in rows and the crowd overflowed into the back hall. She was pleased with the turn-out, especially since her latest book had been pub-lished last October. Normally, Gabrielle spoke only when she had a new book to promote, doing readings at local libraries, signings and chats at bookstores.

Tonight's talk was different. She wasn't here to sell books. She was here to use her expertise to sway people's thinking. She'd stop short of endorsing Richard Stern's mayoral campaign, and she definitely wouldn't mention the much visible Mary Perkins.

Gabrielle started on time. She'd watched the flow of people walk in, keeping an eye out for Derek or his gun-toting father. Thanks to that searing kiss earlier today, she'd been too distracted to ask Derek if Holly had been serious about her grandfather. But so far, neither man had showed.

Though she was disappointed, she reminded herself she hadn't expected him to be here tonight. Still, she'd be a liar if she didn't admit that she'd hoped the kiss had stayed with him long enough to lure him out, anyway.

Shaking off her disappointment, she began an animated talk. She started off stating the amount of study she'd done in the area of the paranormal and followed by discussing how it related to her books. In *Future Stars,* she'd debunked fortune-tellers and in *Her Mind's Eye,* she questioned the validity of psychics.

She continued her speech by addressing curses, which she'd dealt with peripherally in *Disenchanted,* last year. She referred to theories such as the

Theory of Suggestibility, which detailed how people experiencing intense emotions regarding certain subjects, like a curse, were more receptive to ideas surrounding them. Referring to the towns of Perkins and Stewart, she explained that the emotions surrounding the curse were so high, any event that seemed to meet the criteria of the curse was automatically pegged as a result. She also explained the notion of crowd psychology and how group mentality often came to overrule an individual's personal thought and belief system.

Though careful not to mention the Corwins or the Perkins families by name, and even more cautious not to meet Mary's and Elizabeth Perkins's stares, Gabrielle finished by pulling together the towns' collective experience with the curse. She tried to impart the notion that just because every male within a cursed family line that had fallen in love had suffered financial loss and emotional devastation didn't mean the curse existed. Individual circumstances coincidentally met the same criteria as the curse, and it was possible that even the power of suggestion played a role in the choices key players made.

Gabrielle received a standing ovation for her talk, then she took questions. Finally, she glanced at the clock and realized an hour had passed.

"Last question?" A quick glance at the back row told her Mary Perkins had left unnoticed.

However, when she turned her gaze to the back door, she was surprised to see Derek and his father had arrived at some point, as well.

Pleasure wrapped over her at the sight of him. In nothing more than dark jeans and a basic T-shirt, he still stood out in a crowd.

His gaze met hers and heat stirred in her belly, distracting her from anything except him. Her lips curved into a smile.

Suddenly he raised his hand, which reminded her she'd been about to take her last question. She swallowed hard. "Yes?" she asked, pointing to him. "Derek?"

"I was wondering what your next book was going to be about."

Wow. She'd expected the question at some point. Just not from him.

"Thank you for asking." His interest warmed her as much as the fact that he'd shown his face at a public discussion on curses. But she didn't know how he'd take the answer to his question. "Growing up here, I'm well acquainted with the rich history of the area, and of Salem in particular." Again, she had to tread carefully for Derek's family's sake. "I plan to take a look at specific family curses."

An overwhelming round of applause followed. Apparently people liked the idea of her taking on a subject so close to home. Gabrielle hoped that meant they'd be open to being questioned about their ancestors.

Derek listened to her answer in dismay. He wouldn't have asked had he known the answer ahead of time. He couldn't believe she'd be delving into something so deep and personal. Yet, who was he to interfere in her career? He didn't have to like it, but apparently the crowd did.

"The hell you are!" Derek's father stepped up from behind him.

Derek glared at his father. Though Hank had been the one insisting they show up tonight, he'd been fidgety for most of the lecture. Close to the end, he'd slunk out and Derek assumed his father had gone to the men's room. He'd been relieved, and he'd hoped his father would stay there for the duration of Gabrielle's talk.

"Is there a problem?" Gabrielle asked.

"Darn straight there's a problem!" Hank bypassed Derek and waved his hands as he spoke to both Gabrielle and the crowd. "It's bad enough you're standing up there trying to tell everyone curses don't exist when my family's living, breathing proof they do. But now you're going to make money off of our story?"

Gabrielle's cheeks flushed red. As red as her temper, Derek would bet, cringing at his father's accusation.

She drew her shoulders back straighter. "Excuse

me, Mr. Corwin, but I object to the notion that I'm out to make money off of other people's misery. I write about factual situations and how the choices people make play into the outcome. The hope is that other people will learn lessons from these situations they can apply to their own life. In this case, I want people to see that the power of suggestion is as strong as any curse."

"Sounds to me like you're mocking us, as sure as anybody who tells tales about us around town," Hank said.

"Mr. Corwin, I assure you, I'm doing no such thing," Gabrielle said hotly.

"Hah! If you mock the curse, something worse will happen to us. You just watch." Hank turned beet-red.

Derek was surprised his father wasn't foaming at the mouth. He placed a calming hand on his dad's shoulders. "Getting worked up isn't good for your blood pressure," he said quietly but sternly, warning his father to back off.

"I'm not mocking anyone or anything," Gabrielle said. "What I'm doing is debunking something that has ruled your family's life for too many years."

Derek knew Gabrielle. She wasn't about to back down.

"Hah!" Hank said, obviously warming up for another tirade.

Without warning, Sharon stood up in the center

of the room. "Relax, Mr. Corwin, or I'll have Roger show you out," she said, pointing to the uniformed officer who'd only come in case he needed to direct traffic.

"It's a public library, missy. I can stay and have my say."

"It's *my* library and you're insulting my guest!" Sharon perched her hands on her hips.

Before things could get any more out of hand, Derek grabbed his father's arm. "Shut up and leave on your own before you embarrass us any further." Derek clenched his jaw.

Hank muttered under his breath.

And Holly inched closer to Derek's leg.

"That's my point!" Hank said, not finished arguing. "Look how she's humiliating us in public!"

Hank was the only one humiliating the Corwin family, but before Derek could let his father in on that fact, Chaz, the town drunk who showed up at any public gathering in case there was free liquor, rose to his feet.

"Maybe that's because Derek dumped her before he went off to college," Chaz said.

The dig got chuckles from the crowd. Chaz had been in Derek and Gabrielle's graduating class. And even though he'd been drunk for most of his life, he was right about what had happened.

Derek didn't appreciate the public reminder and clenched his hands into tight fists at his sides.

"You did?" Holly pulled at his shirt. "You dumped Gabrielle?" his daughter asked.

Derek groaned. "Way to go, Pop."

"What'd I do?" Hank asked.

Derek shook his head. It was useless. His father wouldn't understand that he had taken a calm, quiet talk and turned it into a mudslinging, embarrassing mess. Not until he'd calmed down and reflected on it, Derek thought.

Gabrielle cleared her throat. "Tonight's lecture is finished. Thank you all for coming," she said, as she collected her notes from the podium in front of her.

"Daddy?"

Derek bent closer to his daughter. "Are you okay?" he asked her.

She nodded. "Tonight was more exciting than I thought it would be!"

At least she seemed unfazed.

"Tell me about you and Gabrielle," Holly said, wide-eyed.

"Listen, I told you that Gabrielle and I were friends in high school. I'll explain more to you later, but right now I need to talk to her and make sure she isn't upset."

Holly nodded, wise for her years. "Please do. I'm sure Grandpa didn't mean to hurt her feelings."

Derek gave his naive daughter a hug, then rose. "Dad? Take Holly home for me."

"How will you get home? You drove here with us," Holly reminded him.

Derek cupped her chin in his hand. "I can get a ride with somebody here. Don't worry, okay?"

Holly shrugged. "Okay. But tell Gabrielle I said hello?"

"I will. I'm sure she'll really appreciate it." He kissed her forehead and placed her hand in her grandfather's. "Take her home."

"I only meant to protect our good name," Hank said, his bluster gone.

With people still snickering around them, Hank seemed to realize he'd embarrassed himself, the family and Gabrielle.

"She was always a nice girl. I never meant—"

"I know." Derek ran a hand through his hair. "Take Holly home. I'll handle things here." He'd done it before.

Like his cousins, Michael and Jason, Derek had spent most of his youth responding to kids making fun of his family—how they weren't real men since they couldn't hold on to a woman. When Derek couldn't ignore the taunts any longer, he'd fought back. While he didn't appreciate his father's approach, he totally understood the reasons for it.

Derek watched his father wrap his arm around Holly's shoulder and lead her out of the library, not pausing to talk to anyone.

He blew out a deep breath and made a beeline

for Gabrielle. Her friends, Sharon and Richard Stern, had circled around her in protective fashion, preventing anyone from heckling her further.

Derek wasn't just anyone. "Hi, Sharon."

She narrowed her gaze. "Derek. Haven't you and your family done enough? Wouldn't it be smarter to just go home?"

"Give a guy a break. I just want to make sure she's okay." He gestured to Gabrielle by tipping his head toward her.

Sharon frowned, keeping her body between Derek and her best friend. Even in high school, she'd been Gabrielle's protector, even though Gabrielle hadn't needed anything of the sort. These two women had a bond the likes of which he'd never seen. Though Sharon had been friendly enough to him since his return, now that Gabrielle was back in town, Sharon left no doubt as to where her loyalty lay. She'd shown it tonight.

Still, he wasn't about to let anyone dictate whether or not he could see Gabrielle. He and Sharon wanted the same thing—what was best for Gabrielle.

With a determined step, he strode around Sharon and came up behind Gabrielle. "Gabby?" he asked, calling for her attention.

She turned toward him.

He spoke before she could say a word. "I'm sorry for my father's behavior."

She waved off his apology, her expression warm despite the circumstances. "You aren't responsible for what someone else does."

It didn't feel that way to him. "I tried to convince Dad to stay home."

"His shotgun might have hurt less," she said, laughing.

He stepped closer. "You're really okay?"

She nodded. "Sticks and stones and all that. I'm tougher than I look. But thanks for asking."

He nodded, knowing when to let something go. "Holly said to tell you she says hi. She was here, but I sent her home with my father."

"I didn't see her in the crowd."

"She's short."

"I'm so sorry she heard all that." Gabrielle sobered quickly.

Derek nodded in understanding. "She's been through a lot, but she's tough. She'll deal with it. I'm more worried about whether I can handle her questions later," he said, only half joking.

Gabrielle smiled. "I'm not an expert with kids, but she seems pretty smart to me."

"Which is why I'll have to do some fancy footwork in answering." He couldn't very well admit that Gabrielle was his first and only true love to his daughter.

She playfully tapped his face with her hand. "I'm sure you can handle it."

He grinned, meeting her gaze. The heat smoldered, reminding him of their kiss earlier today. The one he'd promised himself he couldn't repeat. But, man, how he wanted to.

"The room's emptied out." Sharon joined them, diffusing the sexual tension.

At least for the moment, Derek thought.

"I appreciate you running interference for me," Gabrielle said to her friend.

Sharon nodded. "I invited you here to speak, not to get thrown to the wolves." She scowled at Derek. "Can't you control your father?"

He cocked his head to one side. "Would you believe me if I said I tried? Short of tying him up, there wasn't much I could do."

Gabrielle picked up her tote bag. "Let's just go home and forget about it. Who's walking out with me?"

"Richard and I came together, but I need to straighten up a few things and lock up before we can go," Sharon said. "Besides, he's busy talking to one of his campaign people." She pointed to the corner, where her fiancé remained deep in conversation with another man.

Derek had already decided he wasn't going to leave without talking to Gabrielle alone.

"I'll walk you out," Derek said.

He needed to make sure she knew where things

stood. He couldn't rekindle a relationship with her no matter how much he desired her. She might not believe in curses. But he did.

SHARON DIDN'T HAVE TO straighten up her office tonight, but she did need to blow off steam before heading home. Besides, Richard wasn't ready to leave yet, so she might as well make good use of the time.

"Ready to go?" Richard stepped into the room. Dressed immaculately in a suit and tie, he looked like the consummate politician. As he was handsome, as well as smart and compassionate, she thanked her lucky stars she'd found a man like him. Few women were offered second chances in life. This time she intended to get it right.

"I'm all set. Tonight was a huge success, wasn't it? I think Gabrielle did a great job of making people think twice about believing in an old superstition."

He stepped around her desk. Coming up beside her, he wrapped his arms around her waist and she snuggled closer.

Richard wasn't into public displays of affection. He'd hold her hand or touch her back, but his reserve in public meant she had to take advantage of every chance for intimacy whenever they were alone.

"I think Gabrielle was great and I have you to thank for inviting her. But I think you were even better. The way you stood up for your friend—" he shook his head "—you did me proud."

She smiled, pleased. "I just couldn't believe Hank Corwin attacked her that way."

"I'm glad to see you felt confident enough to do it."

She didn't want to talk about herself. "I'm just glad I could contribute to the cause."

He smoothed his hand over the back of her hair. "We're a team. It's *our* cause. You know that having you by my side only makes me look better."

"And more intelligent." She laughed and kissed him on the cheek.

"Speaking of intelligence, I spoke to some people on their way out the door tonight," Richard said. "Most mentioned they'd never thought much beyond the curse before tonight. They just believed in its power. They're rethinking those views now," he said.

"Did you see the way *she* sat there tonight? Not saying a word, just making sure people don't forget she exists?" Sharon shivered at the memory. "She even tried to con Gabrielle by requesting she autograph a copy of her book."

"Mary's devious, all right," Richard said. "There's no question she gets things done. It's her means of doing them that are questionable."

"Well, hopefully her days of subtle threats are coming to an end. If nothing else, Gabrielle has gotten people to think about whether putting

Mary Perkins back in office is something they want or something they feel compelled to do because they're afraid of her." Sharon was definitely pleased with tonight's outcome.

"I really appreciate all you do for me." He tipped her face and kissed her, keeping things slow and sensual, the way she liked it.

"Mmm." A purr escaped from the back of her throat.

"Please tell me you can come back to our home for a while tonight," he said in a gruff voice.

"I think I can manage that as long as you drop me off at my parents at a semirespectable hour," she teased.

He let out a long-suffering groan. "I hate that we have to be apart."

"Another couple of weeks and we'll be married. Then I won't have to leave you ever again."

He hugged her tight.

"Well? Will you get me home early?" She knew that meant setting an alarm so neither of them fell asleep.

"Let's see. Take you home now or squeeze in a few hours alone with you and live without sleep." He devoured her with his eyes. "You drive a hard bargain."

She wiggled her eyebrows. "I've only just begun," she said, promise rich in her voice.

CHAPTER FIVE

GABRIELLE STEPPED INTO the muggy summer air, a
direct contrast to the air-conditioned library. Yet
despite the humidity outside, she breathed more
easily. It helped that she had Derek by her side. She
stepped closer so her arm deliberately brushed his
as she walked. A ripple of awareness shot through
her and she inhaled deeply, only to be surrounded
by his masculine scent.

His overpowering presence enabled her to focus
on the more positive parts of the evening, including her successful speech and the fact that she'd
openly revealed the idea for her next novel.

Because it was summertime, the sun hadn't yet
set and there were still vestiges of light in the sky.
In the meantime, the streetlamps were already
turned on in anticipation of darkness.

"Can I hitch a ride home?" Derek asked.

She smiled, happy to have more time with
him. "Sure."

His steps slowed but they continued their walk,
pausing at her car. "I need to talk to you."

Something in his tone had her stomach churning uncomfortably. "What is it?" She shielded her eyes from the setting sun, squinting as she met his gaze.

"Here." He held her arm and moved her around so he could swap places with her, taking the brunt of the glare. He leaned against the car and shaded his eyes with his hand.

She waited for him to speak.

Finally he cleared his throat. "This afternoon? That kiss?"

Gabrielle's entire body stiffened in automatic denial. "Oh, no. No way are you going to tell me it was a mistake." Not when everything about it, and them, had been—and could still be—so right, she thought.

"Maybe I should tell you more about my past few years so you'll understand why I still believe in curses. Now more than ever." The set of his jaw told her he wasn't kidding.

She stepped back, needing space so she could think. Argue. Fight. Because she wasn't going to let him go as easily as she had the last time. She was older now, wiser. Stronger emotionally and at a point when she'd experienced more of life, and she knew what she wanted. She wanted Derek and she wasn't going to let him use ancient history as an excuse not to try again.

"Look, I'm only in town for another few days, but I only live an hour from here. We have all the time in the world to talk things out. It's been so long, can't we just enjoy getting to know each other again?" she asked, in an effort to buy herself time before he made a final decision.

She turned around to see his face and caught sight of her car. Her beloved black convertible, purchased with her first big advance, had been keyed. An ugly scratch mark split the paint from below the handle across to the end of the single door. "Bastard!"

"Hey, I'm just looking out for you," Derek said, clearly upset.

"Not you! My car. Someone keyed my car!" She pointed to the long, jagged mark in the paint.

He jerked around in surprise and studied the damage for himself. "That wasn't an accident," he said under his breath a few moments later.

"Merde!" She cursed in French. "Who would do such a thing?"

Derek ran a hand over his eyes. "I have no idea." But he didn't like the fact that someone thought nothing of doing this with a huge crowd inside.

"Come on. Let's get you back to the Rhodes Inn. I'll call Harry at the garage and talk to him about getting it painted."

She shook her head. "I'll take it into the Lexus dealer when I get home," she said, her mood deflated.

She pulled out her keys and unlocked the doors. The beep echoed in the night air. She climbed inside.

He joined her around the other side, unsure of what to say. He sure as hell wasn't going to upset her any more by bringing up the curse. He leaned back against the seat and heard a crunching sound of paper beneath him.

He reached down and pulled out a piece of paper. "Sorry," he muttered, smoothing the crumpled paper in his lap.

Gabrielle reached to snatch it back but it was too late. He'd already read the red scrawl. *Go home or else*. "What the hell is this?"

"It's nothing." She leaned back in her seat and exhaled hard.

"I don't call a threat nothing." If someone had a problem with Gabrielle, they were going to have to deal with him first.

"It's hardly a threat. It's more like a welcome note I received this morning." She put the key in the ignition and started the car.

"It's still a threat. Did you tell Sharon? The police? Anyone?"

She laughed. "Come on, Derek. It's written in crayon, for God's sake. Nobody in their right mind would take this seriously."

She backed out of the parking spot and started to drive.

"I want to go back to your room with you. I want to make sure you get inside okay." Derek reached out and brushed her hair from her face.

She glanced at him from the corner of her eye before returning her gaze to the road. "I appreciate that, but I can take care of myself."

"Did I say you couldn't? I'd just feel better knowing you were locked safe and sound inside. In case the note and the damage to the car are related."

"Do you think that's possible?" She gripped the steering wheel harder, causing the muscles in her arms to tense.

"Anything's possible. What's more probable is that someone didn't want you to speak at the library tonight and left you a note, while stupid kids keyed your car as a prank." At least that's what he hoped had happened.

But because he couldn't be sure, he was going to keep an eye on her. Just in case.

"How will you get home?" she asked.

"I can walk. I'm just a few blocks away."

She nodded. "I'm sorry I took my anger out on you. It's just been a crazy night ever since…" She trailed off.

"Ever since my father opened his big mouth." He shook his head. "I wish the night had ended with the standing ovation. You deserved it."

He'd been so proud of her in that moment. His heart had swelled at the sight of her speaking to her hometown. He'd even been able to overlook the personal subject of curses and just enjoy her the same way the crowd had.

"Thank you." The beginnings of a smile curved her sensual lips. "I was happy with the way the talk went."

He nodded. Having distracted her, he continued talking about her speech and her books. He didn't bring up the subject of the kiss again, either.

Even though at the moment, her lips were the only things he could focus on.

Gabrielle drove straight to Rhodes Inn. From the set of her jaw, Derek knew she didn't think she needed his protection, but he felt better giving it, anyway. She parked out front in one of the few unpaved spots and together they walked around back to her room.

"It's not well lit back here," he said, concentrating harder so he wouldn't trip on a rock or tree branch.

"That's an understatement. I tried to get a room at the Quality Inn but they were booked."

"Tourists and vacationers," he muttered.

"It's fine. Mrs. Rhodes still rents out rooms because she likes having people around, but she only lets relatives of local residents stay here. She feels safer that way," Gabrielle said as she found the key to her room.

She opened the door and they walked inside. She turned on an old bedside lamp and waved her arm around the room. "See? Safe and sound," she said to Derek. "Do you feel better now?"

"I'd feel better if there were lights out in the parking lot and that lock wasn't a hundred years old."

She tossed her bag onto the bed and her keys onto the nightstand. "Home sweet home," she said.

He glanced around the small room. "Where are you living now?" he asked.

"Boston. I bought a brownstone in the Back Bay."

He raised an eyebrow. "That's an impressive area. The book business must be treating you well," he said, unable to squelch the pride in his voice.

She nodded. "My first release hit the *New York Times* bestseller list. It's difficult to get authors on prime time or morning shows, but right now, anything paranormal is hot." She shrugged. "I'm smart enough to know it may not last. But real estate is a solid investment, so I feel good about putting my money there."

"I agree. I've advised my clients to diversify and real estate is something you can count on, or at least ride out over time. Especially in the area you bought in."

She grinned, obviously pleased he approved. "It's great to be back home. Florida is nice but I love New England. How 'bout those Red Sox?" she asked, laughing. "Maybe you, Holly and I can catch a Red Sox game before the summer is over?"

"Baseball," he said reverently. He slapped a hand over the left side of his chest. "A woman after my own heart."

"I could be persuaded to sit through a football game in the fall…for the right price," she teased.

"And what would that be?" he asked.

"Something delicious, something decadent, something—"

"Chocolate," he said, as soon as he realized what she meant. "I didn't realize you were so easy." He chuckled, enjoying their easy banter.

"Only with you. And only because you know me so well. How did I get along without you for the past fourteen years?" she asked lightly.

He stepped closer. Her warm scent settled over him, causing a distinct stirring inside his chest. "That's a good question." His mood changed from teasing to serious in an instant. "How *did* you get along?" he asked, suddenly needing to know.

"Not easily," she admitted, as she reached out and linked her hands behind his neck.

As she looked into his eyes, she aligned her lower body with his. No way could she miss the evidence of his wanting her. If she remembered him mentioning that he wanted to talk about the kiss, about not getting involved, she obviously wasn't going to bring it up now. And although he should, he couldn't.

He could use the threats against her as an excuse, but in his heart, he knew that's all it was. An excuse to be near her. He grabbed on to it as tightly as she held on to him now.

"I'm assuming you had relationships."

She nodded. "More than a few. I was searching for someone who…" She paused and bit down on her lower lip. "Someone who could live up to the memory of you. Of us."

His heart slammed hard against his chest. "Did you find him?" He must be a glutton for punishment to ask such a thing.

"What do you want to hear?" she asked, a teasing smile on her lips. "That even at eighteen you set the standard by which all other men fell short?"

She slid her hand up the back of his head and played with the ends of his hair with her fingertips. Her touch was electric. Her words seductive.

Selfishly that was exactly what he wanted to hear, but he'd been the one to do the leaving. "I wanted you to go on with your life. To be happy."

She tipped her head to one side. He loved the sassy sway of her hair. He couldn't resist running his fingers through the strands. "I went on. I've been successful in my career. Not so much in my personal life."

"I shouldn't be happy that you didn't find someone special. But I am."

"I shouldn't be happy that you're divorced," she countered. "But I don't think I could have handled running into you again and knowing you belonged to someone else." Her voice sounded like a husky purr.

Every fiber of his being was on alert. His skin was hot. His body strung tight. He desired her in a soul-deep way. He was dying to reconnect with her now and worry about the repercussions later. But mention of his divorce reminded him of the reasons he needed to be careful how far he let things go. "I still need to tell you about Holly's mom and what happened between us." Why the curse ruled his life now more than ever.

"Mmm. You do." She touched her forehead to his. Her mouth hovered close, tantalizing and tempting him.

Finally, she allowed their lips to touch, featherlight but enough to send his pulse racing. She toyed with him for a while, a few light pecks at first, but each one lasted longer than the last.

He grasped her waist, his grip tightening with his desire until nothing mattered but the here and now. His head spun with her scent, her taste, his need.

"I want to hear everything you have to tell me. But not tonight," Gabrielle said, her voice cutting through his fuzzy thoughts.

"Hmm?"

She stepped back. "You need to get home to Holly," she reminded him. "I'm sure she's confused by what she heard at the library."

She was throwing him out? After reeling him in, she was kicking him out?

He swallowed hard. "You're right. Holly is

probably waiting up for me." He stepped back and tripped over nothing. He righted himself quickly.

"Say hi for me."

"I will."

Gabrielle clasped her hands behind her back and grinned.

At that moment, he realized she'd played him. She'd deliberately seduced his senses, reminding him of their potent chemistry, all so he would be too consumed by her to worry about why they couldn't be together.

He met her gaze. "I'm on to you, you know."

"Moi?" She raised an eyebrow in fake innocence. "I don't know what you're talking about." But the smile pulling at her lips told him she was lying.

"Good night, Gabby," he said softly.

"'Night, Derek." She walked him to the door.

"Lock up behind me," he instructed.

She nodded. "I will."

He meant to reach for the door. He reached for her instead. Next thing he knew, she was in his arms, melting backward as he caught her in a hot, searing kiss. His tongue tangled with hers and a low, sexy sigh escaped from the back of her throat, driving him crazy.

It took everything he had to step away, keeping his hand on her back as she caught her balance.

"Sleep tight," he said. Then he walked out before he picked her up and carried her to bed.

He'd wanted to one-up her in her sensual game. A light, teasing moment to prove to both of them that he was in charge, that he might want her but he could still walk away.

Instead he'd learned a hard lesson. She was definitely the one with the upper hand.

GABRIELLE WOKE UP EARLY. She'd called Sharon the night before and asked if she wanted to take a ride into Boston for the day. Gabrielle needed to pick up clothes from her apartment. Despite the threats, she had decided to stick around her hometown for a little while longer.

Derek Corwin, watch out, Gabrielle thought wryly. But he wasn't her only mission. Talking to people about the Corwin Curse was.

Gabrielle stopped at the Dunkin' Donuts in town, a new addition to Main Street, and headed for Sharon's parents' place. She pulled up front just as her friend was putting letters in the mailbox at the end of the driveway.

Sharon waved. She pulled out a stack of mail, placed her envelopes inside, flipped the door closed and the flag up, before joining Gabrielle inside her car.

"Good morning," Sharon said, her mood upbeat.

"'Morning. Coffee?" Gabrielle asked, pointing to the cup in the passenger-seat holder.

"Love some. Thanks."

"It has milk and sugar, the way you like it."

Sharon took a sip. "Hot and good. Thanks!"

"No problem." Gabrielle pulled onto the street and they began the hour's drive.

"How are you doing?" Sharon asked. "Still upset over last night?"

Gabrielle brushed her hair out of her eyes, but the wind from the open convertible blew it right back. "I'm okay. Derek's father has always been crotchety. I didn't take it personally."

"You're a better person than me. I think I'd be devastated if Richard's family spoke to me that way."

Gabrielle nodded. "I'd probably be hurt if I didn't know how badly that curse affects the whole family." It was something she wanted to explore in more detail, for her book and for herself. "Know what I mean?"

"Hmm," Sharon said, sounding distracted.

Gabrielle glanced out of the corner of her eye. Sharon was opening a large manila envelope.

"What's that?" Gabrielle asked.

"I'm not sure. There was no return address." Sharon pulled out a photograph with a note clipped to it. "Oh, my God."

"What?"

"I'm going to be sick." Sharon laid her head against the window and shut her eyes.

Worried, Gabrielle pulled over, into the nearest side street. They were still fairly close to home.

She parked the car and turned to her friend. "What's going on?" She reached for the pictures, but Sharon smacked her hand on top of Gabrielle's. "Don't," she said in a hoarse voice.

"Then you tell me. What's got you so upset?"

Sharon met Gabrielle's gaze. "Remember Tony DeCarlo?"

"Your ex-boyfriend from college," Gabrielle said carefully, not wanting to stir up too many bad memories.

"Oh, please, just call it what it was. My big mistake. While I was blindly in love with him, he was in it for blackmail."

Gabrielle remembered. Tony had put something in Sharon's drink, drugged her then taken sexually explicit photographs that he'd threatened to turn over to the dean of the college and any magazine who'd take them unless she came up with one thousand dollars.

He'd hit up the wrong girl.

Sharon, though mortified, had gone to her father, who was an attorney. He'd hired a private investigator. It turned out that Tony DeCarlo had a history of being the perfect boyfriend until he'd drugged, photographed then blackmailed other women. Sharon hadn't been his first. She had, however, been the only one to press charges, putting Tony behind bars.

"I thought it was over. I thought all the photographs had been confiscated by the police." Her voice shook as hard as her hands as she lifted a grainy copy of a photograph. "The police obviously didn't find them all," she whispered. "Someone got hold of one and is threatening to turn it over to the newspaper unless I pay."

"Is it from Tony?" Gabrielle asked.

"There's no signature, but who else would have the old photos?"

"That son of a bitch," Gabrielle said, her temper rising. "He obviously didn't learn from his time in jail. He's still underestimating you. Do you want to drive straight to the police station?" Gabrielle relished the idea of turning this guy in.

Sharon shook her head. "Are you nuts? Do you know what these pictures would do to Richard's campaign?" She shivered at the prospect. "We live in a conservative small town. The only reason there wasn't a huge scandal all those years ago was because Tony pled to a lesser charge for reduced time in jail!"

"He'll get thrown right back in for resorting to extortion again." Gabrielle had been so proud of her friend for having the guts to tell her parents what had happened and for following through with pressing charges.

But Tony had taken that confident part of Sharon's personality with him when he'd been carted off to jail. The incident had changed Sharon from being a bubbly, outgoing person to little more than a shell of her former self. Gabrielle had talked her friend through many difficult, sleepless nights. Only lately, with the patience and love of Richard Stern, had the old Sharon begun to reemerge. It had showed up tonight when she'd defended Gabrielle at the library. Gabrielle shuddered to think what this would do to her friend's self-esteem.

She wouldn't let Sharon backpedal. "You can press charges again," she said, urging her friend to do the right thing.

"It's different now. I don't have just me to think about. I have Richard."

"Exactly, and he loves you for who you are."

Richard had grown up in Perkins, rivals to Stewart in football, basketball and other sports. Gabrielle and Sharon had seen Richard around a lot, considering he was Perkins's star basketball player. And they'd made sure he had seen them. So Richard knew the woman Sharon had been. And he seemed to love everything about her.

When Sharon remained silent, Gabrielle continued. "It's not like you haven't confided in Richard about what Tony did. He'll support you."

"He knows about my past, but he's also very traditional. He doesn't blame me, but he's never been interested in the sordid details." Sharon shivered as she spoke.

Gabrielle considered herself a decent judge of

character, and Richard seemed like one of the good guys. "I'm sure he just doesn't want to put you through the pain of reliving it," Gabrielle assured her friend.

"Or maybe the thought of it just disgusts him." Sharon ran her hands up and down her arms. "So far we've been lucky that nobody's dug up that old dirt on me. But if these photos get out, his political dreams will be ruined and I'll be to blame."

"Honey…"

Sharon's eyes filled with tears. "As much as it goes against what I believe in, I'll just have to pay whoever it is to keep this quiet."

"No!" Gabrielle slammed her hand against the steering wheel. "You can't give in to blackmail."

"Unless you have a solution that doesn't involve this photo and God knows how many more becoming public, I have no choice." Sharon smoothed out the paper with the note. "It says here that I should go to the Wave, a nightclub in Stewart, tomorrow night at eight. I'm to bring the money with me."

"How much does he want?"

"Five thousand dollars." She swallowed hard. "If it's Tony, he's raised his price."

Gabrielle narrowed her gaze. "That doesn't seem like all that much money these days, even with inflation," she said, trying for levity.

It worked. Sharon smiled. "I know, but that's his MO. Last time Tony only asked for a thousand.

He'd planned on stringing it out, asking for more each time. I'm sure he's got the same plan now. He'll keep me on edge by making me wonder if and when those photos will show up in the next day's paper." Her face had grown pale at the notion.

Something wasn't sitting right in Gabrielle's mind, but she couldn't put her finger on what was bothering her. "When did Tony get out of prison?"

Sharon shrugged. "I don't know that he did, but it has to be him, right? Nobody else would have the pictures but him."

"I don't know." She drummed her fingers on the steering wheel. "It seems odd that your old pictures would resurface around the same time I'm not so politely being asked to leave town," Gabrielle mused.

"You think the two things are related?" Sharon shifted in her seat, curling her knee beneath her so she faced Gabrielle.

"Yes. No. I don't know. It's just weird to have two separate threats against each of us going on at the same time." She paused. "What if Tony sold the pictures to someone?"

"Anything's possible."

"This stinks. Even if you pay, you can never be certain that you have all the pictures. This could drag on forever." Gabrielle turned and stared out the window, trying to come up with some way to help her friend.

They needed to track down Tony, but Gabrielle

didn't think her friend was up for that conversation just yet. Maybe after the shock wore off. In the meantime, she'd do some digging herself. Research was what she was good at, after all.

"Do you have the money?" Gabrielle asked.

"For this payment and maybe one more. I obviously can't afford to keep this up indefinitely. I just wish I hadn't been so stupid."

"Hey!" Gabrielle whipped around in her seat. "Do not blame yourself. You were drugged. It's not like you were a willing participant," she reminded Sharon.

With that, Gabrielle realized what had been bothering her. "You were a victim. Surely nobody will hold that against you or Richard. I say you call his bluff. Refuse to pay and ride out the scandal. Richard loves you. He'll stand by you and so will I." Gabrielle reached out and squeezed her friend's hand. "It's the least I can do for the woman who went toe to toe with Hank Corwin for me."

Sharon glanced out the window. "I think you're forgetting who Richard's opponent is. Mary Perkins won't hesitate to use this as ammunition to hurt Richard and convince people to vote for her."

Mary Perkins and that damned curse she wielded like a magic wand with the power to bend people to her will. Gabrielle decided the incumbent mayor would be high on her list of people to interview, if for no other reason than to dig into the psyche of someone willing to use other people's weaknesses against them.

"At least tell Richard what's going on so he won't be caught off guard if this leaks," Gabrielle suggested.

"No." Sharon swung back around. "Not yet. I need to go to the Wave tomorrow night and see what and whom I'm dealing with first." Sharon's voice shook at the idea, but with her decision made, she drew her shoulders up straighter.

"*Merde.* You are stubborn." Like Gabrielle herself, once Sharon set her mind on a course of action, like pressing charges against Tony years ago, nothing would deter her. At least some of her spunk remained, despite the fear.

Gabrielle cleared her throat. "Fine. If you insist on going to the Wave tomorrow with five thousand dollars, you aren't going alone. But we still need to go to Boston today because I don't have any clubbing clothes with me here." Gabrielle restarted the car.

Sharon blew out a relieved breath of air. "Thank you. You're the best. Now, just promise me you won't tell Richard about any of this."

Gabrielle frowned. She wasn't a fan of keeping secrets, but it wasn't her choice. "I won't tell him if you insist, but—"

"I do. So you promise?"

"Fine." She put both hands on the wheel. "I don't like it, but I promise not to tell Richard."

But that didn't mean she had to keep it to herself. Just like in the old days, when something serious happened, there was just one person Gabrielle wanted to turn to. One person she trusted with anything, one who she knew in her heart would help her with any problem.

Derek.

And not just because he'd been back in town long enough to know someone who could quietly help her find Tony. If she and Sharon were meeting a crazy man who'd drugged a number of women, taken nude photos of them and gone to prison for his actions, they weren't going alone.

She wanted a man by her side that she trusted.

She wanted Derek.

CHAPTER SIX

DEREK BURNED THE PANCAKES he'd made Holly for breakfast. He really couldn't cook and should have known better than to try. Back in the city, he'd lived on takeout.

Scraping the destroyed remains into Fred's dish, he glanced at his daughter. "Want me to try again?"

She shook her head and made a disgusted face. "Can I have cold cereal, Dad?"

He laughed. "Smart move."

"Yeah, I know. Even you can't ruin corn flakes." She climbed onto the counter and pulled out a cereal bowl. "Dad?"

"Hmm?" He poured the flakes from the box, then added milk and handed her a spoon.

"You promised to tell me about you and Gabrielle. That man said you dumped her. You said you didn't. So what's the real story?" she asked between slurping cereal and milk from a spoon.

He pinched the bridge of his nose, wondering how to explain adult behavior to a preteen. "We dated in high school and broke up before going away to college," he said, proud of his concise summary.

"Who broke up with who?"

"I broke up with her."

"Why?"

"I had my reasons. Finish your cereal. Grandpa's coming by to take you to feed the ducks at the pond. You want to be ready."

She glanced down and focused on eating what was left. "There. I finished my cereal. I'm just working on the milk." She picked up the bowl, clearly intending to drink it down in one gulp.

He shot her a warning look.

"Okay, okay." She retrieved the spoon and slowly sipped at the milk.

"That's better."

"Can Fred come with us to feed the ducks?" she asked.

"I don't see why not. Just talk to your grandfather."

She finished two more spoonfuls, then asked, "So what are you doing today?"

Boy, was she talkative this morning. "I'm going to get some work done here." He had clients in the city who had left messages he needed to return. He didn't need to go to the office he rented in town, though.

She finished her cereal with a last, loud slurp

and walked the bowl over to the sink. "Do you still like Gabrielle? 'Cause I really like her a lot."

He swallowed a groan. "Of course I like her."

"Will you marry her the way Mom married John?"

Derek's palms began to sweat. Suddenly, without warning, the front door creaked opened and Hank's voice bellowed throughout the house.

"Who wants to go feed the ducks?" he called out to announce his presence.

"I do!" Holly swiveled around and ran into the other room.

Derek followed her out.

"Can we bring Fred? Please?" Holly asked her grandfather, questions of marriage and Gabrielle temporarily forgotten.

Bullet dodged, at least for the moment, Derek was grateful for his father's interruption. "Hey, Dad," he said, joining them by the front door.

"Grandpa said Fred can come because he's a lazy old bastard who'd chase his tail before he'd worry about running after a duck," Holly said, pleased both with her grandfather's answer and herself for getting to repeat the curse word without reprimand.

Derek scowled. "Can you both watch your language?" He turned to his daughter. "Holly, go put on some sunscreen and make sure you take your oldest sneakers. Duck poop and dog poop are hard to get out."

"Will do!" She ran upstairs to the loft, giving Derek some time with his father.

"I need to talk to you before she comes back down," he said immediately.

"Yeah, yeah. I already apologized to you for my behavior last night. Isn't that enough?" Hank didn't meet Derek's gaze, looking down at his feet instead.

At least the older man was contrite, even if he hid it behind his bluster.

"An apology to Gabrielle next time you see her would be even better. But I have an important question for you right now. When you walked out in the middle of her speech, where did you go?" Derek watched his father carefully for signs of dishonesty.

His father raised both eyebrows, clearly surprised at the question. "I told you when you got home last night. I went to the john. Why are you asking?"

Derek walked to the sofa in the family room and Hank followed.

"Someone deliberately keyed Gabrielle's car during her talk. Someone also put a threatening letter under her windshield yesterday afternoon. It sure looks as if somebody didn't want her to speak about curses," he said, pointedly looking at his father.

"Hey, I resent the implication. I've got a temper but I'd never threaten a lady."

Derek didn't bring up the shotgun Hank had planned to take to the library. He wanted to believe his father. Besides, he couldn't see Hank deliberately destroying someone's property or threatening anyone.

"Just watch yourself," Derek warned him. "If anyone but me had seen you with that gun, you'd be answering to someone other than me—someone with a badge."

"You need to show some faith in your own family. Holly, are you coming?" Hank called upstairs.

She ran down the stairs and rounded the corner, a baseball cap on her head and another in her hand.

"Is that for me?" Hank asked.

"No, it's for Fred." She walked over to the oversize sausage roll they called a dog and plopped the cap down on his head.

Derek laughed. "How do you expect him to see where he's going?"

"He has me, silly! Ready, Grandpa!" She clipped Fred's leash on just like Derek had taught her and grabbed Hank's hand.

Together they walked out, Fred lumbering along with them.

Alone, Derek let out a sigh and turned back toward the kitchen. He'd left the burned pan soaking and he needed to try to clean it, but the telephone rang, interrupting him.

"Hello?"

"Derek?" Gabrielle asked in that breathless way she had.

Just hearing her voice sent tremors of awareness rocketing through him. "Hey there." He tightened his grip on the receiver.

"I only have a minute," she said, talking low. "I came home to pick up a few things and Sharon's in the other room. I need to see you tonight. It's important."

He didn't hesitate. "Sure. Do you want to come here?"

"I don't want Holly to hear what I have to say. Could you come by my room? Say around seven?"

"Sure thing. Can you give me a clue what it's about?"

She laughed. "Wish I could, but you'll have to wait until tonight. It's serious, though."

His body tensed immediately. "Did you receive another threat?"

"Not exactly. I promise I'll explain everything when I see you, okay? Hang on."

He heard her say something to Sharon in the other room.

"I'm back. Oh, one more thing. Can we get dinner? There's nothing to eat at Mrs. Rhodes's inn and I'll be *starving*," she said, drawing out the word.

"Not a problem."

"Thanks!" She disconnected the line.

Dinner with Gabrielle tonight.

He'd heard the urgency in her voice, so he knew

she had something big on her mind. But he'd also been intimately acquainted with the seductress side of Gabrielle and he was certain dinner had nothing to do with her needing to speak to him—and everything to do with a need of another kind.

DEREK ARRIVED AT GABRIELLE'S room to find her waiting with a picnic basket in hand. He decided not to question her intentions and drove them in his SUV to the public beach as she'd asked. Although there were still people enjoying the end of the day, they managed to find a quiet spot.

From the minute he'd picked her up, he couldn't tear his eyes off the strapless sundress she wore—or rather the bare skin she revealed. She was more tanned than he'd realized, and her shoulders glistened beneath the setting sun. Despite all his good intentions, he was all wrapped up in her again. He was finding it damned hard to say he minded.

They ate the chicken-salad sandwiches she'd picked up at the café in town and made small talk.

Once they'd finished, he asked, "So what did you need to talk to me about?"

At the same time, she said, "I really need to talk to you."

They both laughed.

"Great minds think alike." She wiped her mouth and helped him put the remnants of the food and garbage back into the basket. "There was a time we used to finish each other's sentences." She met his gaze as if daring him to remember.

He did.

"Anyway, I thought you should finish eating first because this situation isn't pretty. I didn't want you to lose your appetite." Then Gabrielle launched into a description of Sharon's past, her unsavory ex-boyfriend, the pornographic pictures and how Sharon had thought it was all behind her. Then Gabrielle finished by explaining that the photographs had resurfaced and Sharon was being blackmailed.

He clenched his jaw, his blood boiling. "What kind of scumbag does that to a woman?"

"Beats the hell out of me," she muttered. "But not only does Sharon refuse to tell her fiancé about the blackmail but she's insisting on dealing with this guy herself." Gabrielle's voice rose in pitch. "She's going to the Wave tomorrow night to exchange money for photos, if you can believe that!"

"I can't."

"Well, I said I'd go with her." She spoke softly, probably hoping he'd miss that last part.

His hearing was better than she'd hoped. "The hell you are. You two have no business handling a blackmailing bastard by yourselves."

Gabrielle drew a deep breath. "Listen, friends don't let friends get blackmailed alone. But you're right. We shouldn't go by ourselves. That's why I'd like you to come for backup." She patted his cheek with her palm.

"You're just trying to stroke my ego so I'll forget I'm upset with this whole situation."

"Maybe I am." She grinned. "And you're much more astute than I gave you credit for. You have to know I can't let her handle this alone." She paused and arched her brows at him. "But I have another idea, though."

He kicked at the sand with his heel. "I'm listening."

"I thought you and I could do some investigating tomorrow, look up her old boyfriend. Maybe we can head this off. What do you say?" Her eyes were wide and imploring, yet excited at the prospect of doing some digging.

"My cousin Mike's a cop in Boston. I'll ask him to see what he can find out about Tony DeCarlo."

"Excellent idea!" She wrapped him in her arms. "Thank you!" She tipped her head back and met his gaze.

Her eyes darkened immediately.

His thoughts turned to long hot kisses. But now he was preoccupied with her safety, as well. The fact that Sharon was being blackmailed was bad enough. But Derek hadn't forgotten about Gabrielle's two threatening incidents, either. He wanted to get to the bottom of everything going on, but since Sharon's threat was more imminent, he'd start there.

"I really appreciate your help." Gabrielle released her hold and settled back onto the blanket.

"Not a problem."

"Hey." She reached out and smoothed his forehead with her hand. "Relax, okay? I didn't want to put you in a bad mood and ruin the whole night, but it was important enough to tell you about."

He nodded. "I'm glad you trusted me," he said gruffly.

She smiled. "I do. Now, let's change the subject."

He exhaled hard. "That's a good idea."

"So how much of a grilling did Holly give you about us?" Gabrielle asked, doing a one-eighty.

Reminded of his precocious daughter, he laughed. "*Grilling* is a good word for it. She's a master interrogator. I told her we dated in high school and broke up before college."

"And she accepted that without asking anything else?" Gabrielle stretched her legs out in front of her and wiggled her toenails, which were painted a hot pink.

"Oh, she asked for details, all right. She asked if I was going to marry you the way her mother had married John."

Gabrielle jerked her head toward him, her eyes open wide.

Now, whatever had possessed him to admit such a thing?

"What did you tell her?" she asked.

"Nothing. She got distracted before I had to answer."

"Derek?"

"Hmm?"

"What would you have told her? If she hadn't been distracted?"

He propped his hands behind him and leaned back, settling in for an honest discussion. "I would have told her that I left you, but it hadn't been easy."

"Then why did you do it?" She glanced out over the ocean, her expression sad.

A warm breeze blew her hair back and his fingers itched to run through the silky strands, but he refrained, closing his fist instead. "You know why. I couldn't let it touch you," he said, referring to the curse.

Gabrielle bit on the inside of her cheek to keep from tossing back a sarcastic reply. She knew from experience if she baited Derek, he'd withdraw. And she needed to hear what he had to say.

"Tell me about Holly's mom." She couldn't bring herself to call her his ex-wife.

"She's a good woman who deserved better than me." He groaned. "I already told you how we ended up together."

A group of kids ran by their area of the beach, laughing and talking loudly.

He waited before he continued.

He met Gabrielle's gaze, the pain in his eyes as great as the one in her heart. "Go on," she said.

"That's where I started to think about the curse and how it related to my future. I loved you, so I broke up with you to protect you from the fallout that all men and the women they loved in my family have suffered. But I didn't love Marlene." He never broke eye contact with her. "Not the way I loved you."

He'd said it the other night, but hearing it now caused her breath to catch in her throat and her heart thudded heavily in her chest. As bad as she felt for the other woman, this was exactly what she'd always needed to believe. That he'd never been able to move past loving her, just as she'd never been able to fully commit to someone else.

He needed to know she'd felt the same way. "Derek—"

He placed his hand over her mouth. His touch was electric. Her body tingled and every nerve ending came alive.

"Let me finish explaining first."

She nodded.

"After the shock of Marlene's pregnancy wore off, of course I offered to marry her."

"It was the gentlemanly thing to do."

He inclined his head and looked up at the sky. "That wasn't the only reason. I realized that Marlene was giving me a chance to have a future—a wife, a family."

All the things she'd wanted with him, Gabrielle thought, but said nothing. What good would it do now? They could only move forward from here.

"It might not have been the situation I would have chosen, but that's what made it so perfect. I thought that since I cared about her but wasn't in love with her, the curse wouldn't ever come into play. The wording specifically said—*Any Corwin male who falls in love would be destined to lose his love and his fortune.* Because I didn't love Marlene, I thought I was safe." He exhaled hard. "I was wrong."

Gabrielle's heart picked up speed. This was her chance to question the curse, the opportunity she'd been waiting for to change Derek's way of thinking.

She scrambled to her knees and inched closer to him. "Derek, listen to me. I need you to think," she said, knowing her future depended on his reaction to her words. "Tell me why your marriage broke up and how you think it was because of some ancient curse." She intentionally sounded as sarcastic as she felt.

"Gabby, I know the curse isn't rational. But in my family history, facts are facts. And I watched it play out again in my own life."

"How?"

"Marlene came from a family that didn't have a lot of money. Her father was a solid working guy un-til he died when Marlene was in junior high. Her mother was an Italian woman who stayed home to take care of the kids, but after her husband passed away, she had to get a job as a housekeeper to make ends meet. Marlene was the first one to go to college. Getting pregnant wasn't in her plans, but we agreed to keep the baby and make it work between us. I tried." He sounded tired and weary, as if relating an old story he could no longer quite believe.

She placed her hand over his. "I'm sure you did everything you could to stay together for Holly's sake."

He nodded. "I worked damned hard to make enough money to stem Marlene's childhood insecurities about being poor. But she didn't understand about the long hours I had to put in. And the more strained things got at home, the harder I worked. By the time we divorced, there was nothing left of the friendship we'd shared." He shook his head, his frustration obvious.

Gabrielle squeezed his hand tighter. "Did you ever think it was something as simple as two people who aren't in love might not be able to make a marriage work?"

"I sure did. Until I took a huge hit financially. I'd worked my way up at a large securities firm. I did well, made big money for my clients and for myself. Later, I began investing capital in companies I thought were going to do well. Start-ups like JetBlue Airlines among others. Around the same time as my divorce, I put a large chunk of cash into what was supposed to be a sure thing." He shook his head and laughed wryly. "That's when I learned there's no such thing."

As Gabrielle listened to him, her frustration grew. "It would have happened, anyway! A financial miscalculation has nothing to do with a curse. Don't you see how each incident—your divorce, your money problems—they're not related. There's a logical, rational explanation for each!"

He remained silent so she continued. "Let's say for the sake of argument, there is such a thing as a curse. It kicks in if you fall in love. But you weren't in love with Marlene. No love, no curse!" she yelled at him.

"Well, if things got that bad with Marlene, I sure as hell am not going to take that chance with you!" His brown eyes flashed with determination.

But she was equally determined to make her point. "Well, I'm not going to give you a choice." She settled into his lap, wrapped her arms around his neck, pulled him close and planted a warm, hot kiss on his lips.

CHAPTER SEVEN

DEREK HAD NEVER BEEN able to win an argument with a determined Gabrielle. And the woman now straddling his lap was equally strong in her resolution to come out on top. Pun intended. Although, he wasn't laughing. He was completely, thoroughly aroused.

Her lips were hot and seductive as she made her point. A point he couldn't remember, thanks to the pulsing in his groin and the desire flooding his body. He couldn't focus on anything except the delicious woman seducing him on the beach, so he did what any sane man would do.

He kissed her back. Slid his hands up the bare skin on her back and kneaded her soft flesh, all the while deepening the kiss. He slid his tongue around her mouth, losing himself in sensation. Need surrounded him.

A haze of pure enjoyment rushed over him when suddenly, she cupped her hands around his face and slowly ended the kiss.

He breathed out hard.

"I missed this," she said softly, her gaze meeting his. "I missed you."

"Yeah. Me, too." More than he'd wanted to admit.

Even now, the tremors in his body continued, along with the sound of desire filling his ears. Of course, it could be the ocean behind him, but he chose to believe Gabrielle's effect on him was that potent.

"What are we going to do about it?" She wiggled her hips against him, and though her dress covered all his sins, her eyes darkened, telling him she felt him grow hard between her thighs.

She certainly wasn't going to accept "nothing" as an answer.

"We need closure," she said.

"I agree." He couldn't just let her walk out of his life. Not yet. He needed more.

She raised her eyebrows in surprise. "You do, huh?" Her lips curved upward in a pleased and somewhat smug smile.

For once they were on the same page.

"Excuse me," a stranger said.

Startled, both he and Gabrielle jerked their gaze upward.

A woman stood over them. "This isn't a private beach. And it's not the place for public displays of affection," she said, toe tapping in disapproval. "I suggest you get a room." She sniffed and strode off, her nose in the air.

"I'm mortified," Gabrielle said, her voice rising in horror.

Derek couldn't help but laugh. "Relax. She's a stick-in-the-mud. We're off in our own corner, not bothering anyone."

Gabrielle bit down on her lower lip. "Well, still. There are kids around. You wouldn't want Holly coming across a couple doing what we just did on a public beach." She delicately climbed off him, careful, he noticed, not to look at the lingering evidence of his arousal bulging in his jeans.

"Good point." He pulled her toward him again and placed a brief kiss on the tip of her nose. "It's just that you can make me forget everything but you."

She grinned and rose to her feet.

He followed, straightening his clothes and thinking about Gabrielle's effect on him. Decision made, he had no choice. He was finished denying the attraction. Nothing in the curse prohibited a short-term affair.

Closure, as Gabrielle had said.

Together they packed up the blanket and basket, when suddenly he turned and faced her again. He wrapped his arm around her waist, but instead of letting himself get caught up in another embrace, he turned her around and playfully swatted her behind.

"No more PDA," he said, laughing. "Let's get our things and get moving." He grabbed the basket while she picked up the blanket and they started up the beach.

He couldn't help but think about the implications of their talk as he walked to his SUV. Tonight had changed the dynamics between himself and Gabrielle. He'd agreed to find closure between them. And considering he knew how Gabrielle's mind worked, he had no doubt private displays of affection were going to play a large part of that closure.

DEREK WOKE UP EARLY the next morning and was on the phone with his cousin Mike by nine. Derek was deliberately vague with his story, omitting the fact that Sharon was being blackmailed. He didn't want to put Mike in a position where he had to act, nor did Derek want to betray Gabrielle and Sharon's confidence. Mike was happy to dig up information, but he warned Derek to be careful.

A short while later, Mike called back and Derek had some solid facts. Sharon's ex, Tony DeCarlo, was out of jail and living in a small suburb outside of Boston. As far as Mike could tell, Mr. DeCarlo was a model citizen—or he just hadn't been caught.

Although Derek would have liked to pay the man a visit by himself, he wasn't about to risk going solo and facing Gabrielle's wrath. He could handle her anger, but if she stopped trusting him, she'd go off on her own next time.

Gabrielle seemed to appreciate his efforts—she

was chatty and upbeat the entire trip. He didn't want to take her expensive convertible, which was an attention-getter, and so he drove his SUV, pulling up to the address Mike had given him, a small rented garden apartment in a surprisingly nice area. Gabrielle immediately jumped out of the truck.

"Hey, wait up." He caught up to her on the walkway. "Let me do the talking, okay?"

She shook her head. "No, it's not okay. I have a few questions for him and I'm going to ask them." She strode ahead of Derek and headed for the first-floor apartment, ringing the bell before he joined her.

"Who is it?" a male voice called out from behind the door.

"A friend of a friend," Gabrielle said.

Derek folded his arms across his chest, resigned to letting her handle things and acting as backup if she needed it. Obviously she wasn't going to give him a choice.

The door opened halfway. "What friend?"

Gabrielle recognized the man from old photos Sharon had sent her while in college—before her new boyfriend had turned into a nightmare. "Hi, Tony?"

"Who wants to know?"

"Me. I'm a friend of someone you used to date. I believe you remember Sharon Merchant?" Gabrielle asked in a sweet voice.

Tony's wary expression turned dark. "I don't have anything to say to Sharon or to you." He started to shut the door but Derek slipped his sneakered foot inside.

"That's no way to treat a lady, buddy. At least hear her out."

Gabrielle shot Derek a grateful look. "How've you been, Tony?"

"Busy. I work and I come home. There's no time for chitchat."

"So why aren't you at work now?" According to Derek's cousin, Tony had been stocking shelves at the local supermarket. He had positive employment reviews and no complaints against him.

"It's my day off. What's it to you?"

She shrugged. "Just curious. This is a nice apartment. Mind if I ask how you afford it? I mean, stocking shelves doesn't pay that well."

"My sister lives with me and shares the rent. Again, what's it to you?"

"Some of those pictures you took of my friend resurfaced."

His face turned pale. "I had nothing to do with it!"

"So you say," Derek said, stepping forward. "But she received a package that has your MO. It's hard to believe someone else is behind it."

"Believe what you want, but it wasn't me. You think I'd risk going back to jail?" he asked incredulously. "No way, man."

Gabrielle narrowed her gaze. "Did you keep extra copies of the pictures?"

He shook his head. "The cops took them all." He stepped outside, joining them as if he had nothing to hide. "Look, I was young and stupid. I saw a quick way to make money by taking advantage of naive women. And I paid for it. That part of my life was over a long time ago."

Gabrielle glanced at Derek, silently asking what he thought.

"If you don't believe me, that's your problem. But you're not going to pin this on me." He tipped his head to one side. "Are we finished now?"

"For now," Derek said.

Gabrielle nodded. "Just don't leave town," she said, turning her back on the other man and walking away.

Derek jogged after her. "Just don't leave town? What kind of bad TV cop language was that?"

"So sue me. It was all I could think of on short notice." She strode to the vehicle, her hair swaying as she moved. "God, that was useless."

Derek shook his head. "Maybe not. He'll be nervous now. If he's behind it, he might make a mistake."

"Do you think he's the one blackmailing Sharon?"

Derek leaned against his car. "I have no idea. I guess we'll know more after we hit the Wave tonight."

"Speaking of the Wave, will you dance with me tonight?" she asked, her eyes sparkling with anticipation.

"I'm surprised you'd want to. The last time we danced together—"

"We had fun at the prom, didn't we?"

He'd bet Gabrielle deliberately cut him off before he could discuss their last night together—and the horrible way things had ended the next day.

"We did." He still remembered picking her up at her parents' house. She came down the stairs wearing a gorgeous off-white ruffled dress that bared one shoulder and draped her curves perfectly.

He hadn't gone to the prom that night knowing he was going to break up with her right afterward. As a result, they'd enjoyed a very special evening. The next day, a letter he'd sent to his birth mother had been returned to him, unread and marked Return to Sender. Obviously, she hadn't wanted to hear from him.

That was when he'd decided he had to insulate himself and the people he loved from the pain associated with the curse. Breaking up with Gabrielle had seemed like the only way to protect both of them from imminent future anguish.

"Well, I want to dance tonight, so be ready," she said, obviously not thinking about what had happened after the prom.

"You got it," he said. If she could put it behind her,

then so should he. "What are you doing this afternoon? I'm taking Holly swimming. Want to come?"

"I'd love to. Unfortunately, I promised Sharon I'd come by and keep her calm this afternoon. She'll be climbing the walls waiting for tonight. Although I can't imagine this guy showing up now that we've confronted him." Gabrielle glanced back toward the apartment building.

Derek shrugged. "He's not just going to drop his plan. Let's take it one step at a time, okay?"

"Okay."

"So how about you invite Sharon? There's nothing like some sun, sand and preteen chatter to get her mind off her problems."

"Good idea!"

Later that afternoon, he was forced to rethink the wisdom of his invitation when he caught sight of Gabrielle in a sleek one-piece bathing suit, looking sexier than any woman had a right to. With his daughter around, he had to keep his hands to himself, and he realized he'd signed up for an afternoon of pure torture. And he had only himself to blame.

GABRIELLE HAD PROPOSED THEY arrive early at the Wave so her friend could have a drink or two to relax. Sharon was a basket case, and Gabrielle didn't blame her. She'd told Sharon that they had found and questioned Tony DeCarlo earlier this afternoon. Like Gabrielle, Sharon was disappointed they hadn't found out anything and was skeptical about Tony's supposed change for the better. Because if he was telling the truth, somebody else was blackmailing Sharon. And that was an even more frightening concept.

While they waited for Derek to arrive, Gabrielle intended to question the club's owner, George Saybrook. Known as Curious George—as a bartender, he'd asked questions instead of dispensing advice—George knew everything about everyone in Perkins and Stewart. Gabrielle had never met George, but his reputation preceded him.

According to Sharon, that hadn't changed. Neither had the fact that people from both towns gave Curious George's bar their business. Then a few years ago, old George had a heart attack and his son, Seth, had taken over. Based on what Sharon had told her this afternoon, Seth had gone to college, majored in marketing, returned home and immediately renovated the old bar into a nightclub that attracted a younger, hip crowd. But old George still worked the bar, and before Derek showed up, Gabrielle wanted to talk to George about the past. Curses, in particular.

With Sharon by her side, Gabrielle sidled up to the bar and luckily they snagged two seats.

George, whom Gabrielle had never met, immediately noticed two new patrons and walked over.

Despite his cartoon nickname, Curious George was a fine-looking man. Tall and distinguished-looking, at seventy-five George had a full head of white hair and a bright smile. Whether or not the teeth were his own, that was his secret to keep.

"Sharon, how are you and that politician fiancé of yours?" he asked.

"We're doing great, George. Are you still spreading the word to vote for Richard?" Sharon asked.

He nodded. "You betcha. Can't wait to oust the old biddy," he said, laughing. "So who's your friend?" He eyed Gabrielle with his legendary curious stare.

"Gabrielle Donovan, meet George Saybrook, George, my closest friend, Gabrielle," Sharon said.

Gabrielle shook his weathered hand. "Nice to meet you."

"The pleasure's all mine. So what can I get you ladies?"

"A cosmopolitan, please," Sharon said.

"A sour-apple martini for me," Gabrielle said.

He picked up two glasses. "That's what I like about serving women. You challenge my mixing skills more than a beer-drinking guy does."

Gabrielle laughed.

Instead of working on their drinks, George lingered to talk. "I recognize your name," he said to Gabrielle. "You're the author. I heard you gave quite a speech at the library the other night," he added. "It's the talk of the town."

"Which town? Perkins or Stewart?" Gabrielle asked.

"Both. My bar doesn't discriminate." He laughed and turned to mix their drinks.

"I think he means my nightclub," George's son, Seth, said, joining his father by the soda fountain. "Hi, ladies." He nodded at them both.

While Sharon repeated the introductions, Gabrielle compared father and son. They shared height and breadth in their shoulders, but Seth's hair was an inky-black, giving Gabrielle an idea of how handsome George must have been in his youth.

"A pleasure to meet you," Seth said to Gabrielle. "Welcome to my establishment."

"Make sure you don't listen to anything my boy says. He forgets who owns this joint, the bar and the land beneath," George spoke proudly.

But since he looked at his son with pride in his eyes, Gabrielle knew there was nothing but good humor behind the words.

"And he forgets it's the club paying the bills and not the old bar," Seth joked as he put his arm around his father's shoulders. "Pop, why don't you take the night off? Go out and enjoy yourself for once."

Gabrielle had just turned eighteen when she'd left for college. She'd never come to the bar, but everyone knew that George's wife had passed away when Seth was just a little boy. George hadn't remarried and he'd raised his son by himself, moving from their house to a large apartment above the bar where he could keep an eye on his child and his business at the same time.

"This is my enjoyment." He placed the glasses in front of the women. "One cosmopolitan for Sharon and a sour-apple martini for the author."

"Thank you," Gabrielle murmured. She'd have bet George was too preoccupied talking to remember what they'd ordered, not to mention who'd ordered what. She'd have lost.

"I'm not going anywhere tonight," George said to Seth. "Where else can I spend time with beautiful young women like these two? Even if one of them is awfully quiet." George settled his gaze on Sharon.

Lost in thought, Sharon didn't reply. She probably hadn't even heard the conversation going on around her. Not that Gabrielle blamed her for being distracted.

"She has a lot on her mind, don't you, Sharon?" Gabrielle nudged her friend.

Sharon jumped, obviously startled. "Oh, right. My wedding. I have this ongoing list in my head and I just can't seem to concentrate on anything these days." She gave a smile, one Gabrielle recognized as forced. "At least I have until after the election."

"Here. Take your drink. I'm sure it'll help you relax," Gabrielle said.

Sharon accepted the glass and shot her friend a grateful nod. "Thank you. I'm going to call Richard," she said, pivoting away from Gabrielle as she pulled out her cell phone.

"No problem." Gabrielle squeezed her friend's shoulder before turning back to George and Seth. "Would you mind if I ask you some questions about things going on around town, George?"

Something at the other end of the bar caught Seth's interest and his gaze wandered. "Whatever it is, Dad will be happy to indulge your interest," he said to Gabrielle, sounding distracted. "I hope you won't be insulted if I go make sure the other customers are happy. I'm sure I've heard whatever story he ends up telling you at least a hundred times." He winked at Gabrielle. "He's all yours."

"That I am, beautiful. What can I do for you?" George asked.

She lifted her glass for a sip of her martini. The sour taste filled her mouth. "I don't know if you heard the subject of my next book—"

"Of course I did. The Corwin Curse!" George said, a little too loudly.

Gabrielle winced, glad Derek wasn't there to hear. She drew a deep breath. "Since you know everyone, I thought I'd ask you about the families involved."

George nodded. "You've come to the right place."

"I was thinking about starting with the recent past." The rest she could look up at the library or even on the Internet if any records of the curse had been kept. "Tell me what you know of the current Mary Perkins."

Gabrielle already had personal knowledge of the Corwins, and what she didn't know, she hoped Derek would share. Otherwise, she'd have to question his father and his uncles. And though she'd always heard Thomas was a reasonable man, everyone knew Edward was an unstable recluse living on the outskirts of town. And since Hank had been polishing a gun, at least according to Holly, Gabrielle didn't think he'd be quick to answer her questions.

"So, you want to know about Mayor Mary Perkins…" George leaned closer to Gabrielle. "That woman's one nasty piece of work. Not that she'd give you that impression if you met her. No, ma'am. In public, she's so sweet, butter wouldn't melt in her mouth, but in private?" He whistled through his teeth.

"What's going on?" Sharon whipped her head around to see where the noise had come from.

Gabrielle laughed. "Go back to spacing out. I'll be finished in a few minutes."

Sharon glanced at the door. "How will I even recognize the guy if he walks in?" she asked.

Gabrielle patted her hand. They'd discussed this all afternoon and neither woman had come up with any solid answer. They'd just have to see how the evening went.

Gabrielle turned back to George. "Actually, I met Mary the other night. She attended the lecture at the library."

"And? What was your impression?"

"She was extremely polite. She even brought a book for me to sign. She didn't seem upset by the fact that I was discussing something so personal to her family."

"That's Mary, all right. Saying one thing, plotting another," George said. "Watch your back."

"Dad, I'm not sure you should be telling tales." Seth had come back to check on them.

"They're only tales if they aren't true. I'm giving her facts and you know it." George waved a hand, dismissing his son's concerns before turning back to Gabrielle.

"If Seth doesn't want you talking about her—"

"What I want and what Dad does have never been the same thing," Seth said.

George laughed. "Go back to mixing drinks," he said to his son. "Now, where were we? Oh, yes. There's one word to describe Mary's attitude," he said in a low voice. "Entitlement." He shook his head. "Never seen anything like it."

Gabrielle took a sip of her drink and listened. George was a gold mine of information.

"Here's an example of what I'm talking about. Every year Mary comes into my bar and requests the use of the back room for her weekly staff meeting. She says she likes to keep morale high among her workers by feeding them. That's a crock, though." He shook his head. "More like she wants to keep an eye on 'em after hours and eavesdrop while they talk. Anyway, she always comes in like she owns the place. Then, sweet as sugar, she says that since I want to show town loyalty, she's sure I won't mind giving her use of the room. Giving." He slammed his hand against the wooden bar. "Like I wasn't earning a living for myself and my son."

Gabrielle leaned forward on her elbows, closer to the other man. "So how do you handle her?"

"I tell her the fee for the room and the other costs. She reminds me that karma won't look kindly on me and I wave her on her way. But I own this land and always have. She can't do anything to me or my family, so I'm not scared of her. Wish I could say the same for some others." He glanced at Seth, who spoke to the patron a few bar stools down from Gabrielle, then leaned closer. "But Seth gave in and damned if she doesn't come here weekly. For free." He scowled.

Interesting, Gabrielle thought. "Did Seth ever say why?" she asked softly.

George nodded. "He says it pays to do favors for people in high places. I don't agree. He's just caving like everybody else. For people who rent instead of own their homes? There's a strong likelihood Mary's family owns the real estate, so they cave in to whatever she asks. Miller's Pharmacy? It was forced to close their doors just last year. A big-brand joint opened up not one month later."

Gabrielle ran her finger over the rim of her drink, thinking about the situation, wondering if George was giving Mary's power too much credit. "Unfortunately, a lot of mom-and-pop businesses aren't making it anymore."

George shook his head, dismissing the notion. "That may be true in some areas, but it's different around here. A big chain came sniffing around and the Millers told them to take a hike. It's not about money. Miller's was a family-run business and had been for generations. They didn't want to sell. Next thing you know, the landlord invokes some clause in their lease to increase their rent." He snapped his fingers in the air. "In no time the Millers are gone. Mom and Pop Miller are out, Big Name is in."

"And Mary Perkins owns the land?" Gabrielle guessed.

"A corporation owns the land. I bet a search of the records would show the Perkins family owns the corporation, but nobody looked. Nothing illegal was done. Immoral? You betcha. But Mary pulled some fancy PR by giving Mrs. Miller a clerical job in the mayor's office and CVS hired Mr. Miller as their manager."

"You're telling tales," Seth chimed in.

Gabrielle hadn't realized Seth had still been listening. "Some things are fact. Others are just hunches. There's nothing wrong with him answering my questions," she said, defending George. She glanced at the older man and lowered her voice. "But we can drop it since it makes Seth uncomfortable."

George winked at her. "Well, as much as I enjoy talking to you, *he* signs the checks." George gestured to his son with his elbow. "I'd better get busy with other customers," he said aloud. Then he added more quietly, "But if you want any more 'hunches,' you know where to find me."

Gabrielle smiled. "Thank you so much, George. You've been a huge help."

He inclined his head. "Good luck with your book."

"Thank you," she said. But her mind was already focused on what came next tonight.

She placed a hand on Sharon's shoulder. Next up, they'd deal with the blackmailer.

Then if all went well, the night was about to belong to Gabrielle and Derek.

CHAPTER EIGHT

THE BLUE NEON LIGHTS surrounding the dance floor matched the aqua-blue of the Wave's logo and decor. From the beat of the music to the welcome sign over the bar, everything at the Wave was customer friendly. Everything except their reason for being there, Sharon thought.

She'd sat beside Gabrielle and half listened as she'd questioned George and then some of the cocktail staff about Mary Perkins and their feelings on old curses. Sharon couldn't help her friend. She couldn't think about anything but those photographs and a time in her life she thought she'd put behind her forever. That, and what would happen if those pictures became public.

Because they'd arrived so early, she and Gabrielle had been able to snag an empty table with a good view of the front door and the bar.

For the umpteenth time, Sharon glanced at her watch.

Gabrielle treated her to an understanding smile.

"Within half an hour, we'll know something," Gabrielle assured her.

"Right." She nodded and began drumming her fingers against the tabletop.

"You know, it isn't too late to call the police in on this," Gabrielle whispered.

"No!" Telling the police wasn't any different than making the photos public. Sharon knew that from previous experience.

"Then at least tell Richard."

"I can't." Sharon glanced down.

Every time Richard mentioned how good she was for him or for his campaign, her heart did a little flip. She didn't want to disappoint him and she definitely didn't want to ruin his political chances.

"What's going on? Is this about more than his campaign?" Gabrielle asked. "Come on. It's me. You can tell me anything." Gabrielle placed her hand over Sharon's. She found the warmth comforting.

Sharon drew in a deep breath. "Richard loves me and accepts me for who I am and he knows what happened with Tony."

"But?"

"He's…uptight, you know?"

Gabrielle raised her eyebrows. "Sexually?"

"It's hard to explain. He's such a good man. He's sweet and gentle." Her throat filled up as she spoke about the man she was supposed to marry.

After Tony, she'd felt so stupid, so dirty. Some

therapy and a solid family had brought her pretty far, but her relationship with Richard had helped heal her the rest of the way. He treated her like a china doll he wanted to love and protect forever. She was so afraid of losing him and the life they planned together.

"Those are all good things about Richard. I've seen you two together. He obviously adores you. He isn't going to hold something he already knew about against you." Gabrielle squeezed Sharon's hand tighter.

"It's one thing for him to know a man I trusted took advantage of me," she whispered. "It's another for him to see it firsthand. Especially for a man who is as conservative as Richard. I'm afraid he'll never look at me the same way again." Sharon's voice caught. Despite her best efforts, a tear fell and she brushed it away with the back of her hand.

"I really don't think you're giving Richard enough credit. A man who loves you as much as he does will do anything to keep you."

Sharon shook her head and laughed. "You're a good friend." She inhaled a shaky breath. "Listen, let's get through tonight and I'll think about telling Richard. Okay?"

Gabrielle nodded with a short jerk of her head. "Okay."

"Hey, ladies, you're both looking exceptionally

beautiful tonight," Derek said as he strode up to their table.

Despite her position facing the front door, Sharon had been so engrossed in conversation, she hadn't even seen Derek come in.

"What are you doing here?" Realization dawned and Sharon looked from Derek to Gabrielle. "You promised to keep this between us," Sharon said, feeling betrayed.

Gabrielle's cheeks flushed red. "No, I promised to keep it from Richard. I never said I wouldn't tell Derek."

Sharon closed her eyes and shook her head.

"Come on. Don't tell me you aren't more comfortable knowing we have backup in case it's necessary," Gabrielle said, her voice close to Sharon's ear.

She exhaled slowly and forced herself to think. "You're right," she said at last. "I feel better knowing we're not alone," she admitted. She lifted her head and faced her friends.

Derek placed his hand on the back of her chair and leaned in close. "Your secret's safe with me. And so are you." Since there were no empty chairs, he stood beside Gabrielle and gestured to the cocktail waitress weaving between tables and crowds. "We'll get you through this," Derek promised her.

She wanted to believe him.

"Ladies? Drinks?" Derek asked.

"I'm fine." Sharon pointed to the half-empty

glass on the table. It was already watered down from the ice and she wasn't interested in another. She just wanted this night to be over with.

She glanced at her watch. Another fifteen minutes to go and even then she didn't have any sort of plan.

She rose from her seat. "I have to go to the bathroom."

"Do you want me to go with you?" Gabrielle pushed back her chair, ready to be Sharon's shadow.

"No." Sharon waved her hand. "Sit back down and relax. I'll be fine. Derek, take my chair, please," she said, walking away.

"Hurry back," Sharon heard Gabrielle call to her.

Sharon headed through the crowd, which was marginally younger than she was, and definitely hipper. She found the ladies' room down a long hallway and was about to push open the door when someone jostled into her.

She whirled around, her heart beating hard in her chest, and bumped into a woman exiting.

"I'm sorry. I tripped," the woman said as she righted herself.

"No problem. Are you okay?" Sharon asked.

"I'm fine."

Sharon walked inside, heading for the mirror and sink area.

Alone, she leaned both hands against the counter and blew out a long stream of air. God, she had to calm down. She consoled herself with the thought that soon enough, this would all be over.

She just wished she knew when.

GABRIELLE KNEW SHE HAD just a small window of time alone with Derek before Sharon returned, the drama of the evening with her.

"I appreciate you being here. So does Sharon despite how she's acting. She's a nervous wreck," Gabrielle said.

"I can't say I blame her. I'm just glad you don't have to face it alone."

She nodded in agreement.

"But Sharon needs us sitting here with her. I don't think you're going to get that dance you wanted after all," he said, not sounding too disappointed. But she was.

"I guess it wasn't realistic to think we could have a romantic evening while Sharon was being blackmailed." She'd just wanted to feel Derek's arms around her again. She needed him to pull her close and press his cheek against hers while they moved to the beat of the music.

The collar on his polo shirt was crooked. She reached out to adjust it and her hand skimmed the razor stubble on his jaw. At the simple touch, her skin tingled and her body burned.

Instead of pulling her hand away, she caressed his jaw, giving him exactly the signal she wanted to send. "Maybe we can't dance here, but there are other places," she said, her voice ripe with innuendo.

His eyes darkened in understanding. Her body craved intimacy and closeness with him in the most basic way.

"I'm back," Sharon said, joining them again.

Gabrielle pulled back. She glanced at Sharon and smiled.

Derek rose from his seat, insisting Sharon take it again.

The rest of the night passed in a drawn-out blur of drinks that turned into diet sodas after a while and anxious conversation from eight until 11:00 p.m. Three hours later, they finally had to accept the fact that nobody was coming to contact Sharon.

"Well, this was a bust," Sharon said. "Now what? I wait until he contacts me again?" Her voice shook.

Gabrielle glanced at Derek. "Unfortunately, you don't have a choice."

She nodded. "Let's get out of here. I just need to find my keys." She dug through her purse, clearly upset.

"If you'd just leave half that crap home, you'd be able to find something in there," Gabrielle said laughing, attempting to ease her friend's tension.

Sharon ran her hand through her hair. "I know. I have got to clean this bag out," she muttered. "Aha!" She pulled out her keys.

Together they walked to the parking lot. Derek walked them to Sharon's Ford Escort.

"Call me," Gabrielle said to Derek, her gaze lingering on his. What she really wanted to say was, *Meet me back at my room,* but she refrained.

Sharon opened her car door. "Oh, for God's sake. Derek, take Gabrielle home, will you? You two want to be alone so badly, I can feel it."

"But we didn't do anything," Gabrielle protested. Derek merely shook his head.

"You didn't have to do anything. It's obvious. I spent the afternoon at the beach, watching you two stare at each other, remember? It was just like when we were in high school and I was the third wheel."

"You were never the—"

"Relax. I'm kidding!" Sharon laughed. "Besides, I just want to go home, crawl under the covers and pretend none of this is happening." She waved her hand toward them, indicating they should leave. "So go."

"Don't be silly. I want to make sure you get home and inside your house safely," Gabrielle said.

"Which you wouldn't be able to do since I'd be dropping you off at Rhodes Inn, anyway. Stop worrying and acting like my mother. I appreciate it but I'm fine." She turned Gabrielle around and pushed her toward Derek.

"But…" As much as Gabrielle wanted to be with Derek, she did not want to leave Sharon alone.

"We'll follow you to your house and make sure you get inside safely. Then I'll take Gabrielle home," Derek said, appeasing both women.

Gabrielle smiled at him. "He's a true diplomat."

"No, you're just easy to please," he said in that deep voice she loved.

Sharon rolled her eyes. "Oh, brother. You two have it bad."

Gabrielle grinned. Her friend was right. She did have it bad for Derek. And it was time he discovered just how bad.

DEREK FOLLOWED GABRIELLE into her room. She flipped on the lamp beside the bed, illuminating a sparsely decorated area. He'd been here before, but this was the first time he'd really looked around. Besides the bed and a night table, there was a dresser and a TV stand with a small television on top. In the corner, her suitcase was propped open on a chair.

All in all, there wasn't much living space. "Aren't you getting tired of being so cramped?" Derek asked.

She shrugged. "I haven't spent much time in here so it hasn't been too bad. Anyway, I'm enjoying catching up with you and Sharon. Who cares where I sleep?"

He cared. A lot. He wanted her sleeping with him, in his bed. Or hers. He wasn't fussy as long as they were together.

"I'm enjoying spending time with you, too."
Not that getting out of the house had been easy
tonight. Holly had wanted to spend more time with
Gabrielle and a nightclub had sounded fun to her.
She hadn't appreciated being left behind, and he
had a feeling she'd be heaping on the guilt for a
while.

"I just wish we'd had a more productive night."
Gabrielle interrupted his thoughts.

Derek agreed, but he didn't want to spend the time
they had thinking about Sharon's problems. "Since
we can't change it, let's try to forget it for a while."

"You have a point," she said, her voice suddenly
more sultry. She stepped toward the nightstand
and pushed a button on travel-size iPod speakers.

Soft music filled the air.

"Do you want to dance with me now?" she
asked, reaching her hand out to him.

He grinned. "You know I do." This was her fantasy and he intended to give it to her. He linked his
fingers through hers and pulled her close.

Her breasts pressed into his chest, her hips
swayed in unison with his, and her soft curves
cushioned him in molten heat. His groin hardened
and swelled thick in his jeans. They moved together slowly, with an ease born of familiarity. It
seemed his body had never forgotten hers.

"Mmm. This feels good," she said, splaying her
fingers across his back. "I've missed holding you."

"Same here. Reminds me of prom."

"Minus the rented tux, the fancy dress and the chaperones." She laughed.

"You're such a brat," he said, chuckling. He eased her closer. Burying his face in her hair, he inhaled deep. "Chocolate?" he asked, guessing her scent.

"Mmm-hmm. Isn't it delicious?"

He breathed in again and groaned. "You're delicious." He swept her hair off her neck and nuzzled the soft skin there. She swayed against him, her body sensuously brushing against his, deliberately provocative.

Remaining still enough to continue the dance wasn't easy, but he was determined to pace himself.

She cupped her hands around his cheeks and pulled his face to hers, capturing his lips in a long-awaited kiss. It wasn't their first since her return, but because they were alone, because there'd be no interruptions, he savored it.

Prolonged it.

Made it last.

She didn't rush it, either. She slid her lips back and forth over his, teasing with her tongue, heightening the foreplay and his arousal until he slanted his head and deepened the kiss.

She took the lead in the dance, easing them toward the bed. She braced her hands on his shoulders and pushed him down before stepping away.

"Going somewhere?" He patted the space beside him, encouraging her to join him.

"I'll be right back. Why don't you get undressed in the meantime?" Her eyes gleamed in anticipation as she sashayed toward the bathroom, stopping only to open a drawer and pull out something that looked like flimsy lingerie on the way.

CHAPTER NINE

GABRIELLE HAD GONE BACK to her apartment for clothes and for the garment in her hands—baby-doll-style lingerie with lace covering her breasts and a pleated fall of silky material that ended high on her thighs. The peach color complemented her tanned skin and gave her a boost of confidence. She quickly slipped into the sexy negligee, needing all the confidence she could get.

She dusted shimmery powder on her chest in the fragrance Derek had noticed earlier before opening the door and stepping back into the room.

She'd hoped to blow him away, but when she found him lying on the bed, she was the one undone. Sure, she'd seen Derek in a bathing suit earlier today. She'd marveled at how much his body had filled out, how he'd matured and changed. But they hadn't been alone. She hadn't had time to drink him in, remembering the past while hungry for a future.

He leaned back against propped pillows, resting

comfortably against the headboard. She'd think he was relaxed…if not for the erection tenting the black cotton briefs. Her mouth grew dry and she swallowed hard.

In her dreams, he was always the boy she'd lost. But now she was facing the man—a sexy man wearing nothing but short black boxers.

"I've never known you to be speechless," he said as he held out a hand.

She'd never lied to him before and she wasn't about to start now. "You're suddenly real." She walked toward him and placed her palm in his. "I'm overwhelmed."

"Same for me." He ran his fingers over the pulse point in her wrist.

She knew he could feel her heartbeat pounding through her veins.

"I can't wait to be inside you," he said, his voice husky and deep.

Her pulse skyrocketed even more and moisture pooled between her thighs.

Unexpectedly, he closed his eyes and groaned, a sound of frustration, not pleasure. "I don't have protection," he said through clenched teeth.

Derek couldn't believe now that he was here with Gabrielle, finally about to make love to her, he'd have to call a halt. He'd been so busy thinking about how not to act on his desire, he wasn't prepared.

She reached over and put her hands on his. "I'm on the pill."

He raised an eyebrow, surprised. "I thought you hated the thought of putting hormones into your body," he said, repeating what she'd told him when he suggested that form of birth control when they'd been teens.

She smiled. "You'd be amazed how quickly terrible monthly cramping will change a woman's mind," she said wryly. "So don't worry about pregnancy. As for the rest, I'm safe."

He understood what she meant. He wasn't sure he wanted to discuss her love life at the moment, but then, he couldn't think of a better time.

Before they shared anything else, he needed to know. "What *has* your love life been like?"

She tipped her head and laughed. "Helluva question right now."

"Humor me."

"Well, after you, there wasn't anyone for a good long while. I went to the University of Miami and majored in psychology. I threw myself into school."

"Miami has its share of athletes," he said, knowing there had to have been guys in her life.

She shrugged. "There were men, Derek. You didn't think I would become celibate, did you? It just took me longer than it took you."

He winced, but he deserved the dig.

"But there wasn't anyone serious for a long time."

"And once there was?"

"There was an assistant to one of my professors, but he was too uptight. No sense of humor."

He held on to her hand. "You need a man with a sense of humor," he said gruffly.

She nodded. "After him, there was a publicist I met while on a book tour."

He bit the inside of his cheek. "What were his flaws?"

"He was too slick."

"Slick?"

She nodded. "I couldn't trust him." Her eyes twinkled as she spoke.

Damn, but she was enjoying this. "And then?"

"Another author. My editor introduced us at an awards ceremony."

"Too messy, being in the same profession?" he guessed.

She shook her head. "Too needy. I want a man who's independent and doesn't have to know where I am 24-7. Besides, he worked at home and he was around. All. The. Time." She groaned at the notion. "After that, there was the butcher, the baker and the candlestick maker. The butcher was a slob, the baker too heavy and the last guy always smelled like another woman's perfume," she said, laughing.

"Wench." He realized by the end she was teasing him, although he also sensed there'd been some truth in each of them.

No man had suited her.

"How about me? What are my flaws?" he asked.

"Honestly? The fact that you don't have any. And that brings us back to the issue at hand. Protection and how we don't need any." Her eyes darkened as she met his gaze. "I want you, Derek. I always have."

His body throbbed with anticipation. He'd been hard since he'd seen her again. And he'd wanted her ever since they'd said goodbye years ago.

"The problem is we *do* need protection." He swallowed hard. "Ever since Marlene got pregnant, I've made it a nonnegotiable rule to always wear a condom," he said, more serious than he'd ever been.

She nodded slowly. "I respect that. And it just so happens that I believe in protection, too—with everyone in my past. Even though I was on the pill." She licked her lips. "But I had a hunch you might feel this way, so look what I picked up?" she asked, obviously pleased with herself. She held up a box of condoms.

"You're still thinking ahead," he said, amused that this one character trait hadn't changed.

And though he'd like nothing more than to feel her around him, her hot slick walls cushioning him in moist heat, he couldn't break his rule. He needed to protect them both from the damn curse.

The time for talk was finished. He flipped her onto her stomach in the center of the bed. The hem of her lingerie slipped upward and cool air rushed over her bare buttocks.

He groaned and rubbed his hand first over one cheek, then the next. His body shook over hers and he knew he was building their arousal and anticipation. Knew he wanted her as desperately as she wanted him.

Derek leaned down and pressed a kiss against her skin.

Gabrielle's body trembled, and before she could think beyond the erotic sensation of his lips against her flesh, he straddled her derriere and began to massage her back and shoulders. A delicious pulsing began between her thighs. And as he worked on her shoulders with his hands, he rocked insistently, erotically against her back, his erection obvious. His hard length lay in the crevice of her bare behind and she felt him *there,* an oddly arousing sensation.

"If I let myself go, it'll be over in two seconds," he said, his breath hot in her ear. He swept her hair off the back of her neck and leaned forward to press his lips against her skin. As he moved upward, so did his penis. Rigid and unyielding, he pressed himself against her bare cheeks.

Her thighs clenched of their own volition and her body quaked in reaction.

She attempted to roll over, but Derek placed a hand against her back, stopping her. "Not so fast. I'm not finished with you yet," he said in a gruff voice.

He kissed her neck, nibbling with his lips and tongue, traveling from the sensitive flesh on her shoulders down the length of her back. His touch burned and she writhed beneath him, pressing against the mattress, seeking relief from the building crescendo of need.

There was no relief to be found. With each pivot of her hips, his erection thrust harder against her, heightening her excitement and her desire until she ground herself harder and faster against the mattress, pushing and pressing her lower body until just the right spot hit the bed, sending her closer to the release she desperately needed.

All the while, his movements mimicked hers. His hips rocked faster, harder, his erection exciting her beyond belief. Between her mound grinding against the mattress and his erection thrusting at her back, she could barely catch her breath. She gasped for air, unwilling to choose between breathing and coming apart right here, right now.

Finally, tiny flickers of light danced in front of her eyes. The fulfillment she'd been seeking hit and a fast and furious orgasm followed. And continued until she collapsed against the sheets.

Her body still trembled, her breath still came in shallow gulps, long after the sweet release had ended. When she was able to focus again, she took stock of her surroundings, how her body felt. And she immediately realized something was missing.

He was missing.

She needed him inside her.

But with his delicious weight on her back, he was still calling the shots. She cleared her throat.

With a chuckle, Derek eased off her and she flipped over onto her back. His heavy-lidded gaze met hers.

She let out a contented purr, letting him know she'd enjoyed it. "But it wasn't enough."

"Tell me something I don't know," he said through gritted teeth.

She grinned and decided turnabout was fair play. Through the thin cotton briefs, she cupped his erection in the palm of her hand, sliding up and down his length, pausing only to circle her finger over the damp head.

He leaned back and let out a low groan.

Pain? Pleasure? A mix, she supposed, enjoying watching the play of expressions cross his handsome face.

Her own body was ready again. Dampness pooled between her thighs and her nipples were puckered into hardened peaks. The pulsing had started yet again, as she anticipated finally having him inside her. But she wasn't ready to give up feeling his strength and power pulsing inside her hand.

Wanting to give him just a taste of the sensual torture he'd inflicted on her, she bent down and flicked her tongue over his cotton briefs. She aimed for the tip of his erection and tasted his salty essence through the cotton barrier.

"Mmm." She hadn't let go of his rigid length, nor did she stop at one taste.

His hips jerked upward and his body shook. "That's it," he ground out.

Gabrielle smiled, pleased she was still able to make him as crazy as he made her. So many things hadn't changed. They'd gotten even better with age, she thought as she sat up, meeting his gaze.

Derek couldn't hold out another minute. If she kept up the pressure, he'd come in her hand.

He was finished waiting and thankfully so was she. He pulled her into his arms at the same time she reached for him.

She came warm and pliant, molding against him and making the thin fabric separating them a mere nuisance. He pulled one of the straps over her shoulder and trailed damp kisses down her neck, over the scented skin on her shoulders and arms, before she helped him by wriggling her upper body out of the sexy garment. From there it was easy for her to lift her hips and, with his help, slip off the negligee completely.

He sucked in a shallow breath, stunned at how her body had changed. Either that or his memory had failed him. She was curvier than he remembered, her breasts lush and full. His gaze traveled over her silken flesh to the small triangle of hair between her thighs.

She didn't cover herself in embarrassment but let him drink in the sight of her.

"When is it going to be my turn to look?" she asked, a sultry glint in her eyes.

He'd be happy to release himself from the confining boxers. "Whenever you're ready."

"Now sounds good." She slid her fingers beneath the elastic waist and began to ease them over his hips.

He helped and soon she was the one staring.

"Keep looking at me like that and it'll be over before it begins." He didn't know how he'd held on this far. But giving her pleasure, while holding back his own, had let him feel her orgasm rush through her. It was an incredible sensation, feeling her release, while still surrounded by her warm body and delicious scent. He hadn't been able to resist savoring every moment of it.

She backed up to the top of the bed and beckoned to him with a crook of her finger, her eyes gleaming with delight.

At last he joined her. He ripped the foil open. She took the condom back and together they rolled it over his hard length.

Protected and more than ready, he came down

on top of her, hard and fast. Her skin was warm, her body soft, so opposite of his.

Finesse went by the wayside. He slid his hand through her slick, dewy folds, finding her damp and ready. Her hips twitched and her body trembled as he parted her and pushed hard and fast inside. He found himself cushioned in unbelievable warmth and he exhaled a slow groan, unable to hold back the sound. It wasn't the physical sensations that floored him, but the rampaging feelings he couldn't control. Connected with her, body to body, his heart swelled with deep emotion that shook him to his core.

And when he met her gaze, it was obvious in her eyes and her expression she felt the same.

She shifted beneath him, and the subtle change in position made him catch his breath. He began to move, sliding out, then in again. She synchronized her rhythm to his, as if they'd never been apart, as if they'd made love just yesterday.

The old bed creaked beneath them and Gabrielle laughed. "I hope nobody's going to complain to Mrs. Rhodes. She'll never look at me the same way again." Amusement bubbled in her voice and she grinned.

He propped himself up with his hands and placed a long, lingering kiss on her lips. One she answered by locking her arms around his neck and kissing him back. Once again, their bodies began to move in unison. He didn't remember starting up again, but everything with Gabrielle came instinctually.

Without warning, she raised her legs, locking them tight around his back. She held him captive with her body, and there wasn't another place he'd rather be. He rocked his hips from side to side, thrusting as best he could, seeking the friction their united bodies created.

He succeeded. Waves of desire built higher with each plunge he took deeper and deeper inside her. Her breath was warm and hot in his ear, becoming rougher with every thrust. Just when he thought she was about to come, he deliberately slowed his pace.

It nearly killed him, but he took his time, wanting to see her clearly. He knew it was selfish, but he wanted to mark every moment in time as he plunged in, then out again. He needed her to feel every hard inch of him branding her, inside and out.

He pulled out of her until only the tip of him touched her moist opening. Reaching down, he circled her breast with his palm, cupping and molding her in his hand. Her hips jerked beneath him, her small feminine mound thrust upward, wet, wanting.

"God, Derek!" She reached for him but he remained out of reach.

Instead he leaned down and pulled one hard, distended nipple into his mouth. He suckled on the engorged tip, teasing with his teeth, laving with his tongue. Back and forth until her hips shook in a frenzied rhythm.

A frantic plea.

His groin throbbed desperately and he knew he'd reached his limit.

"Dammit, Derek, *now!*" Apparently so had she, as the words exploded from deep inside her.

She grabbed on to his shoulders and dug her long nails into his skin, and with her heels, she pushed his body back toward hers.

He didn't need any more coaxing. He plunged into her so fast his world spun. He didn't remember anything after that except the heat suctioning all around him and Gabrielle's screams of pleasure. Release didn't hit him slowly but slammed into him with the force of a Mack truck.

At that moment, everything around him suddenly cleared. He inhaled her warm, sweet scent. His face was close to hers and her soft hair brushed against his cheek. He was inside her. She surrounded him. And the explosion that followed rocked his world.

Although he was filling her body, she did the same for his heart, completing him as no woman ever had.

DEREK DOZED BESIDE Gabrielle. She knew she'd have to wake him soon so he could go home before Holly realized he'd slept out, but she wanted a few selfish minutes first. She let her gaze travel over him.

Asleep, he was so much more vulnerable than awake and definitely less guarded. Not that he'd been remotely guarded when they made love, she thought, a smile curving her lips as she remembered.

Their connection had been even stronger than when they were younger and she'd dare him to challenge her on that. When she and Derek joined together, it was a connecting of hearts. She knew it just as she knew now she had something to fight for.

No, she thought, correcting herself. She had *everything* to fight for. Still, she had an uphill battle ahead.

Wanting a little more quiet time before he had to go, she snuggled in to him. He reached out and pulled her close, spooning his body around hers. She shut her eyes and savored his heated warmth until, little by little, her body relaxed and her mind wandered.

GABRIELLE AWOKE WITH a start. Sunlight flooded the room through the window curtains she'd forgotten to draw shut last night. She glanced at her alarm clock and realized it was 9:00 a.m.

Wow, she must have really been exhausted to sleep so late. Then again, Derek had definitely worn her out, she thought wryly. She quickly glanced at the other side of the bed, hoping he hadn't slept through the night along with her. With relief, she realized he was gone, which hopefully meant he'd gotten home before Holly missed him.

She placed her hand on the space beside her. The sheets were cold. He must have left not long after she'd fallen asleep last night.

She wasn't worried that he'd left her bed with regrets. She knew it was Holly that had drawn him away. She trusted Derek enough to know that if anything had changed between them, he'd tell her face-to-face.

But she wasn't going to give him the time or space to panic about what they'd done or the implications. She could work as easily here as she could at her apartment. She was in no rush to get home.

Gabrielle tossed the covers off and headed to shower for the day ahead. Now that she was sure of her own feelings, she planned to include Derek in every area of her life, lavishing him and his daughter with enough affection that he wouldn't be able to deny they belonged together. And if that wasn't enough, she'd arm herself with enough curse-rebuttal knowledge to change his mind.

Because she loved him. Before last night, she'd sensed she had never stopped doing so and now she was certain. They had a lot to learn about each other still, but they deserved the opportunity. She was determined to give it to them.

WHEN SHE COULDN'T FIND her car keys again the next morning, Sharon decided to change purses. She was going to move everything she'd put in the small open-topped handbag she'd taken to the Wave into her work tote, giving her more room.

Sitting at her kitchen table, she dumped the contents of the smaller bag onto the table. Yes, she was a pack rat. Even her dress bags were stuffed with unnecessary items she *might need* and couldn't leave the house without. Richard, who was much neater, often teased her about the clutter.

Reminded of Richard, the fear and panic she'd been fighting all morning resurfaced. Nobody had contacted her last night, which meant she'd be constantly looking over her shoulder for the big shoe to fall. The photo would eventually surface, although it wasn't in the local paper, thank God. At least not yet. She'd run to the end of the driveway this morning and scanned the news cover to cover. Not knowing what Tony's next step would be had her on edge.

"Concentrate on your daily routine," she instructed herself aloud. The only way she could function was to ignore her churning stomach and focus on the things she needed to do.

She picked up each item, one at a time—her wallet, makeup case, cell phone and keys—and placed them in her work bag. She also went through the receipts and papers that she'd been accumulating. Tissues went into her tote. Receipts, notes and the like she set aside in two piles, trash and to file later.

"What's this?" She picked up a small envelope she didn't recognize with her name typed on the front. The flap hadn't been sealed.

She didn't have a good feeling about this. With shaking hands, she pulled out a note. "Leave the money in the bathroom hallway, beneath the fake ficus tree outside the ladies' room. Photos will be returned shortly thereafter."

Cryptic and to the point. But she hadn't seen this letter last night and she broke out in a sweat now. He'd expected her to leave the cash and she'd left the bar instead. No money had changed hands and she had no way to contact the person to explain. No way to contact *him* to explain.

She was in so much trouble.

What if Tony—she still believed it was Tony who was blackmailing her—was furious? What if he thought she was playing with him and he got angry? He could very well expose her instead of contacting her again. Those photographs could show up in the paper any day.

No. She couldn't let that happen.

Which meant she needed a plan.

As she stuffed the note in her purse with shaking hands, she realized what her next course of action had to be. And a sudden sense of calm overtook her. She was going to take charge of her life again.

First, she needed to talk to Tony, but she couldn't go in blind. She had to stake him out and see what kind of life he led now. Only then could she consider approaching him.

She pulled out her keys and headed for her car. First stop, Gabrielle's. Sharon needed to come up with a story to cover her sudden upcoming disappearance so her best friend wouldn't worry. She couldn't tell Gabrielle what she had planned. Her friend would definitely try to talk Sharon out of it. And if Gabrielle couldn't dissuade Sharon, she'd insist on coming along. But this was something Sharon needed to handle herself.

With any luck, she wouldn't be arrested with her hands around Tony's neck as she screamed, "Give me my naked photographs, you jerk!"

GABRIELLE GOT A LATER start to the day than planned because Sharon had stopped by to let her know she'd be out of town for a few days. She said she'd received a call late last night from another librarian. The woman had asked Sharon to fill in for her at a regional conference, since she'd come down with some kind of summer virus. Sharon said she'd be gone three or four days tops, but she'd call to check in.

Gabrielle was disappointed. She'd hoped to spend some more time with her friend, but she would have no problem keeping busy. Sharon's trip would give Gabrielle a chance to interview people in town about the curse.

Not to mention, she could spend much coveted time with Derek. They'd just begun to tap into the feelings they needed to explore.

Doughnuts in hand, Gabrielle rang Derek's doorbell. Before she could think beyond the still-delicious tingling between her legs and the aches in body parts long unused, the door swung open wide.

"Gabrielle!" Holly greeted her with a welcoming smile. Dressed in a nightshirt, her hair mussed from sleep, Holly managed to hang on to her normal enthusiasm despite the early hour.

"Whatcha got there?" the young girl asked, eyeing the bag Gabrielle held in her right hand.

"Chocolate frosted, powdered sugar and jelly doughnuts. Any of those interest you?" Gabrielle waved the treats in front of Holly.

Her eyes grew wide. "I love all kinds of doughnuts. So does my dad. Come on in." She waved Gabrielle through the door and into the renovated barn.

This was the first time Gabrielle had seen the inside of the place where Derek currently lived. The barn, which had been behind his house since before Gabrielle had first moved to town, had been renovated, insulated and now served as a guest house. Thomas and Hank Corwin hadn't lost their builder's touch, Gabrielle thought, glancing around the interior, which retained a country charm.

"Dad! Company!" Holly yelled.

Heavy footsteps bounded down the loft stairs. "How many times do I have to tell you not to open the front door unless—" He stopped short when he hit the bottom step and caught sight of Gabrielle.

Unlike his daughter, he appeared freshly showered and dressed. Hours earlier, she'd seen him undressed and aroused, just for her, and she couldn't wipe the memory from her mind. Not even focusing on his khaki chinos and short-sleeved shirt helped dull the surge of warmth suddenly rushing through her.

"Gabrielle's here!" Holly said unnecessarily.

"I see that." His voice sounded gruff, as if his thoughts were as vivid as hers.

"I brought breakfast," Gabrielle said with a smile.

"Which means you don't have to try to make pancakes again today." Holly turned to Gabrielle. "He burns them," she explained.

Derek groaned. "I have no secrets in this house," he said, laughing. "For the record, I'm not much better with eggs. It's usually cold cereal for us."

Gabrielle glanced at the bag in her hand, realizing at that moment how little she knew about raising children. Her carb-loaded, sugar-laden choice in breakfast didn't have the same nutritional value as eggs.

So much for making a good impression on Derek, she thought. "Well…" She cleared her throat. "I didn't exactly bring breakfast. These are doughnuts. So maybe your father will let you have them *after* you eat something healthy."

"Aww—"

Holly geared up for a teenage outburst, something Derek had no intention of dealing with at the moment. Not when Gabrielle looked so crestfallen about bringing doughnuts for breakfast.

"Or maybe I could let you enjoy them now?"

His suggestion garnered him a huge hug from his daughter. As Holly took the bag, Derek winked at Gabrielle, silently telling her to relax.

She grinned and exhaled in relief.

"Let's eat!" Holly ran for the kitchen.

"I think she wants first dibs on her choice of doughnuts," Gabrielle said.

"She can have it. I want first dibs on you," he said in a low voice.

He'd gotten home late last night, long after Holly had fallen asleep. This morning she'd been tired and hadn't asked any questions. A good thing, since he couldn't have answered them without a goofy grin on his face. Despite how wrong it was for him to keep seeing Gabrielle, knowing he was sinking deeper and falling fast, he couldn't deny they were magic together. He wasn't ready to let her go yet.

She stepped closer. "I'm glad to hear you don't have any regrets."

"How could I? You just need to remember where I stand."

She tilted her head to one side. "How could I?" she mimicked his comment wryly, but kept a smile on her face. "Did I ever tell you what my favorite television show is?"

He narrowed his gaze. "What does that have to do with anything?"

"It's *Survivor*," she said, ignoring his question. "Want to know why? The motto. Outwit, outplay, outlast. Something I happen to think I'm pretty good at." She met his gaze with flashing determination.

He'd been warned. She wasn't going to let the curse stand between them this time.

"Are you two coming? I already finished one doughnut!" Holly called from the other room.

"Did you even chew it?" he called back.

Gabrielle laughed. "Come on. If there's not a chocolate doughnut left, there'll be hell to pay."

He led the way into the kitchen, thoughts of Gabrielle and chocolate dancing in his brain. He still smelled the scent when he breathed in, even before she'd shown up this morning.

"I wish I could stay and eat but I have an early appointment in town. I'd planned on grabbing coffee while I was there."

"Where is your office, anyway?" Gabrielle asked.

"I rent a room at Englebert and Rowe, the law firm in town. They have all the office supplies I need, and since they had empty space, it was a win-win situation."

Gabrielle nodded. "I understand. I should have called before showing up, anyway."

"Can you stay and have doughnuts with me?" Holly asked Gabrielle, powdered sugar on her nose.

"I sure can. If your dad doesn't mind?" She paused and glanced at Derek for permission.

He *should* mind. His daughter shouldn't be bonding with Gabrielle any more than he should sleep with her again. "Of course I don't mind if you stay."

"Yes!" Holly pumped her fist in the air. "I want you to meet Fred."

Gabrielle crinkled her nose in confusion. "Who's Fred?"

"My father's basset hound," Derek said.

"He's old and he smells like shi—"

Derek shot his daughter a warning glare.

"Shiitake mushrooms. He smells like shiitake mushrooms," Holly said, giggling as if she had gotten away with the curse.

Derek groaned. Marlene was going to give him hell when she returned and discovered his daughter's new vocabulary, courtesy of Hank.

"I'd love to meet Fred," Gabrielle said.

Derek knew she meant it. He remembered that Gabrielle had always wanted her own dog, but her parents had never wanted the responsibility.

He'd intended to get her one for Christmas, their senior year. But then he'd talked to her parents. They'd been adamant about him waiting. He'd promised her a puppy one day…but then he'd come to his senses. His mother's letter had reminded him about the ramifications of the curse and why he and Gabrielle couldn't be together.

"Did you ever get a pet?" he asked her, knowing he was treading on sensitive ground.

She shook her head.

"Why not?" Holly asked. "Don't you like dogs? You'll like Fred. He's a lazy bas—"

"Hey!" Derek admonished.

"Basset hound! He's a lazy basset hound. Jeez, Dad, relax!"

Gabrielle laughed.

Derek's face flushed hot. Time for him to go to work, he thought, before he made a bigger ass of himself.

"I never got a dog because it wouldn't have felt right." As Gabrielle spoke, she never broke eye contact with him, giving him a view into her soul.

After he'd left her, Derek had been selfishly focused on his own torment. He'd convinced himself that she'd move on and be better off without him. As her career had soared, he further patted himself on the back, reassuring himself he'd been right. But suddenly, in her eyes, he saw the pain he'd inflicted and accepted that the dreams he'd crushed hadn't just been his own.

He swallowed hard, facing his actions for the first time. Then and now he wanted everything she had to offer. But he could give her nothing in return.

He needed air. Work was the perfect excuse. "You'll like Fred. Just watch out for your shoes."

"He likes to chew them, sometimes he even pees," Holly said. "Grandpa says it's a wonder he doesn't poop there, too."

"I'll keep my shoes on." Gabrielle curled her toes into her sandals.

"I've got to get going. Uncle Thomas is next door," he told his daughter. "I was going to drop you off there, but Gabrielle can do it when she's ready to leave. I'll let him know you'll be over a little later than planned, okay?"

She nodded.

"Your father isn't around?" Gabrielle asked.

Derek caught the hopeful note in her voice.

"No, he's out. It's his week to do the grocery shopping," Holly said.

In other words, she had no need to worry about the old man and his shotgun, Derek thought, but he didn't say the words aloud.

He left his two best girls alone and headed out to work.

CHAPTER TEN

BY THE TIME GABRIELLE finished breakfast with Holly, she'd discovered just how precocious Derek's daughter could be. As they walked across the land that separated the barn and the main house, Holly continued the inquisition she'd begun over the doughnuts.

"So have you ever been married?" Holly asked.

Gabrielle liked this question better than *Were you in love with my father back in high school?* It was young love, Gabrielle had said. And she much preferred this question to *Are you in love with him now? He's a really good guy even if he does snore.* That one had stumped her and she'd deflected the question by focusing on the snoring instead of the love.

Did she love Derek?

Without a doubt.

Was that the same as them having a future? Not just yet. But she wasn't going to let him walk away without fighting this time.

"Gabrielle, did you hear me? I asked if you've ever been married." Holly nudged her with her elbow.

"Nope, never been married." Grass connected the one large piece of property and Holly enjoyed skipping as they walked.

"Why not?"

Gabrielle glanced up at the warm sun in the cloudless sky. "Because no one I loved ever asked me," she said honestly.

"Would you say yes if my dad asked?"

"You are a nosy one." Gabrielle shook her head and laughed.

"That's what my mom says, too."

"I'd like to meet her one day." Gabrielle was surprised to realize she wasn't just saying it to be nice to Holly. She did want to meet Derek's ex-wife.

Not only to get a better view into Derek's past but to meet Holly's mother. "I bet she's a great lady. After all, she's got a kid like you."

Holly laughed. As they reached the house, the girl caught sight of Fred and ran toward him, leaving questions about Gabrielle loving Derek far behind. Thank God for the kid's short attention span, Gabrielle thought.

"Gabrielle, come meet Fred!" Holly waved her over.

Gabrielle knelt down and greeted the old basset hound with a pat on the head. "You are as smelly as promised, old man." But his sad face and long ears were so sweet, Gabrielle couldn't help falling in love immediately. "How old is he?"

Holly shrugged. "Grandpa says he doesn't remember."

"He's about ten," a deep male voice said.

Gabrielle glanced up.

"Thomas Corwin," he said, extending a hand.

She rose to greet him, wiping the dust off her walking shorts. "Gabrielle Donovan." She shook his hand.

Unlike his brother Hank, Thomas had freshly trimmed hair, also dark like his brother's, and a buttoned-down collared shirt with khakis.

"We met when you were younger," Thomas said.

"At Derek's. I used to have dinner at his house when we were in high school." Before the brothers had moved in together.

He smiled. "I remember."

"Uncle Thomas, can we give Fred a bath?" Holly asked.

He nodded. "I think that's a great idea. I'd love to see the look on your grandfather's face when he comes home and finds Fred smelling like a rose."

Holly grinned. "I'll go get the shampoo!" She took off at a run, leaving Gabrielle dizzy.

"She's a bundle of energy, that kid. And she switches topics faster than the speed of light."

"She's a special little girl," Thomas said, nodding. "Thank God she is a girl. In this family that's a blessing, as you well know." His voice turned somber at the subject matter.

The curse.

He'd given her an opening to question him, and Gabrielle glanced around to make sure they were alone. Holly was busy finding shampoo to wash the dog, Derek was in town and Hank wasn't home, either. She might not get another opportunity.

"Do you mind talking about it?"

"The curse? Why not? You're going to write this book, so you might as well hear the true version of our family history. Besides, I've read your work and I know your history with Derek. I don't believe you'd hurt us."

"Thank you," she said, warmed by his apparent faith.

"Let's sit." He gestured to an old scarred picnic table with benches on either side.

She lowered herself onto the hard wood.

Fred ambled up to her and plopped himself on the floor at her feet. She gave the dog's head a few strokes before turning to Thomas, who sat beside her on the bench.

"I know about your generation. Who married who and when, who passed away, who got divorced. The dates and specifics I can get from county records. What I can't figure out is the rationale behind the belief."

"Why grown, intelligent men believe in witchcraft?" he asked, surprising Gabrielle with his deep laughter.

"Exactly." She nodded, glad he'd put it that way and not her. "Why would all of you prefer to believe your family was cursed rather than see your history as an unfortunate set of circumstances?"

Thomas rested against the table. "Because those circumstances keep replaying themselves in every generation. That adds up to a curse, if you ask me."

Fred pushed his nose into her calf, insistently urging her to give him more attention. She leaned over and petted him some more. "You know the expression, when it rains it pours?" she asked Thomas.

"Of course."

"Isn't it possible that your family's just had more than its share of misfortune? That this is the hand you were dealt?"

He glanced out at the yard. Together they watched Holly retrieve the bucket and shampoo from the garage, along with other things for Fred's bath.

Thomas met her gaze. "My father laid eyes on my mother and it was love at first sight. My mother said the same thing about him."

Gabrielle placed her elbow on the table and propped her chin in her hand, listening intently.

"Like the Corwin males before him, my father was determined to beat the curse. His father, my grandfather, died not long after catching his wife cavorting with the neighbor, a widower who'd lost his wife and was lonely. My grandmother would go help him with the kids. A little too much helping went on, if you get my drift. My grandfather walked in on them when he came home from work early one day. He shot the neighbor and my grandmother died of a heart attack right there on the spot."

Gabrielle blinked. "Seriously?"

"Sounds like a comedy of errors, doesn't it?" He tapped his foot against the dirt on the ground, discussing the tale as if it had happened to another family.

Gabrielle had seen that kind of behavior before in her interviews. Subjects often found it easier to detach themselves from things that haunted them, rather than let themselves face the emotion. Especially men.

Gabrielle inclined her head. "It does," she admitted.

"We haven't even gotten to my parents' story," Thomas said. "Mom and Dad married and had their kids pretty quickly. They were happy. Even they thought they'd conquered the original Mary Perkins curse."

Gabrielle knew what was coming next. "Until…"

"A huge storm hit the East Coast. A nor'easter, probably, though I'm not sure if they called it that back then. Wiped out most of the town and my father's business."

"What did he do for a living?" Gabrielle asked.

"He was a blacksmith, an extremely talented one. His shop, his tools and equipment—all gone." Thomas slashed his hand through the air.

Nature, Gabrielle thought. A storm, which she knew from growing up in New England, often devastated the coastline and businesses along with it.

But before she could point that out, Thomas continued. "The storm hit late afternoon. We were all home except for my father. Since my grandmother—my mother's mother—lived with us, Mom left us kids with her mother so she could go out and look for my father. She never made it."

"What happened?"

"A flash flood hit and she drowned." He spoke without emotion, but pain flashed in his eyes.

"We pretty much raised ourselves after that. Grandma wasn't much help, since she was getting on in years and died soon after she lost her daughter. Dad spent most of his time doing repairs for a little money in and around town. He never could replace the tools and equipment he lost that day. And mentally, he was never the same."

"How so?" Gabrielle asked, although she could hazard a guess.

"He blamed himself for Mom's death. He said if he had pushed her away instead of marrying her, the curse wouldn't have kicked in. She'd still be alive."

"But—"

He shook his head. "We all said what you're probably thinking. We told him it was a storm, an act of God. Nobody could control it."

Gabrielle nodded, glad he'd agreed. "Which is logical and true!"

"Except that over time, each one of us ignored the curse and lived to disprove its existence. You already know my brothers' stories of love and loss. I'm sure you've heard mine. Why wouldn't we believe it was predestined?"

She exhaled hard, realizing as she'd listened to Thomas recount his family's past, how the history had built upon itself, working against rational belief.

Yet she tried to counter his argument, anyway. "Because as much pain as you've all had in your life, you must realize other people suffer, too. Bad things happen. You can't always explain it away."

"Uncle Thomas!" Holly called out to him. "I'm ready!" She pointed to the bucket and the hose she'd run from the spigot and dragged to the pail of water.

Fred lifted his head from his resting position on the ground beside Gabrielle.

"Fred, come!" Holly called.

The dog took one look at the bucket and the running water and rose to his short feet.

"Come!" Holly called again.

The dog turned and headed the opposite way.

Gabrielle chuckled. "That dog is smarter than he looks."

Thomas grinned. "Go grab Fred's leash. I'll be right there," he called to his niece before turning back to Gabrielle. "Don't you think I want to agree with you? I have a son who deserves the best in life, but it just isn't in the cards. Look at Derek."

Gabrielle's head began to hurt at the other man's obstinance. It was a family trait. "I have looked at Derek and so far all I see is a man who broke up with me before anything bad could happen. A man with a failed marriage and business, both of which can be traced back to human error," she said, frustrated.

Thomas surprised her by reaching out and placing his hand over hers. "I can understand why you feel the need to disprove a curse that affects your own life. But take it from me and my brothers. It can't be done." He patted her hand compassionately, which only made her more determined to get Derek over the negative mind-set held by his male relatives.

"At my age—"

"How old are you, if you don't mind my asking?"

He grinned. "I'm fifty-six. Hank's fifty-seven and Edward is the baby at fifty-five," he said, his frown returning at the mention of his brother and rival. "Why?"

"Because you all look young. You *are* young.

Too young to have sworn off love," Gabrielle said, knowing she was discussing something intensely personal with a man who was basically a stranger.

But this man wasn't a stranger to Derek. Thomas Corwin and his brothers' choices all affected how Derek viewed life, and love.

He shrugged. "I can't speak for the others, but I enjoy my life."

"And you're prepared to spend another thirty or so years alone? With just your brother for company because things didn't work out for you the first time?"

Once again, he patted her hand. "Young lady, I may have sworn off love but I'm not devoid of companionship, if you get my drift."

Gabrielle was sure she blushed about ten shades of red.

"I'm smart about no longer wanting things I know I can't have."

"Like love," she said.

He nodded. "Like love."

Gabrielle sighed. She was surprised at how easy it was to understand where Thomas and the rest of the Corwin men were coming from.

And that scared her.

Because unless she could prove the curse was nothing but coincidence, circumstance, she'd have a fascinating true-life paranormal book…but she and Derek wouldn't stand a chance.

SHARON FELT LIKE AN ASS. Dressed in running wear, shorts and a T-shirt, her hair pulled back in a ponytail and dark sunglasses covering her eyes, she waited outside the building where Gabrielle had said Tony lived. But feeling stupid and giving up were two different things. Someone was torturing her, and she intended to find out if her ex-boyfriend was that person. The first part of her plan was to discover what Tony's life was like now. To see if he'd changed, or if he was the same self-centered bastard she'd known in college.

Back then she'd been in love and blind to his faults. His expensive tastes—designer sunglasses, finer restaurant choices and a budget too high for a college student should have been her first clue something was wrong. But at nineteen, she hadn't cared to look too closely.

Now her eyes were open and her patience was abundant. She'd been sitting by a bench near a tree for the better part of the afternoon and still there was no sign of Tony.

As the hands of her watch neared 4:00 p.m., her patience was finally rewarded. A man resembling Tony rounded the corner and headed for the building entrance. He wore a uniformed T-shirt with a logo on the breast, sunglasses and khaki pants. He wasn't the immaculately groomed man she'd known, but then a lot had changed.

She supposed prison had not only humbled him

but changed his circumstances since his release. Unless he was resorting to blackmail again to fund his expensive taste. Sharon hadn't paid him yet, but had other women? If he'd held on to Sharon's photos, surely he'd kept some of the others. Those victims hadn't wanted to come forward the first time around. They'd feared Tony's retaliation later on. Once Tony had pled guilty, those women had had no need to take the risk. What about now?

As he strode closer to the front entrance, a woman exited the doorway, caught sight of him and waved. From behind him, a young boy ran toward him and Tony caught him in a hug. Sharon narrowed her gaze, watching him closely. Gabrielle had said he lived with his sister. Sharon and Tony had met and dated in college. She'd never met his sister and wouldn't recognize her now. And Gabrielle hadn't mentioned his sister having a child.

Sharon edged closer. Near enough to see and maybe hear, but she kept her head down so Tony wouldn't notice her.

"How was your day?" the woman asked him.

He lowered the little boy back to the floor. "It was fine. Yours?"

His voice was deeper but essentially the same. Sharon shivered despite the heat of the summer sun.

"My day's been busy." She pointed to the toddler and laughed. "Tell Daddy what we did today."

Daddy?

A wife? A child? A life?

Sharon licked her suddenly dry lips.

Could Tony really have straightened out his life this much? Or could his wife and child, the sense of normalcy, be a cover? And if he wasn't her blackmailer, *then who was?*

GABRIELLE LEFT HOLLY with her uncle and headed back to her room at the inn, feeling surprisingly glum. She had thought that the more she explored the history of the curse, the simpler it would be to explain it away. The easier it would be to convince Derek nothing bad would happen if he fell in love with her all over again.

On the surface, it *should* be simple. She had Mother Nature to blame for the destruction of Derek's grandfather's life. It was horrible, but it could happen to anyone. In the next generation, Hank, Thomas and Edward, the matter came down to plain bad luck and human jealousy. It didn't matter that in Gabrielle's mind, those kinds of things happened. That was life.

To the Corwin men, though, those things could all be traced back to the curse. Thomas seemed intelligent and logical. Derek was the same. Yet both men deeply believed. She was beginning to wonder if anything could change their minds.

Frustrated, she went back to the inn. But before she even let herself into her room, she realized something was wrong. Her door, which she'd locked before leaving, was ajar. A glance at the door frame told her it had been wedged open.

She nudged the door open the rest of the way with her foot. "Hello?" she called out.

Nobody answered.

She didn't see anyone in the small room. She quickly checked out the area. The bathroom door was open. Even the shower curtain was pulled back, so she could be sure nobody lurked there.

Heart pounding, she stepped inside. At a glance, she didn't see anything missing, but how could she really know? Until she packed, she couldn't be certain. The only jewelry she'd brought with her was on her body. Her watch, favorite ring, the diamond earrings she loved and the bracelet that her mother had given her.

And her laptop was in her car. Out of a sense of security, she kept it—and all her manuscripts and notes—with her.

So whatever was missing, it couldn't be anything of real value, sentimental or otherwise. Still, someone had been in her room and ransacked the whole place. Drawers had been pulled out, clothes from the suitcase scattered everywhere.

Feeling violated, she backed up one step, then two until she got outside and felt less confined.

She glanced at the two doors to the other rooms, then knocked on each. No one answered. Both were shut tight, with no evidence of someone breaking into either one. She headed around the path to the front of the house and knocked on Mrs. Rhodes's door, ringing the bell persistently at the same time, with the same result. Nothing.

Forcing a deep breath, she pulled her cell phone from her purse and dialed 9-1-1. They instructed her to wait in the car until the police arrived. Gabrielle was more than happy to oblige.

CHAPTER ELEVEN

DEREK'S MORNING HAD BEEN a success. An older couple whose money he'd been managing for the past six months brought their newly married son and daughter-in-law to meet with him. They had a substantial sum from their wedding, and with both parties working high-end jobs, they were a definite bonus to his portfolio. Of course he'd had a difficult time concentrating on business when all he could think about was the night he'd spent in Gabrielle's bed.

By the time he returned to his father's house to pick up Holly, he was on a definite high.

He let himself inside. "Who wants lunch?" he called out with Holly in mind. He was in the mood for a celebration.

"Dad!" She came running, skidding in front of him on the hardwood floor.

"Whoa!" He held out a hand in case she didn't stop in time.

"You're just in time!"

"For what? What's the hurry?" he asked.

"Grandpa's radio went off!"

"What radio?"

"My police scanner," Hank said, joining them.

"You have a scanner?"

"From my days as a volunteer fireman."

"Day," Derek said. "You lasted one day." Derek shook his head. "Never mind. What's burning?" Derek asked.

"Nothing's burning. Gabrielle's in trouble!" Holly said, her voice rising.

Derek's nerve endings went on alert. "What?"

"The chief said something about a break-in at Mrs. Rhodes's inn," Hank said, translating for Holly.

Derek refused to panic. "There are three rooms at Mrs. Rhodes's place. It could be one of the other people staying there." But even as he suggested it, he vetoed the idea. Gabrielle had already had her car vandalized and received a threatening note. This wasn't a coincidence.

He curled his hand tighter around his keys.

"Chief mentioned a home invasion at the famous writer's room. Want me to watch little missy here?"

Holly shook her head. "Oh, no. I'm going with to check on Gabrielle." She folded her arms across her chest and a mutinous look crossed her face.

Derek grasped Holly's forearms gently and lowered himself to her level. "Listen to me. I know you're worried about Gabrielle. I am, too. But if I take you with me I'm going to worry about you, as well, and then I won't be any good to either of you. What if I promise to call you as soon as I know she's okay?"

"I guess." She glanced down. "If you won't take me, take Fred with you."

He paused. "Dare I ask why?"

"Lots of reasons. Protection, for one thing." She raised a finger in the air. "And he can be your drug-sniffing dog, for another."

Derek stiffened. "Who said anything about drugs? Dad, have you been letting her watch your *Scarface* DVD again?"

Hank ignored him, placing his hand on Holly's shoulder. "Want me to take you for that lunch in the meantime?"

She shook her head. "I won't be able to eat until I know Gabrielle's okay." She glanced up at Derek. "What are you still doing here? Go!" she ordered him, pointing her finger at the door.

She didn't have to tell him twice.

BY THE TIME THE POLICE arrived, Gabrielle had gotten over being scared and had moved on to being furious. This was the third time someone had threatened her since she'd returned to town and she was finished putting up with it.

After examining her room, the police had two pieces of evidence to work with—the door that had been jimmied and a message left in the bathroom, which Gabrielle hadn't gotten close enough to see when she'd first walked into the room.

You were warned! The words had been scrawled in red lipstick on the bathroom mirror.

"Ma'am?" a young police officer, the one who'd already questioned her when he arrived, asked.

Gabrielle turned. "Yes?"

"Are you okay?"

She nodded. "What did you find?"

The officer scratched his head. "Nothing at a glance. We'll have to see what Forensics uncovers."

Gabrielle hoped Forensics was sophisticated in her old hometown.

"In the meantime, I suggest you don't stay here." He tipped his head toward her room. Two other officers remained inside.

"I thought as much myself." But she didn't want to go home.

Going back to Boston would be tantamount to admitting defeat. Giving the person trying to run her off exactly what they wanted. She didn't see that she had much of a choice, though.

"I'll need to know where I can reach you," the officer said.

"She'll be staying with me."

Gabrielle turned at the unexpected sound of

Derek's voice. She might be an adult capable of handling things herself, but she couldn't deny she was happy to see him.

"I'll be right back," she said to the policeman.

"Take your time." He nodded and returned to her room.

Once the police were finished investigating, she'd have to pack up her things, but for now, everything she owned was on display for prying male eyes.

She took Derek's elbow and led him to a private spot outside, beneath a tree. "What are you doing here?" she asked.

"Checking on you." He cupped her cheek in his hand.

She turned her face into his palm, letting his strength calm her. "How did you know I needed checking on?"

"Intuition."

"Seriously."

"Dad's police scanner. What happened?"

She shrugged, still not sure herself. "I dropped Holly off with your uncle Thomas and then I came back here. Someone had broken in while I was gone, tossed stuff all over and left a lipstick-scrawled message on the bathroom mirror."

Derek clenched his fists. "What did the note say?"

"Nothing important."

"Gabrielle…"

"It said, *You were warned*. But—"

He shook his head. "But nothing. Did you tell the police about the first note on your windshield?"

She nodded.

"And your car?"

She nodded again. "But we can't be certain those things are related."

"No, they're coincidence," he said, his sarcasm making his frustration clear.

"Fine." She splayed her hands in front of her. "I'm just trying to calm you down. You're getting all worked up."

He was. His heart was beating hard against his chest and his palms sweat at the thought of someone wanting to hurt her in any way.

"Gabby, you're coming home with me." Where he could keep an eye on her. "I won't take no for an answer."

"As much as I appreciate your concern, you need to think this through." She propped her hands on her hips, obviously ready to chastise him. "Someone is obviously after me. I don't want to bring trouble to your doorstep."

"I can handle it," he said.

"You can, but do you really want to put your daughter at risk?"

That took the wind out of his argument. He ran a hand through his hair and groaned. "I can't believe I didn't think of Holly first."

Her gaze softened. "You're worried about me

and I appreciate your concern. I do. But it's better for everyone if I go back to Boston."

He took her words like a punch in the stomach. Having just found her again, he wasn't ready to let her go. "How do you know you'll be any safer at home?"

"Because leaving is exactly what my tormenter wants me to do." She bit down on her lower lip. "I can't say it's what I want to do, but I don't see that I have any choice."

He racked his brain for an alternative, but he couldn't come up with one, either. "Maybe you're right."

She stepped closer, tipping her head back and meeting his gaze. "Will you miss me?"

He pulled her close and planted a long, sizzling kiss on her lips. One that made her light-headed and dizzy.

"I'll take that as a yes," she said, when she'd finally come up for air. "It's a good thing I'm only an hour away. I might sleep at home, but I'll be in town during the day. I still have research to do."

He frowned. "I'm guessing that's going to make someone even more unhappy."

She nodded, a pleased smile on her face. "Exactly what I'm hoping for. I want to push them into showing their hand. How else can I find out who's behind this unless I keep doing what I'm doing?"

"Unless you bait them, you mean?" Derek was beginning to like this scenario less and less.

"You might call it that." She clasped her hand behind her back and swung from side to side, apparently pleased with her idea.

"I don't like it. You're deliberately trying to provoke this person?"

"I'm going to do my job. In the meantime, if you're nice and supportive, you can visit with me while I'm in town."

And keep an eye on her while he was at it.

He waited with Gabrielle until the police let her back into her room. In the meantime, Mrs. Rhodes had returned from her grocery shopping. The older woman was overcome by the news, so the police took her inside and they called her sister to come help her.

Now Derek sat on the bed while Gabrielle began packing up her things.

It shouldn't feel final, but it did.

He shouldn't be upset. But he was.

Neither one of them mentioned the words on the bathroom mirror or the mess she had to clean as she sorted through the clothes and papers that had been tossed around the room.

"I don't have all that much to pack. I've been living out of a suitcase since I got here."

He'd already taken all of her toiletries out of the bathroom and placed them on the edge of the bed so she wouldn't have to go in there and see the bold words again.

She paused at the foot of the mattress and sealed each bottle in its own bag before placing everything in the female version of a dop kit and laying it on top of all her clothes.

She zipped the suitcase closed. "That's it." She turned back toward him.

"Let me help you to your car."

To his surprise, she let him lift the suitcase off the chair and haul it out to the street. He wedged it into the back of the trunk and slammed the door closed.

"Thank you." She treated him to one of her sweet smiles.

"I didn't think you'd let me help." She'd always prided herself on her ability to do things on her own.

"Do you want the truth?"

"Of course."

"After last night, I'm a little sore in body parts I didn't know I had." She curled her hands around his shirt and pulled him closer. "Since you caused it, I figured it's only fair that I let you do the heavy lifting for me today," she said playfully.

Leaning forward, she planted a kiss on his lips.

He cupped his hands around her face and reciprocated, his tongue slipping easily inside her willing mouth. His heart kicked hard inside his chest and he tilted her head to the side, delving deeper into her sweetness.

She broke the kiss first. "I think you're going to miss me," she said, sounding extremely pleased.

She should be, Derek thought. Because he wasn't just going to miss her, he was going to worry every second she wasn't in sight. Which meant he'd be thinking about her.

Day.

And night.

DEREK ARRIVED BACK HOME in no mood for an inquisition, but resigned to answer Holly's questions, anyway.

Sure enough, she greeted him as soon as he stepped in the front door. "How is Gabrielle?" his daughter asked. "What happened at her place? Did someone really break in? Did they take anything? Is she hurt?"

He slung an arm over his daughter's shoulders and steered her toward the kitchen. "Gabrielle is fine. Someone ransacked her room, but the police don't think they took anything of value. Does that cover all of your questions?" he asked, unable to contain a grin.

"Just the first few. Where is she? Is she scared to stay alone? I can't imagine being by myself after something like that happened to me."

He lowered himself into one of the kitchen chairs. "Gabrielle went back to Boston," he told her.

"What? Why?"

"Because it's safer there for her. Besides, that's where her home is." He glanced at Holly. "Would you mind getting me a Diet Coke?"

She shook her head and headed to the fridge, pulled out a plastic bottle and handed it to him.

"Thanks." He twisted off the top and took a long, cold drink.

"Dad, why didn't Gabrielle just come back here with you?" Holly looked up at him with her big, inquisitive eyes and asked the question he'd hoped she wouldn't think about asking.

"I offered, but it seemed smarter for her to go home."

Holly narrowed her gaze. "Smarter how?"

Sometimes he really wished she wasn't so darned bright. "She didn't want to bring trouble to our doorstep," he said carefully, trying to find a way to phrase things without making her feel guilty.

"You mean, whoever broke into her place could break in here if she was staying with us?" Holly asked.

"That's right." He lifted the bottle for another drink.

"But you could handle anyone who broke in! So could Grandpa Hank," she said, pride and certainty in her expression. Just as quickly, the light in her eyes dimmed. "She was worried about me, right? I'm the reason she didn't come back to stay here?"

Derek ran a hand through his hair. "Baby, she

lives in Boston. She belongs at her place. She was never going to stay here permanently, anyway."

"But she never took me to Target like she promised." Disappointment tugged at Holly's lips. He hoped she wasn't about to cry.

"Hey! Boston isn't the other end of the world. Gabrielle has every intention of coming back here often. She's working on a book and she has people to interview here. And I know she'll take you shopping. She wouldn't miss that." He rose and ruffled Holly's hair, hoping he was cheering her up.

It was difficult to force a smile when he was worried about Gabrielle going home alone. Still, whoever had a grudge against her obviously wanted her gone from Stewart. They'd have no reason to bother her in Boston.

"Uncle Mike can look after her in Boston, right? He kicks bad guys' butts all the time!"

Derek shot her a warning look, but he let her get away with the comment. Because for an eleven-year-old, she was smarter than her dad. "Yeah. Uncle Mike can keep an eye on her."

Derek might not like the distance between them, but he had to admit she was safer in Boston than she would have been here.

GABRIELLE PLANNED TO GO home, get some sleep, wake up and be back in Stewart the following morning. Life and routine got in the way.

She awoke, showered, made herself a cup of coffee and called her mother, just as she did every day. She'd spoken to Juliette while she was in Stewart, but now that she was home, her mother had *plans* for them.

"So I thought we'd have an early lunch at Le Petit Croissant and then we could go shopping at Neiman's at Copley. Your father is teaching summer classes and so he won't be joining us."

"I won't be able to make it, either, *Maman*. I have interviews I have to do back in Stewart." Gabrielle tucked the phone between her ear and her shoulder, wrapping her hands around a big mug of coffee as she spoke.

"Then we can have breakfast early and you go do your interviews later in the day. I miss you," her mother said.

Gabrielle smiled. "And I miss you, too. I'll meet you in an hour." Breakfast with her mother turned into a two-hour chat fest centered around Derek.

The small café was a favorite of her mother's. Even when Gabrielle was a little girl, they'd often come into Boston and stop here on their shopping trips. Now that her parents lived in the city, her mother frequented the quaint café almost daily.

Juliette reached across the table and placed her hand over Gabrielle's. "He hurt you badly," her mother said, concerned.

She didn't need the reminder. She'd lived it.

"Not because he didn't love me. I know what I'm dealing with now." At least she hoped she did.

"Well, I always liked him. Derek was a nice boy. He treated you well while you were together. He made you happy and that is what counted then," she mused. "But now? I want for you what your papa and I have."

Gabrielle smiled. Her parents had a happy marriage. They understood each other. It was exactly what she wanted for her own life, Gabrielle thought.

Just as their brunch ended, her father called and invited his favorite women to dinner, which Gabrielie ended up accepting. She was an independent woman who lived her own life, but when her parents invited her, she always felt compelled to go. As if she didn't want to miss out on any time with them.

But spending time with her parents didn't mean she'd forget about Derek. And she certainly didn't intend to let him forget about her.

Her first night home, she climbed into bed and called him before falling asleep.

The phone rang and rang. She was about to hang up when she heard his voice. "Hey, there," she said.

"Hi, yourself." His voice sounded huskier than usual.

"Did I wake you?" she asked.

"Not really."

Gabrielle grinned. He never used to admit she'd

woken him in the past, either. "I'll take that as a yes. I'm sorry. I just didn't want to go to bed without hearing your voice," she said honestly.

"I'm glad you called."

She curled on her side and snuggled into her pillow, the phone cradled against her ear. "And why's that?"

"Your voice will be the last thing I hear before I go to sleep." His deep tone rumbled through her.

Closing her eyes, she let herself imagine him lying in his bed, wearing nothing but the boxers he favored. She could almost feel her fingertips gliding through the coarse hair on his chest.

"Gabby?"

His voice brought her back to reality. "Hmm?"

"I asked how your parents are doing. Are you falling asleep on me?"

She licked her dry lips. "Not a chance," she murmured. "My mother is fine. We had a nice breakfast. And we talked about you."

He let out a groan. "I can only imagine how she feels about me these days."

"She remembers you as a nice boy. I assured her that hadn't changed. And my father is doing well, too. He loves teaching and I think he finds the summer even more challenging because the classes are smaller and his students really want to learn."

Derek chuckled. "I do remember him trying to

engage me in academic debates. I wasn't much good against him."

"Don't feel bad. Nobody is. Anyway, they both said to say hi," she said, fudging the truth.

In reality both of her parents were wary about her getting involved again with the man who'd broken her heart years ago. It didn't help that he now had a child. An eleven-year-old child who only reinforced their opinion that he'd moved on and she hadn't. Since Gabrielle wasn't about to get into personal issues—or curses—with her academic-oriented parents, she decided to let it go. They'd been critical of the beliefs most of the people in town had even back when they'd lived in Stewart. She wasn't about to assume their feelings had changed.

She'd just have to let time and Derek prove them wrong. Or so she hoped.

"Tell them I say hello, too."

"I will."

"When are you coming back?" he asked.

A touch of longing sounded in his tone. It matched the way she felt, too. She missed him. His laugh, his smile. His touch.

"Tomorrow. I'd like to conduct some interviews for my book." And she hoped by stirring the pot, she'd smoke out whoever was after her.

He cleared his throat. "With whom?" he asked gruffly.

She curled her hand into a tight fist as she answered, knowing he wouldn't like her reply. "I called Mary Perkins's office today to make an appointment. Her granddaughter, Elizabeth, answered the phone. She said the mayor was out of the office and she didn't have access to her appointment book." But Gabrielle didn't believe it for a minute. Elizabeth was totally anal, Gabrielle doubted the mayor could breathe without the younger woman knowing about it. Gabrielle knew she was being stonewalled and she'd decided to just show up tomorrow and wait until the mayor made the time to speak with her.

Derek expelled a harsh breath. "Why would you bother with her? She's an old, bitter woman with an unreasonable hatred for my family and an unbelievable need for power."

"That's exactly why. She masquerades as a politician who wants the best for her town and constituents, but the more people I talk to, the more I learn that she's almost universally disliked. She uses her family name to manipulate people. It's part of the ramifications of believing in curses. I want to get into her psyche," Gabrielle said.

"What you're going to end up doing is upsetting whatever nutcase ransacked your room." His voice rose in frustration.

"Shh! You're going to wake Holly," she said, hoping to calm him.

She pulled herself into a half-sitting position in bed, leaning against the headboard and pillows. "You knew I was going to interview people affected by the curse. I can handle myself. I promise."

"I'm not sure I can handle you," he muttered.

She smiled, knowing he'd given in. He might not like her choices, but his tone indicated he wasn't going to fight them.

More relaxed, she eased back down into the bed. "I think you can handle me just fine."

More important, he obviously still wanted to.

"How's Holly?" she asked.

"Fine. I kept her busy planning her birthday party. Since her school friends are in New York, it'll mostly be family, but she seems happy with it."

"When is her mother coming back?"

"Two weeks."

Gabrielle nodded. She understood how important this summer with his daughter was for Derek. "I'm happy for you."

"Thanks. I'm pretty happy myself, considering things were so different this time last year."

"Tell Holly I haven't forgotten about our shopping trip."

"Even if you had, she wouldn't hesitate to remind you," he said, chuckling.

Unable to control herself, Gabrielle let out a yawn. Her eyes were growing heavier with each passing minute.

"You should go get some sleep," he said.

"No. I'm fine." She wasn't ready to let go of him just yet.

"Call me when you get to town tomorrow, okay?"

"'Kay," she said sleepily.

"And remember if you have any problems, call my cousin Mike. You have the number I gave you?"

"Mmm-hmm."

"Gabby?"

"Hmm?"

"Remember when we used to talk like this back in high school?"

She smiled at the memory. "We'd argue over who was more tired. Neither of us wanted to hang up first."

She always used to fall asleep thinking that she loved him but couldn't ever say so. He feared the word as much as the men in his family feared the curse. But she hadn't had to say it. In her heart, she believed Derek had known she loved him back then.

Just as she loved him now….

GABRIELLE AWOKE WITH A start as the first rays of sunlight flowed through her bedroom window. She stretched and rolled over, her hip hitting a hard object.

She reached down to move…the telephone.

She'd fallen asleep while still on the phone with

Derek last night, just as she'd done so often in the past. Smiling, she climbed out of bed, showered, put on her makeup and was getting dressed when her cell phone rang.

She dug her phone out from her purse and answered. "Hello?"

"Hi. It's Sharon."

"Where *are* you? I haven't heard from you since you left for the conference. You librarians must be heavy-duty partiers," Gabrielle said, laughing.

Sharon didn't laugh. "I'm not at a conference."

"Just where are you, then?"

"At the moment? I'm about half an hour from Stewart. My car broke down at the motel I'm staying at and I need you to come get me. I'll explain when you get here."

Gabrielle grabbed a pen and a pad she kept next to her kitchen telephone. "Give me the address. I'll be right there."

Sharon repeated the name of the motel and then, reluctantly, gave Gabrielle the address—which just happened to be in the same town she and Derek had found Sharon's ex, Tony.

Gabrielle expelled a long breath, holding back from chastising her friend until she could do it in person. "Sit tight. I'll be there as soon as I can."

"I knew I could count on you," Sharon said.

Almost an hour later thanks to traffic and a miscalculated exit, Gabrielle pulled into the motel parking lot where Sharon's car had died. Sure enough, Sharon's sedan was in one of the parking spots.

Sharon walked out of a side motel entrance. Dressed in dark pants and a black tank top, sunglasses perched on a baseball hat, she joined Gabrielle. "I called AAA and they should be here soon. We can leave after they've towed my car."

Gabrielle nodded. She seated herself on the curb and waited for Sharon to do the same. "Since we have time, do you want to explain why you look like a cat burglar? And make it good because I'm about to have you committed." She raised an eyebrow and waited.

Sharon took a long breath. "I went to stalk Tony," she said on a rush.

"You what!" Gabrielle jerked around to stare at her friend.

"It's more rational than it sounds, I swear. I just wanted to see what he was up to. What his life is like. If it's possible he's reformed, as he claims."

Gabrielle opened her eyes wider in disbelief. "Why didn't you say something? I would have come with you!"

"That's why. I had to do this for myself. I had to see for myself."

"And?"

Sharon met her gaze. "He has a wife and a child!"

"Whoa. He said he lived with his sister. He lied?"

Sharon nodded. "Apparently so."

"Now, that's a shock. A convicted felon who's also a liar." Gabrielle bit the inside of her cheek. Now she understood why he'd stepped outside and hadn't wanted to let them into the house. "So if he lied about that, what else is he lying about? He obviously didn't want his family to know what he did to you."

Sharon shook her head. "I don't think so. It's weird, but I've watched him for a couple of days and he's different. Mellow. More at ease than he ever was before. I actually do think he's changed."

"Or maybe he hasn't and this life is a cover." Gabrielle placed her hand over her friend's.

"I considered that, too. There's only one way to find out."

"And that is?" Gabrielle was almost afraid to ask.

Sharon smiled grimly. "I'm going to have to confront him."

Before Gabrielle could respond, the tow truck pulled up in front of them. She couldn't continue this talk now, but once the car situation was settled, Gabrielle had every intention of nixing Sharon's suicidal idea.

CHAPTER TWELVE

GABRIELLE PROMISED SHARON she'd drive her back to Stewart right after Gabrielle stopped at her apartment in Boston to pick up some notes regarding her upcoming interview with Mary Perkins. Since Sharon was preoccupied, Gabrielle didn't mention that her room at the Rhodes Inn had been ransacked and she'd been forced to return home for good. She didn't want to add to Sharon's already high stress level.

And since Sharon was upset enough, Gabrielle didn't even chastise her for stalking her ex. There would be time for that during the ride back to Stewart.

"What's wrong?" she asked her friend, instead.

Sharon sighed. "I'm just wondering how much it's going to cost me to get the car fixed, how I'm going to afford it on top of the blackmail." She glanced out the window, pressing her forehead against the heavy glass.

Gabrielle's heart went out to her friend. "It goes without saying…"

Sharon cut her off with a sharp wave of her hand. "I appreciate it, but unless I've exhausted all my options, I'll make it work. I just need to vent and think things through," Sharon said, her tone soft and full of appreciation.

Gabrielle nodded. She respected her friend's independent streak.

Both women knew Gabrielle's writing provided her with a surplus of income and she could more than afford to help Sharon with both the blackmail money and the repairs. But Sharon had a little too much pride. Her refusal to tell Richard about the blackmail was an example. If she needed help, financial or otherwise, Sharon understood Gabrielle would be there.

"We're here." Gabrielle pulled up to the curb by her brownstone. "Wait here. I'll run in and get what I need."

Sharon shook her head. "I'll come in with you. I need to use your bathroom before we start the car ride home."

Gabrielle left the car in the illegal No Standing zone and the women ran up the flights of stairs to Gabrielle's unit, a two-bedroom apartment she'd leased upon her return from Florida.

When they reached the top of the stairs, Gabrielle noticed her door was open and an uncomfortable feeling of déjà vu assaulted her.

"Did you leave this door—"

"No. Definitely not." She cut Sharon off and halted in her tracks, not wanting to go any closer.

"You're sure? Because sometimes I forget to lock my parents' house, you know?"

"I'm positive. I locked it." After her last night in Stewart, Gabrielle had diligently locked her door whenever she left.

She met Sharon's worried gaze. "I guess now's the time to tell you my room at Mrs. Rhodes's was broken into and ransacked. The person left a calling card in red lipstick." Gabrielle tried to swallow but her mouth had grown dry.

Sharon raised her eyebrows. "Well? What did it say?"

"You were warned!"

"Jeez, Gabrielle, you should have told me," Sharon chided, her voice rising.

"Shh!" Gabrielle placed a finger to her lips. "We don't know if anyone is still in there."

Eyes wide, Sharon nodded.

"Follow me."

Slowly and quietly they made their way back down the stairs. From the safety of her car, Gabrielle once again called 9-1-1.

DEREK WAS GETTING TOO OLD for these kinds of scares. Gabrielle had just called and informed him about the break-in at her Boston apartment. This time her computer had been stolen, as well as notes and papers on all her books.

She'd called 9-1-1, for which he was grateful, but she'd avoided calling his cousin. Derek had a hunch she didn't want to involve his family and he let it go. As long as she'd brought the police in, he was satisfied.

It was obvious to Derek that someone wanted to send her a message—and they weren't going to let a little thing like distance stop them.

Clearly, she wasn't safe alone.

She hadn't asked Derek for anything, but he knew she had nowhere to stay where she felt safe. She wouldn't put her parents in danger any more than she would put Sharon and her parents, or Derek and Holly in harm's way.

He'd had one helluva time convincing her to move in with him until the person harassing her was found. But eventually she'd gratefully relented.

He gathered his family together. Uncle Thomas, Hank and Holly sat in his large living room and listened as he explained what had happened to Gabrielle over the past few days.

"So I'm wondering how you'd feel about bunking with Grandpa and Uncle Thomas for a little while?" Derek leaned down on one knee as he asked his daughter's opinion.

Since Holly had just recently come to stay with him and they were just starting to build a relationship, he didn't intend for her to feel displaced or unwanted.

"Par-ty!" Holly said, obviously not upset by the request.

Derek rose to his feet, ignoring the stiffness that reminded him he had stopped going to the gym since his move back home.

"Are you sure?"

Holly swung her head around to look at her grandfather. "Can I stay up late? Eat cookies in bed? Watch whatever movies I want?"

Hank winked at her.

Derek shook his head, amazed at her sunny outlook. Bless her, she wasn't hard to get along with, Derek thought.

"That was easy."

Hank shook his head. "Not so fast. I'm not sleeping in the same room with her. She snores."

Holly giggled.

Once again Derek was reminded of what a good man his father was when it came to his granddaughter. He always knew how to make her laugh.

"So nobody minds?"

"Of course not. You know we can take care of Holly without a problem. It's Gabrielle's safety that's important," Uncle Thomas said.

"Thank you," Derek said.

Hank muttered something under his breath.

"Dad?"

Hank raised an eyebrow. "What?"

"That's what I want to know. What's bugging you?"

His father leaned his elbow against the arm of the sofa. "Nothing."

"Then what were you mumbling about?"

Hank frowned. "You aren't going to like it."

Derek raised an eyebrow. "Tell me, anyway." He'd rather have things out in the open.

"I'm just thinking that Gabrielle wouldn't be in danger if she minded her own business. Digging into other people's lives isn't a very nice way to earn a living."

"Holly, let's go take Fred for a walk," Uncle Thomas said. Rising from his seat, he gestured for her to follow him.

"But…" Holly remained sitting until her uncle forcibly pulled her up. "Fine," she said, grumbling, clearly not happy about being left out of the conversation. "You know Grandpa's just going to tell me later," she said, shuffling her feet as she made her way out the door.

Derek would have laughed if he wasn't so intent on dealing with his father. He strode over to Hank, who had risen to his feet.

"I think it's time we have this out once and for all," Derek said. "What do you have against Gabrielle? Please don't tell me it has to do with her career choice or the subject matter of her newest book."

"Fine." He exhaled a harsh breath. "It's not about the book. It's about her. And you."

Derek narrowed his gaze. "You always liked Gabrielle. So what gives now? Especially since you haven't seen her in over ten years?"

Hank stomped over to the window and glanced out at the yard between their two houses. "When she first came back, it was about the curse. I didn't want her dragging up old issues that should remain dead and buried."

"Not possible, but go on."

"When I saw how many people showed up for her talk, I realized you were right about that. People are fascinated by our love lives, or lack of them." Hank braced his hands on the window-sill. "I resigned myself to her writing the damn book. Because whether she does or not, people around here are still going to gossip about the Corwin men."

Derek nodded. "Agreed. So…?" He prodded his father, wanting him to get to the point. "What's your problem with Gabrielle?"

"She's setting you up for another fall, that's what."

Derek had a feeling he knew where his father was going. To a place he'd been avoiding thinking about since his night with Gabrielle.

"You've been spending a lot of time with her and now she'll be living with you. You'll fall in love with her all over again and it'll make what you went through with Marlene seem like child's play in comparison."

Derek's head began to pound. "I won't fall in love with her." He clenched his hands into tight fists at his sides.

"Good." Hank turned to face him. "I hope you mean that. You weren't in love with Holly's mom, isn't that right?"

Derek nodded. "She was a good woman, a good friend and a good mother. She deserved better than what I was able to give her because I wasn't in love with her."

"And yet?" Hank asked, obviously pushing him to say the words.

"And yet I lost my fortune, my marriage and I nearly lost my daughter," Derek muttered, hating like hell having to discuss the curse out loud.

Hank wrapped a fatherly arm around his shoulder. "I know it hurts, but ignoring the truth will end up hurting even more."

Derek breathed in deep. "I won't fall in love with Gabrielle," he said to his father, wondering how he'd keep his promise when he feared he'd already broken it.

SHARON PACED THE SMALL bedroom of the house she and Richard had bought together. After Gabrielle had dropped her off, she'd called her fiancé and asked him to meet her after work. They needed to talk.

She'd decided to level with him about what was going on. She only hoped he could handle it.

Expecting him around five-thirty, which was when he usually left work at his law firm, Sharon was surprised to hear his key in the lock late that afternoon.

She met him at the front door.

He stepped inside, and though she started forward to embrace him, he walked past her and placed his briefcase down on the floor.

Uh-oh.

She swallowed hard. "You're home early."

He inclined his head. "You said you needed me."

Yet he remained at a distance, emotionally and physically. And she hadn't even confided in him yet.

"So how was your conference?" he asked.

She rubbed her hands up and down her bare arms, but the chill remained. "There wasn't one."

He turned toward her, his handsome face more a mask of disappointment than confusion. She shivered even more.

"Would you care to explain?" he asked.

"Come. Sit down." She led the way into the small study they would one day share. They planned on building bookshelves to line the walls, her own little library, his desk and home office.

He sat on the couch while she chose a chair across from him. Elbows resting on his knees, he stared at her, his gaze intense. He didn't say a word.

She studied him, too. His dark hair, neatly combed, gave him that air of propriety she both loved and feared would be the end of them.

She drew a deep, fortifying breath. "A few days ago, I received an anonymous letter in the mail." She glanced down at her hands, not surprised to see they were shaking. "And though I'm not sure who sent it, it was clear what was in it."

He met her gaze. "What was it?" he asked, his voice steady.

He was everything she loved and wanted in her life. But there was obviously more separating them than the story she had to tell. Not knowing what it was scared her beyond belief.

"A picture," she whispered. "An old photograph. One of *those* old photographs, if you get my drift."

"Oh, I get it, all right," he said, clenching his jaw.

"There was also a note demanding five thousand dollars."

"That bastard." He rose from his seat in a burst of sudden, angry energy. "I'm going to kill him."

She came up behind him and placed her hand on his shoulder. "No, you're not. Because then I'd lose you to prison instead of just…losing you." She stepped back, easing away from him.

This time *he* came up behind her and she felt his body heat close. Reassuring.

"Why would you say that?" he asked.

She faced him again. "Because I didn't get the letter today. I got it a few days ago."

"And you didn't tell me." His disappointment spoke louder than his words.

Nausea rolled through her and she wished she'd listened to Gabrielle's advice about telling Richard sooner.

She shook her head. "You had so much on your plate between work and the campaign. I thought, I hoped, I could make it go away."

"How?"

"The note had instructions. A drop point for the money. So I withdrew the cash from the bank and Gabrielle and I went to the Wave."

He stared at her in disbelief. "You two went to meet with your blackmailing ex-con boyfriend alone?"

She winced at the fury in his voice. "Not exactly."

He ran a hand through his hair. "Then what, exactly, Sharon? Spell it out and be clear."

She knew what she'd say next would only make her keeping him in the dark even worse, but she had no choice. "Gabrielle was thinking more clearly. She knew better than to go there alone, so she told Derek. He showed up before the set meeting time."

He stared at her in silence. She could almost hear his thoughts. *Gabrielle trusted Derek but you couldn't trust me?*

"I trust you," she assured him. "I just didn't

want to burden you with my problems when you have so many of your own." God, her words sounded lame.

Why hadn't she shared this with him earlier? She knew why. She hadn't wanted to see the disgust in his eyes. Every time she thought about those photographs, about that time, she felt it. She was sure he did, too.

"Burden. Right." He muttered something else under his breath. "Go on. What else don't I know?"

"At some point during the night, someone slipped a note in my bag telling me where to leave the money, but I didn't find it until the next morning. I panicked. I thought for sure they would expose the photo and it would kill your campaign. Gabrielle said Derek called his cousin, who is a police detective in Boston. He told Derek where Tony was living since his release and they spoke to him. He claimed to know nothing about the sudden resurrection of the pictures, but they weren't sure if they should believe him. I needed to know."

"What. Did. You. Do?" he asked.

She ran her hands over her eyes, trying to hold it together and not cry. "I stalked him. Sort of. I mean, I stood behind trees and buildings and I watched. He has a wife now. Can a man who has a wife and a child be a blackmailer? I was going to confront him in front of his family, but my car died. I had to call Gabrielle to come get me. We stopped by her place and someone had broken in there, too—" Sharon knew she was rambling, but the stony look on Richard's face had her in a panic.

She didn't know what else to do except to keep talking. If she explained, maybe he wouldn't be angry. Maybe he'd understand and forgive.

She forced herself to look into his eyes and that's when she realized. "You already know something. That's why you've been acting so strange. What is it you know?"

He gestured to his briefcase in the hall. "I also received a photo and a note."

The blood in her veins ran cold. Her legs grew weak and she stepped back to the nearest chair, collapsing into it. "Go on."

"The note said you didn't pay up the first time so now the burden was on me. But the blackmailer didn't want money. No, the terms were that I had to drop out of the race or the photo would be made public. Guess what *my* first reaction was?"

"What?" she whispered.

"To find you. To confide in you. To see if you were okay and to fix this together. That's when *I* realized. If you didn't pay the money the first time, *you already knew* about the photo. You were being blackmailed. But you hadn't confided in me." He turned away from her. "How in the hell do you think that made me feel?"

Sharon pushed herself to her feet. "Don't you think if I thought I could confide in you, I would have?"

He stared at her in disbelief. "What is that supposed to mean?"

She straightened her shoulders and forced herself to face him head-on. "Just that every time I brought up my past with Tony, you brushed it aside. You said you didn't want to hear about it."

"I didn't want to put you through reliving it," he said, correcting her. His eyes flashed angry sparks.

She blinked away tears. "That isn't what you said. You said you didn't need to hear it. As if it disgusted you. As if I disgusted you." Her voice broke on the last word.

"Disgusted me?" Suddenly he was in front of her. He tipped her chin up, making her meet his gaze. "Whatever gave you that idea?"

"You did! Every time you kissed me softly and started to get excited, every time I thought you'd become more aggressive, treat me like you *wanted* me, you'd back off. Get gentle. And it didn't feel like you *wanted* me anymore. Not as much as you should," she said, her voice rising.

She didn't recognize the words coming out of her mouth. She didn't believe she was saying them, yet she was. She was talking from the depths of her soul, admitting things to him she'd never even admitted to herself. Because she was afraid.

Afraid if she said them aloud, she'd lose him.

But, she realized now, she just might have lost him, anyway. So really, maybe she had nothing left to lose.

Nothing and everything, Sharon thought.

DEREK HAD LIVED ALONE for the past couple of years so he wasn't used to worrying about others. He'd always known Marlene was taking good care of Holly and heaven knows his father took care of himself. But now that he had two women in his life, he thought about them constantly. At least Holly was safe with his father and uncle.

Where the hell was Gabrielle?

He glanced at his wristwatch. "Almost dinnertime," he muttered. He tried her cell phone, but it went straight to voice mail and he left a message.

She said she would drop Sharon off at home and come right over. Thirty minutes from Boston with no traffic, an hour with traffic max. Half an hour tops to drop Sharon off, to walk her inside and chat with her parents. Five minutes to get here.

All told, an hour and forty-five minutes, two hours at the most. Instead three hours had passed since he'd gotten her call and rearranged his and his daughter's lives in order to keep Gabrielle safe.

So he asked himself again. Where the hell could she be?

IT HAD BEEN OVER AN HOUR since Gabrielle had pulled up to Mary Perkins's mayoral office, located in an old Victorian mansion on the border of the two neighboring towns. The house was painted a grayish blue with white trim, common in the New England landscape.

Grabbing both her handbag and her laptop for safekeeping, she walked to the front porch. The screen was closed, the main door open.

Taped to the screen was a typed note, not sleek perfect computer ink but old-fashioned typesetting, complete with dropped letters: *Back soon. Let yourself inside. M.*

Although Mary wasn't expecting her, Gabrielle did as the note suggested and stepped into the front hall. There was no receptionist waiting behind the messy, paper-strewn desk.

"Hello?" Gabrielle called out in case someone was inside.

Nobody replied.

She walked around, peeking into various meeting rooms, only to find those empty, as well.

At the far end of the only long hall, a set of heavy-looking double doors were shut tight. She didn't have to read the sign to know what it said— Mayor's Office.

She bit the inside of her cheek and knocked.

Silence.

She jiggled the handle.

Locked.

Mary Perkins didn't have a problem leaving the outer office open, but the doors to the inner sanctum were practically vaulted shut. She wouldn't be surprised if the room was soundproof, she thought wryly.

She couldn't decide what to do. She could leave and head to Derek's, but based on the note on the door, someone was due to arrive soon.

Gabrielle exhaled hard and eased herself into a chair in the sitting area in the front of the house. She crossed her legs, leaned back against the old velour couch and picked up a fan, which had been left on a table. She shut her eyes and fanned herself, hoping to ease the heat and humidity that seeped into the old house and into Gabrielle's pores. Logically she knew waving hot air into her face wasn't going to help, but it couldn't possibly hurt.

She didn't know how much time had passed when she finally heard the creaking of the hinges on the screen door. She rose from her seat without letting go of the fan. At some point she'd become convinced the hot air was somehow cooling her off.

"Grandma?" A female voice called.

"Nobody's here but me," Gabrielle said, feeling like an intruder.

"Who's me?" A pretty brunette stepped into the main area where Gabrielle stood.

Gabrielle lifted her free hand in a half wave.

"My name is Gabrielle Donovan. I came by to see Mayor Perkins. Nobody is here, but the door was open and the sign said someone would be back soon so I thought I'd wait."

"I'm Lauren Perkins," the woman said, extending her hand.

Gabrielle shook it. "Mayor Perkins is your grandmother?"

She nodded.

"Doesn't she have another granddaughter? Her assistant?" Gabrielle asked, thinking of the Mary Perkins clone.

Lauren smiled. "That's my sister."

Gabrielle narrowed her gaze. She just didn't see the resemblance between the two women.

"Don't tell me. We look nothing alike," Lauren said, laughing. "I hear it all the time."

Gabrielle grinned. "You read my mind."

"Yes, well, my grandmother is expecting me as you can tell by the note on the door. I'd recognize Grandma's old Smith Corona type anywhere."

"A typewriter?" Gabrielle asked. "Wow."

Lauren laughed. "Not many people know what those are anymore."

"I'm a writer. I'm into research and old things."

Lauren wrinkled her nose in thought, then snapped her fingers. "Gabrielle Donovan! The author. You're *that* Gabrielle Donovan! I'm a huge fan of your work," she said.

"Well, thank you." She thought about the notion of someone still using an old typewriter today. "I take it your grandmother isn't into the computer age?"

Lauren shook her head. "Although it would be easier for her if she was. Arthritis makes it difficult for her to write. I can't say that typing is much easier, but she says at least it's more legible. I hope my sister is planning to bring her into the technological age soon. But Gran is very set in her ways, I guess you'd say. It makes her hard to please sometimes," Lauren confided.

"Who says I'm hard to please? Shame on you for talking about your grandmother that way!"

Both Gabrielle and Lauren turned at the sound of Mary Perkins's voice.

"Grandma!" Lauren exclaimed, obviously happy to see the older woman and not at all concerned at being caught talking behind her back.

And Mary had obviously not been upset with her, since contrary to her normally restrained demeanor, she held out her arms and pulled her granddaughter into a warm hug.

"How's your arthritis?" Lauren asked.

"Nothing can keep your grandmother down, you know that," Mary said.

"Where's my sister?"

"Running errands for me in town. She left the note for you, but she said to tell you she'll be back soon." Mary stepped back from her granddaughter and turned to Gabrielle. "Ms. Donovan, how nice to see you. What brings you by?"

"I've been wanting to make an appointment, but Elizabeth said she didn't know your schedule, so I thought I'd take a chance and stop by." Gabrielle decided not to mention her upcoming book unless asked. She didn't want to discourage the other woman from setting up a time to talk. Obviously, since her granddaughter was here to see her, she was too busy now.

"Well, Elizabeth can be overprotective of my time." She smiled, but the smile didn't reach her eyes. "What did you want to discuss?" Mary asked.

Gabrielle drew herself up straighter. "Actually, I'd like to talk to you about the curse, how it's affected your family from the original generation on. Whatever you can tell me, I'd love to hear it."

"For your book?" the mayor asked.

"You're writing a new book? About what?" Lauren asked.

Gabrielle glanced at the mayor.

"The Corwin Curse," Mary said.

Lauren shook her head, a skeptical look crossed her face. "Have fun," she said lightly.

"I take it you don't believe in it?" Gabrielle asked.

"Oh, no." Lauren waved away the notion.

Mary frowned.

"Yet Elizabeth does?"

Lauren inclined her head. "My sister and grand-mother are cut from the same cloth."

Mary turned back to Gabrielle. "I'd be happy to discuss my family with you," she said, surprising Gabrielle. "Let me make the appointment myself."

She pulled a set of keys from her purse and walked over to the double doors, letting herself into her office. Since she didn't invite them in, Gabrielle waited where she was, despite her curiosity.

Mary returned with a leather-bound appoint-ment book in her hand. They agreed on a morn-ing appointment during the week and both wrote it down.

Gabrielle glanced at her watch and realized, with a start, how late it had gotten. Derek was ex-pecting her. "I really should be going," Gabrielle said. "Nice to meet you, Lauren."

"Same here." The other woman nodded. "I'm only here for a short time, but hopefully I'll see you again soon."

Considering this woman was related to Mary Perkins and could offer insight into her psyche, Gabrielle nodded. "Count on it," she said, before heading out the door.

CHAPTER THIRTEEN

GABRIELLE DIDN'T HAVE TO ring Derek's doorbell.
He flung it open as soon as she set foot on the front
porch. Grabbing her wrist, he pulled her inside,
locking the dead bolt behind her.

"Where the hell have you been? I've been worried
sick. I thought maybe something had happened to
you!" A muscle throbbed in his left temple.

She winced. "I'm sorry. I got caught up on an
errand. Why didn't you call my cell?"

"I did! Have you checked it lately?"

With a frown, she pulled her phone from her
purse. "Did I forget to turn it on?"

He snatched it out of her hand and fumbled with
it for a few seconds. "You forgot to charge it," he
muttered. "What kind of errand was so important?"

Considering his mood, she didn't think he'd appreciate her answer. "I stopped by Mayor Perkins's
office to make an appointment." She treated him
to her sweetest smile, hoping to ease her way back
into his good graces.

He shut his eyes and groaned.

Obviously it didn't work. He stalked toward her, pushing her back until she hit the wall. His eyes were flashing fire but his gaze quickly darkened, his anger shifting to desire.

"I was so damn scared something had happened to you," he said, his voice husky.

The sound found an answering yearning inside her. Her heart beat faster and her breath quickened. "I'm fine."

"I didn't know that." He placed his palm flush with the wall, his arm bracketing her shoulder.

"I'll call next time."

He tipped his head, his lips close to hers. "You'd better." And then his mouth came down hard against hers.

His touch was electric and welcome.

Today had been stressful and frightening, but she'd held herself together enough to pursue her interview. She hadn't realized how much she'd needed the emotional connection to Derek until now. She wrapped her arms around his neck and kissed him back. A hollow need settled in the pit of her stomach and she knew only he could fill the urgency pulsing inside her.

She wrapped her leg around the back of his thigh and pulled him close, aligning his body with hers. His shirt rasped against her chest. Beneath her tank top, her nipples puckered into rigid peaks and she arched her back so her breasts thrust forward, brushing against the material of both her top and his. Her nipples beaded even tighter, and warm dewy moisture trickled between her thighs.

His hands were everywhere, touching, plucking, caressing her through her clothes until she was beyond thought. Beyond reason.

When he stepped back to undress, she did the same. He didn't suggest the bedroom and neither did she.

"I'll be right back." He darted up the stairs.

She didn't ask where he was going. She knew. And then he was back, condom in hand.

She took the plastic square packet from him and ripped it open, holding the damp sheath in her fingertips. Slowly and with care, she knelt in front of him and rolled the condom over his turgid length. It was erotic, really, to take control and feel him pulsing in her hand, knowing he'd soon be inside her body.

She glanced up to see him watching her intently. She deliberately prolonged the act until he placed his hand at the top of her head.

"Enough. Unless you want this to be over now."

She rose to her feet and met his gaze. The urgency between them was a tangible thing. Gabrielle stood on her tiptoes and placed a gentle, lingering kiss on his stubbled cheek. "I definitely don't want this over too soon."

He laced his fingers with hers and led her to the couch.

"Sit."

This intrigued her and she did as she was told. He placed a hand on each of her thighs and spread her legs open wide. Her leg muscles quivered at his touch.

"Are you okay?" he asked.

She smiled at his concern. "Couldn't be better."

Gabrielle had always loved sex, especially with him, but when they were younger, it had always been a fast, missionary kind of thing. Her experiments with other men had been limited because she hadn't trusted them. With Derek, she felt safe.

He knelt down and eased his big body between her legs. His hands shifted to her waist, his touch burning her sensitive skin. Leaning forward, he pressed a reverent kiss on her belly, pausing to flick his tongue over her belly button, inside and out, then around until his tongue landed on her stomach, taking a damp path downward.

Her legs stiffened and he glanced up. "Relax," he urged with his deep, reassuring tone.

It wasn't that she was nervous. No, she was strung tight and so excited her body quivered of its own volition. But she eased back against the cushion and let him take control.

He lifted her legs over his shoulder, first one, then the other. Before she could react, he dipped his head and touched his tongue to her femininity and she was lost. Desire overwhelmed her as he laved her outer lips, softly, gently, arousing her with every lick, every touch. Up and down, back and forth, he glided his tongue, lulling her into a false sense of security that the sweet-tasting, gentle laving would continue.

Without warning, he switched tactics. He latched on to the tiny bud at her core and began to suckle with insistency. He maintained a determined rhythm that took her from delicious complacency to being on the verge of screaming in delight. Her hips jerked upward and the sensations he evoked rippled into every nerve ending, every distant part of her body.

Her fingers curled into the couch cushion and her hips continued to lift off the seat. And just when she didn't think she could take the light grazing of his teeth and the soothing lap of his tongue against her another second, he thrust one finger inside her, filling her at the same time he worked her into a frenzy.

He thrust into her, then slid out, in again, farther this time, then out. And all the while, he concentrated on the one place sure to make her come…and she did. Every one of his movements was designed to build to a crescendo. The waves built higher until she peaked and a glorious orgasm hit, taking her up and over the edge, spiraling outside of herself.

Her body was still quaking, her breath still short

and quick as he stood. He lifted her off the end of the couch, moving them to the end of the high table right behind the sofa.

"For leverage," he said with a wink.

"You're doing great so far," she told him, her arms wrapped firmly around his neck so she could gaze into the face she adored.

He paused long enough to brush the long strands of hair off her face and place a lingering kiss on her lips, then giving her time to lean back on her elbows before picking up where he left off. He pulled her nearer to the edge of the table and eased himself closer until he was poised at her moist entrance.

"Derek?"

"Hmm?" He met her gaze, his hands drifting to her breasts, toying with them as he spoke.

She glanced down, aroused at the sight of him erect and hard, almost inside her but not quite. "I don't want to know where I begin and you end," she said honestly, pouring her heart into that one statement.

Then he thrust hard.

Fast.

Deep.

And she took all of him, wrapping her feet around his waist and sealing his body against hers. Her eyes shut tight and stars sparkled behind her lids as she let out a heartfelt moan. He felt so good.

"I can't wait." He pulled out, then thrust in again.

Out.

In.

Finally, he ground himself into her, extra hard, extra deep, so she *felt* all of him inside her body. Inside her heart. He was a part of her, a perfect fit. Her other half. Her soul mate.

Her heart swelled and she wished she could reach for him but she needed to keep herself braced. She held on as he moved inside her, a rhythm that was unique and all their own.

The emotions rising inside her defied description as his hips continued to shift and roll against the most intimate part of her until once again, the glorious waves began. She went with them, losing herself to her second orgasm of the night. This one seemed to go on and on and she squeezed her inner muscles around him, wanting to feel every inch of him inside her.

"Oh, yes," he muttered, pumping his hips harder and faster. Then his body stiffened and he thrust one last time, coming along with her.

"I'VE LOST MY MIND," Derek said. "My daughter or father could walk in here any minute." His arms were still braced on either side of Gabrielle, his body no longer inside her. But close.

She frowned. "I thought you locked the door."

"I did. We should still go on upstairs." He held out a hand and she followed him to the bedroom.

"Last one in the shower is a rotten egg," she said, darting around him into the bathroom he and his father had remodeled together.

He stepped into his bathroom to find Gabrielle already in the shower, adjusting the water temperature. "Join me?" she asked, crooking a seductive finger his way.

He figured it was a rhetorical question and stepped under the warm spray along with her.

"I don't have my shower stuff unpacked yet. In fact, my clothes are still in your car. So let's see what you use in the way of soap." She turned to find his plain old bar of Lever 2000.

She wet the bar in her hands, soaping them up, and began to lather her body, beginning with her arms, working her way up to her chest. Her breasts, pale compared to the rest of her tanned skin, called out to him.

"Let me." He took the soap and worked his own hands into a lather. "Turn around."

Her eyes glittered with understanding as she pivoted around. Water sprayed against his back and steam flowed around them. Beginning with her feet, he worked his way upward. He knelt down and slid his hands over her toned calves, her knees, her thighs. He lingered at her luscious behind, cupping her cheeks in his hands and smoothing his palms over and around, letting his fingers dip into hidden crevices.

She wriggled and groaned, then braced her hands against the shower glass. His hands traveled lower, finding her most sensitive spot. He moved his fingers back and forth before easing one inside her.

"Derek," she moaned, and clenched her inner walls tight around him.

His erection throbbed hard against her cheeks and her hips gyrated, the motion nearly taking him over the edge.

"I need you inside me," she whimpered.

He clenched his teeth. "I don't have protection."

"I'm on the pill and I'm safe." She wriggled her backside against his straining hard-on. "Please."

He couldn't resist her plea.

Couldn't resist her.

He wrapped one arm around her waist and positioned himself at her entrance. He already knew she was slick and wet, hot and ready for him.

"Bend lower," he whispered against her ear.

She bent over and he thrust inside.

She cried out his name and pushed her hips backward against him, their bodies grinding together. Nothing had ever felt so good or so right, but he couldn't remain still long enough to savor it. The urgency building inside him was too great.

He pulled out, feeling every inch of her, and lunged back in, cocooning himself in her hot sheath. His movements were frenzied and fast and she met him thrust for thrust, accepting all of him, deeper and harder, inside her.

"Derek, please." Her breath came in faster gasps as she cried out his name.

The sound wrapped around his heart. He wound his fingers in the back of her hair. Maybe it was the fact that he was really inside her, with no barrier separating their bodies. Maybe it was just the effect Gabrielle had on him. But he didn't last long, riding out the orgasm and continuing until he'd taken her up and over, too.

His heart was still galloping inside his chest as he slipped out of her and turned her around, sealing his lips against hers for a long, intimate kiss.

Sated and wiped out, he helped her out of the shower and, wrapped in towels, they made their way to the bed, collapsing together in exhaustion.

GABRIELLE AWOKE TO THE SOUND of distant voices. It took her a moment to realize she was in Derek's bed, in his loft, and the sounds from downstairs were Derek and his daughter. Memories of last night came back and she snuggled closer into his bed, inhaling his scent in the sheets.

He'd shared her bed last night and she'd slept with him cocooned around her. Never had she felt so warm, safe or wanted. But he'd set the alarm early and rose to shower and dress before Holly came. If his daughter asked, he'd slept in Holly's bed last night.

Gabrielle had left her suitcase in the car and she realized she'd have to borrow one of Derek's shirts and, hopefully, a pair of sweats so she could go downstairs and get her things. She stretched and rose from the bed, keeping the sheet over her exposed breasts when she caught sight of her suitcase on the floor near the bathroom.

She grinned, appreciating Derek's foresight. After a quick shower, she headed downstairs to see what the day would bring.

"Gabrielle!" Holly exclaimed, obviously happy to see her. "Dad, Gabrielle's up!"

"I can see that," he said wryly. Derek faced her from across his kitchen, coffee mug in hand. "Sleep well?" he asked, somehow managing a straight face.

She nodded. "I haven't had such a good night's sleep in ages. I'm glad I have a few more nights here, at least. Nice, comfortable bed."

"Can I get you some coffee?" Derek asked.

She nodded. "I'd love some."

"In the meantime, make yourself at home and grab some breakfast." He pulled a mug out of the cupboard.

Gabrielle looked in the refrigerator, the cabinets and pantry. Settling on a bowl of corn flakes and milk, she joined Holly at the table.

"So what are you up to today?" she asked the girl.

She shrugged. "I'm not really sure. I think this girl I met when I first got here gets home from vacation today. Maybe she'll remember to call me." Holly propped her chin in her hand.

She didn't seem like the normally cheerful kid Gabrielle had come to know.

Derek joined them and Gabrielle shot him a questioning look.

"What's wrong?" he asked his daughter.

"I just miss Mom," she admitted. "Not that I'm not having fun with you."

He rose and ruffled her hair before sitting down again. "I understand completely."

After pouring her milk, Gabrielle began to eat her cereal, pausing to enjoy her coffee. Derek had already added milk and sugar to it for her, the way she liked it. She smiled. "Hey, I just had an idea," she said to Holly.

The young girl raised her gaze. "What is it?"

"Well, I need to go grocery shopping for a few things. No offence, but I eat a little differently from the way you and your dad do," Gabrielle said.

"What do you mean?" Holly brushed her tangled hair off her face and resettled herself more comfortably in her seat.

"I use skim milk instead of regular or soy, and have Special K instead of corn flakes for breakfast. That kind of stuff. If you and your dad want to hang out with me today, I thought maybe we could take that trip to Target first."

Holly's eyes regained their sparkle. "Can we, Dad? Please? I want to check out those clothes Gabrielle told me about."

"And I thought maybe we could pick up a couple of DVDs later? I need you to tell me what's out now and what's good." Gabrielle directed her comments to Holly. "If your dad has a DVD player?"

"I do," Derek said.

"Awesome idea. Dad doesn't have *On Demand* like we have at Mom's and I've already missed some of my favorite shows and movies." She put one foot on the floor and began her typical excited bouncing. "Can we do it, Dad? Huh?"

Gabrielle glanced down at her mug, trying not to meet Derek's gaze. She didn't know if he'd appreciate her suggestions without asking him first, but she couldn't stand seeing Holly so sad.

"Sure thing," Derek said. "Why don't you go shower and get dressed?"

She pushed her chair out and grabbed her cereal bowl, placing it in the sink. "Back in a few."

"Take your time! The stores don't open for hours!" he called to her retreating back.

Gabrielle chuckled. "Actually Target opens at 8:00 a.m."

He rolled his eyes and groaned. "Don't tell her that. We'll be finished by nine and have the entire day ahead of us to kill."

"I'm sorry. I should have asked you before I suggested it to her. I don't want you to have to do something—"

"Don't be silly. It's fine. You made her smile and I appreciate it. It's been hard for her being away from her mother for so long."

Gabrielle stared at the lone corn flake swirling in milk. "And you think she's safe with me?" She wasn't worried about her own safety. So far she'd been burglarized twice and been left harassing notes, but there had been no physical threats to her safety. Still…

"I'll be with you at all times, so, yes, I think she's safe with you. I worry about *both* of you," he said, his voice filled with caring. "And as long as I'm around, nothing is going to happen to you."

She smiled, and before she could answer, the phone rang.

He answered. "Hello?"

A few minutes later, he hung up, looking none too pleased.

"What's wrong?"

He held up one finger and called out to his daughter. "Holly, did you get into the shower yet?"

"No!" she yelled back.

"Then don't bother. Fred had a run-in with a

mud puddle and Grandpa wants you to help give him a bath!"

Gabrielle shook her head and laughed. "That's one way to kill time before shopping."

To Derek's surprise, Gabrielle insisted on helping with the dog's bath. They all changed into shorts and old T-shirts and headed outside to meet up with Hank and Fred.

"I got the shampoo," Holly said, running out from Derek's house with her favorite bottle.

"He's gonna smell like a female," Hank complained, turning toward the house to retrieve a different one.

Holly perched her hands on her hips. "And what's wrong with smelling like a lady?"

Derek chuckled. "Nothing…unless you're a man."

Gabrielle laughed. "Come on, let's turn on the hose." With Holly by her side, they walked to the back of the house.

He vividly remembered those long legs draped over his shoulders last night, and he'd woken up with them tangled around him this morning. His groin hardened, ready for another go with her.

"Easy," he muttered as he turned away from the women who were returning, live hose in hand.

Derek grabbed Fred's collar, holding him in place. Hank poured the shampoo over the stinky, mud-caked hound, and Holly scrubbed him down with both hands and the rest of her body until she was covered in soap bubbles. Gabrielle waited patiently with the hose.

Once Fred was soaped down, Hank stepped aside and went into the house for towels, or so he said. Derek had a hunch he was just avoiding the work.

"Let 'er rip," Holly called out to Gabrielle.

She squeezed the hose and ran it over the dog, while Holly again rubbed him, trying to rinse him off. Besides Holly, Derek took the bulk of the dousing, since he was crouched nearest to Fred. By the time they were finished, everyone was soaked.

Everyone except Gabrielle.

She dropped the hose at her feet and wiped her hands on the towels Hank had left on the picnic table.

"Wait, I still see soap on Fred," Derek said.

"I've got it," Gabrielle offered.

He shook his head. "You're dry. I can do it." He picked up the hose before she could argue. "Holly, why don't you dry Fred off?"

"I thought he had more soap on him?"

"No, I just said that because you and I look like drowned rats and Gabrielle is just a little too dry, don't you think?" Hose in hand, he stepped toward her.

Her eyes opened wide as she realized his intent. "You wouldn't." She raised her hands in front of her, as if to ward him off.

He grinned. "Why wouldn't I?"

"Daddy!" Holly shrieked, laughing at the same time. "That's so mean!"

"Listen to your daughter, Derek." Her hands still raised in submission, Gabrielle stepped back.

He stalked forward.

She edged back. "Derek," she said in warning.

He really shouldn't.

But she was so dry and…tempting. "How about I give you some warning? One, two…three." He pressed the hose and directed the long stream of cold water her way.

She squealed and ran, but he was faster. Catching up to her with the hose, he gave her a thorough dousing before releasing the makeshift weapon and letting it drop to the grass.

She was bent over, panting and laughing, while from behind them, Holly was giggling like he'd never heard before.

Gabrielle raised her head and glared at him, but he saw the beginnings of a grin on her face.

"I couldn't help myself," he said.

"I bet." She stood up straight and pushed her wet hair off her face.

He took in her gym shorts and the T-shirt she'd borrowed from him for the occasion. The *white* T-shirt, which was now sheer. Her breasts rose and fell beneath the flimsy material, her nipples rosy and hard, pressing through the light cotton.

He swallowed a groan, unable to think of anything except wrapping her in his arms, pulling her to the ground and making love to her right here, right now. And from the sultry look in her eyes, she knew exactly what he was thinking.

"Dad!"

Holly's voice brought him to his senses.

"Yeah?" he asked, his gaze still focused on Gabrielle.

"Fred's dry and he's trying to get free. Can I let him go?" she asked.

He turned his gaze toward his daughter. "Why don't you take him to Grandpa's house, so he won't get into any more trouble out here?" he suggested.

"Good idea. Then I'll take my shower so we can go shopping!" She pulled on Fred's collar and somehow got the dog to follow her toward the house.

Derek picked up a dry towel from the table and tossed it to Gabrielle, then grabbed one for himself.

Neither of the adults spoke on the way back to Derek's. They didn't need to. Holly did all the chatting for them. His daughter was happy and still laughing over Fred's bath and her father's unexpected fun side.

He was too preoccupied with his own thoughts. They'd all been comfortable with one another. They'd had fun. Holly was happy.

Somehow Fred's hosing had become a *family* affair.

CHAPTER FOURTEEN

To Derek, it was obvious Gabrielle loved Target. She insisted they could find everything they wanted in one place, including food. They didn't, however, which necessitated a trip to the local supermarket. But this was only after they'd loaded up the trunk with all the new clothes, hair accessories and DVDs Gabrielle and Holly had chosen.

Derek marveled at how quickly the time had passed in the store. Even more, how much fun he'd had shopping with Holly and Gabrielle. How often had Marlene asked him to join her on a shopping trip? Too often to count, and she hadn't always been referring to sitting around the women's department while she tried on clothes. As he'd made more and more money, she'd asked for his opinion on items for their new apartment, for Christmas presents for Holly, her parents and his. He'd always rejected the idea outright.

He'd thought his time could be better spent working, even on the weekends. In his job, he'd found an escape from reality—he hadn't had to face the truth of his life. He'd abandoned the woman he loved, married a woman he didn't and he wasn't happy. All because of that damn curse. More than once today, he found himself struck by a twinge of guilt when he found himself enjoying the day.

The three of them strode to his SUV, Holly climbing into the backseat behind Derek, who was seating himself in the driver's seat.

Gabrielle opened the door just as someone tapped her on the shoulder.

She gasped in surprise, then turned.

A young woman with her hair in a ponytail, wearing sunglasses, beige pants and a cream top stood before her.

"Yes?"

"Can I talk to you a minute?"

"Do I know you?" Gabrielle asked.

"Who is it?" Derek asked from inside the SUV.

She held up one finger to stall his question.

The young woman shook her head. "No, you don't know me. I used to be Mary Perkins's assistant before I quit. You're Gabrielle Donovan, the author, right?"

Gabrielle nodded. She was glad she'd already opened the door and Derek was within hearing distance if she had to yell for help.

"How did you know I was here?" Gabrielle asked.

The woman glanced around warily. "I've been

following you since you left the house this morning. I was just waiting for the right time to approach you."

A chill raced through her and Gabrielle rubbed her hands up and down her bare arms. "What can I do for you?" This woman didn't strike Gabrielle as a stalker, nor did Gabrielle think the woman wanted an autograph.

"It's more what I can do for *you*. Here. Take this." She held an envelope out to Gabrielle.

She accepted it warily. "What is it?"

The woman shook her head. "You'll see. I only ask one favor."

Gabrielle tipped her head to one side. "What is it?"

"Forget you ever met me." She started to walk away, then turned. "Good luck," she whispered, then crossed the parking lot and disappeared behind a row of cars.

Gabrielle climbed into the SUV, shut her door and hit the door-lock button as quickly as possible.

"What was that all about?" Derek asked.

She inhaled a deep breath. "Just a fan," she said pointedly to Derek, wanting to wait until Holly was out of earshot.

He nodded.

Meanwhile, she opened the note, but the only thing on the paper inside was a name.

A name she didn't recognize.

SHARON TWISTED HER HANDS together. The closer she and Richard got to Tony's apartment, the more nervous she became. It was one thing for her to stalk Tony from a distance. It was another to confront him, face-to-face, with her fiancé by her side.

And that was Richard's plan.

They still weren't on the best of terms. His disappointment about what he called her lack of faith in him was clear. At the same time, she'd called their sex life and compatibility into question. Their issues were now, officially, out in the open.

But before they did anything else, they had to get to the bottom of the blackmail threat first. They could worry about whether they still had a relationship to save later.

When they got to the apartment and found nobody home, a neighbor helped them out by informing them she'd just seen the entire family depart for the playground behind the building. Sharon and Richard headed there next.

Sharon slowed as they approached the chain-link fence that surrounded a swing set. Mothers gathered around their toddlers, and a couple sat together on the bench by the sandbox.

"Tony," she whispered, pointing to the bench. "That's him?"

She nodded.

Richard started forward, but Sharon placed a hand on his arm, stopping him. "Wait."

"Don't you want to confront him?" Richard asked, appearing confused.

"Of course I do. But *I* want to do it. If you just start asking him questions, he's bound to get defensive. Then we won't find out anything."

Richard nodded. "Fine. Let's go. I'll let you do the talking."

She drew in a deep breath. "Okay." She'd already given a great deal of thought as to how she'd handle Tony when she finally confronted him. She'd had plenty of time while she'd been secretly watching him.

At first, she'd been nervous at the thought of facing him again. Now she was petrified, though it helped to know she had Richard by her side.

She closed her eyes and counted to ten. "Okay."

She stepped forward, but this time he stopped her. "Sharon."

"What?"

"I'm proud of you," Richard said. "It's nice to see some of that spunk return. I was beginning to think all the progress you'd made for yourself had disappeared when the pictures showed up."

She smiled grimly. "I appreciate you saying that." Maybe he really loved her for who she was, after all. "I'm just sorry this is touching your life, your campaign. So. Let's go." She shrugged his hand off, needing all her composure to face Tony.

He inclined his head and together they approached the couple on the bench. Tony wore faded jeans and a red T-shirt. The woman beside him seemed relaxed and happy.

Sharon wondered if she was about to upset the balance in Tony's relationship the way he'd upset hers.

Tony knelt down in front of the young boy Sharon had seen the other day.

She leaned against the chain-link fence separating the road from the playground and cleared her throat. "Tony?"

At the sound of his name, the man's head whipped around fast. She wondered if he recognized her voice, then called herself silly.

He rose to his feet, staring at her as his gaze narrowed in recognition. "Sharon?"

She nodded.

From behind her, she felt Richard slip his hand into hers. She appreciated the silent support.

Warily he approached her. "Watch him?" he said to the woman she assumed was his wife, pointing to the child.

Warily, the other woman nodded. She seated herself on the edge of the sandbox, but her gaze remained firmly on Tony's back.

"I guess I shouldn't be surprised to see you." He stepped closer.

Although rationally she knew she was safe, she

was glad to have the fence between them. "Because my friends were here first."

"They grilled me."

"And you lied to them."

He shoved his hands into his jeans pockets and shrugged. "I have a family to protect now."

"Look, it's because you have a family that I'm hoping I can appeal to your sense of decency. You'll notice I'm giving you the benefit of the doubt by assuming you've developed one."

She studied him. He was still handsome, although his features were more hardened than she remembered, his attitude gruffer. She supposed prison could do that to a man, and she shivered.

Richard released her hand and slid his arm around her back.

"Who's the suit?" Tony gestured to Richard.

Sharon squared her shoulders, meeting his gaze. If he was her blackmailer, he already knew that not only did she plan to marry Richard, but also that he was running for mayor. "My fiancé," she said, still giving him some leeway.

"Well, I'll tell you what I told your friends. I didn't keep the photographs. The cops took them all and there's no way you're pinning any trouble you have now on me."

Sharon hated herself for thinking it, but she almost believed him. The arrogant man she remembered was gone. In his place stood a beaten man who appeared content to live his life simply. He looked too scared of being connected to the photographs to have taken the risk again. Then again, he'd been a good liar once before.

"I hope you realize they're harsher on repeat offenders if you're lying," Richard said.

"Hey, don't make assumptions you can't prove."

Sharon glanced over. A muscle throbbed in Richard's temple, a sure sign he was holding back his anger and disgust at Tony. This time *she* squeezed his hand to calm him down.

"Listen, all I want to know is how someone could have gotten ahold of one of the photos," Richard asked in a controlled voice.

"And I'm telling you the police have them all."

Sharon gripped the fence harder. "Tony, you have a family you want to protect. I understand that. But if I don't find out who's blackmailing me, I won't ever have a family. Don't I deserve that chance? Don't you think you owe me at least that?" she asked, her voice rising.

Tony exhaled hard.

"Honey, don't you think you should tell her?" The woman from the sandbox walked up beside him, holding the child in her arms.

Tony stiffened.

"Tell me what?"

The brunette put her hand on his shoulder. "A few months ago, Tony got an anonymous phone call."

"What did they want?" Richard asked before Sharon could.

Tony groaned. "The same thing you do. The person wanted to know if I had copies of the pictures."

"All the pictures?" Sharon asked. "Of all the women?"

He shook his head. "Just you."

She winced. "And what did you say?"

He slung an arm over the fence. "Again, I told them what I told the rest of you. I have no damn photos. The cops took everything."

"Why keep this to yourself?" Richard asked. "Why didn't you just admit it to us when we asked?"

He rolled his eyes. "For one thing, I didn't know those friends of yours from Adam, so I wasn't telling them anything."

"And me? Why didn't you tell me?"

"Because…" He leaned closer to them, whispering the rest. "The person who called me was an ex-con I'd met in prison. He was trying to make a buck by getting his hands on those pictures for someone and selling them. I'm not supposed to have contact with anyone I met in the joint. And I don't intend to violate my parole and screw up my life again."

Richard nodded slowly, seemingly more satisfied with this answer. "What's the guy's name? The one you met in prison?"

Tony kicked at the dirt in front of him. Obviously he didn't want to get any more involved than he already was.

"Stan. Stan Mancusi," the woman beside him said softly.

"Calls himself Stan the Man," Tony muttered. "He's into petty shit. Anything to make a buck. And he's local," he added grudgingly. "You can probably find him in any one of the seedier bars on the docks in Salem."

"Thank you," Sharon said.

Tony shrugged. "Felicia's right. I owe you," he said without meeting her gaze.

Sharon glanced at the other woman. "I appreciate it." And she hoped Tony would give Felicia the kind of life she deserved.

Sharon and Richard were silent on the way back to the car.

Once inside, Richard turned to her and asked, "Why did you say you might never have the family you want?"

"Because we obviously have a lot to discuss when this blackmail thing is over. If you have to drop out or if the picture or pictures are published, I'll be responsible for ruining your career and your dreams. I don't expect you to forgive me for that."

He shook his head harshly and turned the key in the ignition. "Damn, you don't give me enough credit. Or maybe you just judge all men by that dirtbag's example and I never realized it until now. Do you think that whatever we have to discuss will stop us from getting married? Or that I would really hold something that happened *to* you against you?"

She didn't answer. It seemed every time she tried to speak, she made things worse between them.

All Sharon could do now was throw herself into the search for her blackmailer…and see what happened between her and Richard when all was said and done.

DEREK DROPPED HOLLY OFF with his father for lunch. No sooner was she gone than he turned to Gabrielle. "What was in the note?" he asked. He'd been dying to know for the past half hour.

"A name." She pulled the paper out of her bag. "Does the name Harry Winters mean anything to you?"

Derek narrowed his gaze. "That's the guy who lives near my uncle Edward. His only neighbor. If anyone in town is as much of a loner as my uncle, it would be Harry Winters."

Gabrielle leaned back in her seat. "Any idea why Mary Perkins's former assistant thinks the name would be important to me?"

"As a matter of fact, I do. I'll tell you on the way." He shifted the SUV into Drive.

"On the way where?"

"To pay Mr. Winters a visit. I think we're about to make the connection between who wants you out of town and why."

Ten minutes later, Derek pulled onto the long road that led to his uncle's house. He'd visited Edward on his arrival back home, but he hadn't been here since. He had his reasons.

Gabrielle glanced out the car window at the trees lining the road. "Are those jujus?" she asked, incredulously staring at the items hanging from tree branches.

Derek nodded. "How the hell do you know about jujus?" He hadn't known until his most recent visit.

Apparently his uncle had decided to do whatever he could to ward off the curse and any other impending evil by learning about New Orleans voodoo. He'd decided to obtain jujus—objects made from something that had once been alive, tree bark among other things—as protection.

"You've obviously never read one of my books!" she said, laughing and accusing him at the same time.

His face flushed hot. "Guilty. I've always been curious, but I don't get a lot of time to read."

She shook her head softly. "It's okay," she told him. "I'm just busting your chops. But you can't conduct research on the paranormal and odd cultural beliefs without coming across at least one reference to jujus."

They came to the end of the road where two lone houses came into view.

"Is that a *totem pole?*" She leaned forward in her seat.

He nodded and groaned. "You can get a better look up close. There are several of them. My uncle heard that they offered protection. He took it a little far," Derek said wryly.

"You think?" Her sarcasm and amusement were clear.

He parked and turned her way. "I can't leave my SUV in plain view and not stop in and say hello to my uncle. If he makes you uncomfortable, you can wait here. I won't be long." Derek started to get out of the vehicle.

"Wait!" Her eyes lit up unexpectedly. "I'd love to say hello to your uncle."

"And get a look at his craziness firsthand?" He'd hoped to keep his ornery uncle and Gabrielle far apart. "He may be a recluse, but he isn't so isolated that gossip doesn't reach him. I'm sure he knows by now that you're writing about the curse. You can see how far he'll go to keep it from touching him. I doubt he's pleased you're stirring that pot."

She unhooked her seat belt. "I really don't mind if he's a little gruff with me. I understand his point of view. But even your father softened enough toward me to take Holly so I could stay with you until things blow over. And we washed Fred together without incident. I'll be nice to Uncle Edward. Take me with you, please?" She clasped her hands together in mock begging.

"You don't know Uncle Edward," he warned her.

She rolled her eyes. "I can handle him." She'd already opened the car door and scrambled out.

Derek drew a deep breath and joined her.

They reached the front door and he rang the bell.

"Red dust," she murmured, kneeling down to run her fingers over the dust at the entrance of the house.

"That I can't explain."

"I can," Gabrielle said. "New Orleans tradition holds that if you clean the front steps with red brick dust, it protects the entrance and keeps bad energy and negative people away."

"Figures." He rang the doorbell once more.

The door opened no more than half an inch. "Who's there?"

"It's your nephew, Derek." He shot Gabrielle an "I told you so" look.

Edward opened the door the rest of the way. "You aren't alone."

Derek shook his head. "No. Do you remember Gabrielle Donovan? I went to high school with her."

"The one who's writing about the curse that's destroyed our family?"

Derek tipped his head toward her.

Gabrielle stepped forward. "Mr. Corwin, I'd love to talk to you if you'd let me in. I have nothing but the utmost respect for what you and your family have been through."

"Nope. Not talking. Anything I say can and will be used against me." He slammed the door closed.

"They don't call him a recluse for nothing." With a shrug, Derek grabbed her hand and started back down the walk. He hadn't come to see his uncle, anyway.

"This trip has already revealed a lot," Gabrielle said.

"Such as?" He couldn't imagine what she'd discovered.

They walked across her uncle's driveway and headed to the place next door.

"The jujus, the hermit lifestyle. I've been taking mental notes on what they looked like so I can do some research into exactly what evil your uncle hopes to ward off, how he thinks they'll work, things like that." Gabrielle's voice sounded more animated with each word she spoke. "Since I'm planning to write about the effects of a curse on a real family, I can use everything I saw today firsthand."

"I'd rather you didn't write about the insanity that runs in my family," Derek muttered.

She yanked on his hand, pulling him to a stop.

Turning, he met her gaze.

"There is no insanity in your family." Her eyes flashed with sincerity, which surprised him.

She didn't think his uncle was nuts?

"Look, I was a psychology major and I understand that people react to events in different ways. Your uncle retreated into himself. That's not unusual. People also look for ways to protect themselves. Cut him a break. I promise you I will."

He raised an eyebrow. "I appreciate that."

"I'm glad. What I write will be factual, not derogatory in any way."

"I appreciate that, too." Derek squeezed her hand tighter. "Ready to move on to Harry Winters?"

She nodded. "I hope he's more talkative than your uncle was."

"He wouldn't have to say much in order to do that."

Knocking on Harry Winters's door didn't elicit a response.

Gabrielle let out a sigh of frustration, but Derek knew Winters had to be home. He never went anywhere else.

"Let's go around back. There's a pond there. He might be outside," Derek said, unwilling to give up.

They rounded the back of the house and started down the hill leading to a large pond. Sure enough, a man sat beneath a tree, staring out at the water beyond.

"He can't be any older than his midforties," she said, obviously surprised.

She shoved her hands into her shorts pockets and followed Derek down the rocky path.

Derek drew a deep breath. He knew more about Harry Winters and his background than he'd told Gabrielle. But he wanted her to hear the truth from the man himself. Then Derek could help her put things together and figure out how to solve her problems.

"Mr. Winters?"

The man didn't stop staring out at the water. "Who wants to know?"

Gabrielle stepped forward, but Derek touched her arm to stop her. He wanted to be the one to introduce himself and ease into conversation.

"I'm Derek Corwin, your neighbor Edward's nephew."

"Bully for you. What do you want with me?"

Gabrielle knelt beside to the man. "My name is Gabrielle Donovan. I'm with Derek, but I'm really the one who needs to talk to you," she said softly.

"About what?" he asked in the same monotone voice he'd used since they'd arrived.

Gabrielle swallowed hard. "I've been having some problems since I arrived in town."

"What's it to me?"

At least he was curious enough to ask, Gabrielle thought. "I'm an author and I'm writing a book about Derek and Edward Corwin's family history. The Corwin Curse, to be exact."

Without warning, the placid man scrambled to his feet, his eyes wide with fear. "I don't want to hear any more." He bolted for the house.

Gabrielle rose. but before she could take two steps toward him, she twisted her ankle. "Ouch." She hobbled the rest of the way up the hill and was grateful to see Derek had managed to corner the man before he could lock himself inside his house.

Gabrielle joined them.

"Are you okay?" Derek asked.

She nodded. "I just twisted my ankle getting back up here. I'll be fine."

Derek placed a hand on her back and together they faced the frightened man. "We don't want to hurt you," he said.

"Or scare you." She spoke quietly. "It's just that someone's making things really difficult for me. They obviously don't want me to write about the curse. I've had a note left telling me to leave town or else. Then someone keyed my car and broke into both the boarding house where I was staying and my apartment in Boston. I'm just hoping you can help me."

Harry Winters wrapped his arms around his waist and leaned against the slatted wood of the house. "Why? What's it got to do with me?"

"I was hoping you could tell me that. You see,

earlier today, someone handed me a sealed envelope, and inside it had your name written on a piece of paper.

"Who gave it to you?" Harry asked.

"I don't know. She said she was once Mayor Perkins's assistant."

"So she can join the club." He laughed wryly.

Gabrielle sucked in a surprised breath. "You were the mayor's assistant, too?"

He shook his head. "No, she's just had a long line of fired assistants before one of her granddaughters was old enough to work with her. That family carries power throughout the line, you know. Especially those witches named Mary. They continue the legacy throughout the generations. Make no mistake. One Mary is as evil as the next."

It seemed a ridiculous notion to think any Perkins woman named Mary was a witch, just as it seemed silly to believe the Corwin men were cursed by them.

Gabrielle thought about the mayor's assistant and the obvious flaw in Harry Winters's reasoning. "Mayor Perkins's granddaughter's name is Elizabeth."

He nodded. "*Mary* Elizabeth Perkins. She goes by her middle name so as not to be confused with her grandmother."

Suddenly the note on the mayor's door made

sense. It had been signed "M" and Gabrielle had thought Mary Perkins had signed it. But then the mayor had told Lauren that Elizabeth had left the note for her. Of course the sisters would use their given names with each other. And besides, Mary Perkins would probably have signed "Grandma" when leaving a note for her granddaughter.

But just because the women had a similar name didn't make Elizabeth evil. She wasn't going to argue with a man who'd been driven to living in isolation by his demons.

"Nobody knows what Mary Perkins is capable of better than me," he continued. "I had the misfortune to run against her in one of her early mayoral campaigns."

"What happened?" Gabrielle asked.

He settled his back against the house.

Sensing the man was caving in, Gabrielle joined him, ignoring the dull throb in her ankle. She'd deal with it later. Derek remained standing, more of a lookout than a participant.

"Campaign issues happened. I tried to run a clean campaign on the issues that should have been important to the community, but Mary Perkins didn't play by anyone's rules but her own. Everything came back to her status and power. Power she had no intention of losing."

"I don't understand," Gabrielle said.

"Obviously you *do* understand or you wouldn't be here. She went after me. And now she's going after you. Mary Perkins doesn't care about fairness. The only thing that's important is power and winning *at any cost*."

CHAPTER FIFTEEN

GABRIELLE STARED AT THE MAN in disbelief. "Mary Perkins wants me gone? She's behind everything?" She shouldn't be surprised and yet... "Tell me more."

"She never fails to remind people of the family curse, but not in public. Not in her speeches. In private. When asking for donations. When she's trying to push her own agenda on town council. She achieves her goals by frightening people into submission. And as you've no doubt seen and heard, people need only look to the Corwin men as proof of her point."

Gabrielle winced, not looking at Derek. "Go on."

"I tried to bring her dirty dealings out in the open. There was a Fourth of July gathering in the center of town and we were each making a speech. All I did was say that votes must be earned, and curses were only in people's minds." He cleared his throat, glancing out in a fog once more.

Gabrielle waited him out.

Finally, he continued. "My life went downhill after that. A picture surfaced of me and a prostitute. At first, it came to me alone with a note threatening to reveal it if I didn't drop out of the race. It didn't matter that I swore up and down it wasn't me, I couldn't prove it any more than I could prove Mary Perkins was behind it. *But I knew.*"

Gabrielle shivered because she knew, too. And now she knew who was behind Sharon's pictures reemerging. Mary Perkins had somehow gotten ahold of them. Sharon and Richard were off talking to her ex-boyfriend. If he hadn't sold them to Mary Perkins, she'd found another way to get her hands on them.

"So what did you do?" Gabrielle asked. Because she knew this man hadn't gone from being a mayoral candidate to a hermit over some photographs. There had to be more.

"I refused to give in to the blackmail, of course. I was young and brash and I believed in integrity. I thought I could beat her despite it all. I never got that far. Shortly afterward, my wife had a car accident. It looked like she lost control of her vehicle, even though it wasn't raining and the roads were in good shape."

"You don't believe it was an accident, do you?" Gabrielle asked soberly.

From everything Gabrielle had heard so far, Mary Perkins wasn't just arrogant, she was evil.

And that scared her. Not because Gabrielle believed in witches or curses, but because she feared what the woman was capable of if her power was threatened.

He shook his head. "The police *said* they didn't find anything and I had no choice but to believe them. Personally, I think someone sabotaged the car. At the time, though, I was too busy with my gravely injured wife to give much thought to the car. She recovered eventually, but was left with tremors and paralysis on one side. I stayed by her through the whole ordeal, but she never forgave me for not dropping out of the race and preventing the whole thing."

Gabrielle shook her head sadly. "I'm sorry."

He shrugged. "So am I, but it doesn't change anything."

It did for Gabrielle. She wasn't stupid. She was petrified for Sharon and Richard, who were also in Mary Perkins's direct line of fire. And she was a little scared herself. She now knew who wanted her not just out of town, but away from the subject of the Corwin Curse.

Was she going to give in?

No way in hell.

Gabrielle was more determined than ever to beat Mary Perkins at her long-standing game.

GABRIELLE CALLED A MEETING. Since Holly was already at Hank's place, Derek had asked his father to keep her busy for another hour or so. He also promised her that he'd take her out for a father-daughter dinner later on tonight. Gabrielle knew Derek felt guilty moving her out of his house and she understood why he'd want to hang out with her alone. As for Gabrielle, she'd spend the evening safe in Derek's house, with its locks and alarm system.

Sharon and Richard met up with them at Derek's place.

"It looks like we have a common enemy," Richard said after they'd discussed the situation. He stood in the center of the family room, his suit and groomed appearance giving him an air of authority. A conservative air.

Gabrielle knew he loved Sharon deeply. Yet at the same time she could see how the renewed threat had changed their relationship. Sharon needed to find the strength that had carried her once before if she was going to get through this challenge. Sharon loved and wanted to marry Richard. She needed to have more faith in him and in herself.

Sharon shivered. "It's just hard to believe one woman can be so evil."

Gabrielle nodded. "So addicted to power that she'd hurt people to keep it." Gabrielle rose from the couch. "Well, it's time to bring this all out into the open. Do we all agree on that?"

"Depends on your intended method," Derek

said, leaning forward in his chair. "I don't want either you or Sharon putting yourself out there as a target." His gaze bored into Gabrielle's.

Clearly that comment had been intended more for her than Sharon. Did he really think she'd let Mary Perkins hurt more people? "To start with, we should agree to stay the course. Nobody should change their plans at this stage," Gabrielle said.

"Now, that I agree with," Derek said. "I'm not suggesting anyone pull back or run scared."

Richard nodded. "Certainly not."

Sharon merely listened. She seemed preoccupied with more than just her blackmail situation. Gabrielle would have to have a long talk alone with her friend later.

"The thing is, I don't think staying the course is going to be enough to get the reaction we need from Mary. We need to step things up pretty quickly. Richard needs not to just continue his campaign but to be as vocal as possible about running on merit and not fear," Gabrielle stressed. "Discuss the good mayor's family history with the curse and get people discussing it. Better yet, get people *questioning* it."

This time she let her stare linger on Derek as she lay down the challenge, not just for everyone in the room, but for him and his most personal beliefs.

He raised an eyebrow but said nothing.

But she wasn't finished. "In the meantime, I

plan to start writing my book. I'll interview as many people as possible and make my presence and my topic known." And once everyone began gossiping about Gabrielle Donovan's book on the Corwin Curse and Mary Perkins's desperation to cling to the perception of it, Gabrielle had an even bigger plan.

One she wasn't ready to share with her friends. Especially not with Derek, whose scowl only seemed to grow larger with each word Gabrielle spoke.

"Why in the hell would you want to deliberately antagonize a woman who will go to any lengths to get her way?" Derek asked, furious.

"It seems obvious to me. The only way to prove what Mary Perkins is capable of is to lure her into getting caught. If we keep the pressure on her from both ends, she's going to get nervous and screw up."

"Whether she screws up or she succeeds, someone is going to get hurt. That's her MO and I don't want it to be you."

"Would you rather I sit back and do nothing?"

"Yes!"

"Hold on!" Sharon jumped up and stepped between them. "Fighting with one another is not going to get us anywhere."

Richard nodded. "I agree. Let me see what I can find out about the guy who wanted to buy the photographs. Maybe he'll give us a legitimate connection to Mary Perkins, although I'm sure she's insulated herself. There are probably layers of people between Mary and those who do the actual dirty work."

Derek inclined his head. "I think that's a good idea."

Gabrielle clapped her hands together. "Okay, then, now that that's been decided—"

"You'll do nothing until we see what Richard turns up?"

She gritted her teeth and forced a smile at Derek. "Nothing except what it usually entails to write a book."

Which she knew involved a lot more than sitting behind a keyboard and doing nothing. But what Derek didn't know wouldn't hurt him.

DEREK DROVE HOLLY TO T.G.I. Friday's for dinner. She picked at her chicken fingers and fries, something completely out of character for his daughter, who usually dug into her meals with gusto. Especially meals he had nothing to do with preparing.

"What's wrong?" Derek asked.

She glanced up at him with sad eyes. "I dunno."

"Yes, you do. So out with it."

She laid down the french fry she'd been playing with. "I don't understand why we had to leave Gabrielle home to eat alone."

Derek sat back in his booth, surprised. "Am I such lousy company? I thought you'd want to spend some time alone together, since you've been sleeping at Grandpa's." He'd thought Holly would be feeling left out and maybe even resentful of Gabrielle's sudden presence in his life.

He and his daughter had just started bonding when Gabrielle had returned, and now his former flame was monopolizing his time. He couldn't imagine that his daughter didn't have a problem with it.

"I just think it's rude, that's all." Holly stared into her plate. "And I don't mind being at Grandpa's. Fred is there and it's not like I never see you. It's fine."

"You miss hanging out with Gabrielle, too."

She nodded.

He signaled to the waitress and she walked over to the table. "Can I help you?"

"Would you mind wrapping this up? We've decided to take it to go," he said, winking at Holly.

Her eyes lit up at the idea.

"Can you add a Caesar salad with grilled chicken to the order?" he asked.

She nodded and strode off.

"Thanks," Holly said, smiling.

He returned the grin, but inside his stomach was churning. Holly was turning Gabrielle into part of their family.

And not only was he allowing it, he was even starting to like it.

GABRIELLE HAD BEEN ABOUT to pour a bowl of cereal and curl up on the couch to watch television when Derek and Holly arrived with dinner. She'd been pleasantly surprised, especially when she'd discovered that Holly had been the one wanting to include Gabrielle. She understood Derek's need to spend time alone with his daughter, so she'd happily agreed to do her own thing for dinner. It meant a lot to Gabrielle to realize that Holly didn't resent her for displacing her in Derek's house.

They'd enjoyed a relaxed meal while watching *The Devil Wears Prada,* Holly's choice and current favorite movie. Derek had an issue with the PG-13 rating, but since Marlene had sent the movie along with her daughter's clothes, he couldn't very well argue. Holly was bright for her age and Gabrielle thoroughly enjoyed her. In fact, she had so much fun with the father-daughter duo, she was downright nervous.

Nothing in life came with a guarantee, least of all Derek. And the thought of losing all this as quickly as she'd discovered it scared her beyond reason. Although she couldn't control the outcome, she darn well planned to do her best to sway things in her direction, beginning by *not* manipulating or pressuring Derek in any way.

He'd just walked Holly over to his father's house when his telephone rang. She hesitated a second, then decided, what the hell. She picked up the receiver. "Hello?"

"Um… I think I have the wrong number," a female voice said. "Is this Derek Corwin's residence?"

"Yes, it is. I'm sorry. He stepped out for a minute. Can I take a message?" Gabrielle glanced around the family room and found a pen and paper beside the phone.

"Is Holly there?" the woman asked.

Realization dawned. She must be talking to Derek's ex-wife, Gabrielle thought, a wave of emotion she couldn't name washing over her. "Actually, she's with Derek," Gabrielle said vaguely.

She wasn't sure what Marlene knew about the shift in living arrangements, and Gabrielle wasn't going to be the one to tell her.

"Who is this, anyway?" the other woman finally asked.

Gabrielle swallowed hard. "Um…"

The front door opened and Derek stepped inside.

"Here's Derek now," Gabrielle said gratefully. "Hold on, please."

She covered the mouthpiece and waved the phone toward Derek. "It's Holly's mother," Gabrielle mouthed to him.

He winced and settled onto the couch beside her, taking the phone from her hand. "Hi, Marlene." He glanced at his watch. "Is everything okay?"

He listened, then said, "Why? Because it's late for you to be calling."

Gabrielle rose and started to leave the room to give him privacy, but he cleared his throat loudly. She turned and he waved her back.

With a shrug, she took a seat at the other end of the couch from him, curling one leg beneath her.

A series of "mmm-hmms" followed as Derek listened to whatever his ex-wife had to say.

"I understand, but I have her party planned here."

Gabrielle narrowed her gaze. Obviously the conversation involved Holly.

"That's generous of you, but wasn't the idea for me to spend more quality time with her?" he asked.

"Mmm-hmm. Yes, I'd miss her, too, but—"

His gaze met Gabrielle's, and in his eyes she saw a wealth of pain. "I'll talk to her and get back to you tomorrow." He hung up without saying goodbye.

She was dying to ask, but she didn't want to pry. Luckily, she didn't have to.

"Marlene had planned a four-week trip to Europe. She'd been gone about two and decided to come back early. She misses Holly and wants to take her home to New York when she gets back this weekend," he explained, his tone hard edged, his disappointment obvious.

Gabrielle shook her head. "I'm so sorry."

"I'm not sure I should agree to this. I rarely get time with Holly as it is."

Gabrielle understood, but she also thought he should consider all sides before he reacted in a way that could hurt him even more. "But didn't you say Marlene's just starting to be reasonable about visitation? Do you want a fight that will get her angry and make her be even more difficult again?"

"You're right. She did promise to bring her back up for her birthday party as planned. She also said Holly could come up as often as we could arrange for the rest of the summer," Derek said, the admission obviously difficult for him. "But it still bugs me that just because she misses her, I have to give her up."

Gabrielle eased closer to him and placed her hand over his. "I'm on your side," she assured him. "I just wanted to play devil's advocate."

He smiled grimly. "I appreciate it."

"Um…Derek? Does Marlene know that Holly's living with your father?" And did Marlene know about Gabrielle, period—past and present—she wondered.

He shook his head. "Not from me. I didn't think she'd appreciate the fact that no sooner had Holly moved in than I moved her out."

Gabrielle groaned, her guilt returning. "I am so sorry. I really shouldn't be here. It's wrong. I can get a hotel in Boston and have all the security I need."

"You could, but you won't," he insisted. "I want you here where I can see for myself that you're safe. Besides, after the way Holly reacted when I left you home for dinner, can you imagine how she'd carry on if you moved out?"

Gabrielle shook her head and laughed. "I really do love that kid." The words slipped easily from her lips.

She didn't want to take them back any more than she wanted to spook Derek. She glanced at him. If he'd heard her, he didn't react. No doubt he was more wrapped up in the fact that he was losing Holly sooner than planned. She ought to be relieved he wasn't paying attention to her.

Instead she felt a bone-deep emptiness. One she feared would grow larger over time.

LONG AFTER DEREK AND Gabrielle had climbed into his bed, long after they'd made love and fallen asleep in each other's arms, Derek lay awake, replaying the night in his head.

I love that kid. Derek had heard and processed every word that came out of Gabrielle's beautiful lips. He'd merely pretended he'd been preoccupied.

He didn't know what he was going to do with her, nor did he know what to do with feelings that were growing by the day. Right now, though, he had to keep her safe. And for that reason, letting Holly go home with her mother seemed like the most logical—if painful—solution. But he had no intention of allowing Marlene to think she could continue calling the shots where his daughter was concerned. There would be no more allowing Marlene to schedule silly things on *his* visitation weekends. No longer letting her find convenient excuses not to put Holly on the phone when he called.

In fact, first thing tomorrow, he was getting Holly her own cell phone with a limited calling plan so he could get in touch with her whenever he wanted.

He'd just found his daughter again.

He wasn't about to lose her.

THE NEXT FEW DAYS PASSED in a haze of normalcy. Derek woke up beside Gabrielle, they'd shower, eat breakfast with Holly, then she'd head off to the library to work while he took Holly to the beach. In between, he'd have business appointments while his father took over hanging out with Holly and Fred. Holly had agreed to go home with her mother as long as she could come back as often as she wanted.

Derek knew how much she missed her mother. Because he didn't want her to feel torn between her parents, he'd made the decision an easy one for her. "Fred and I need some alone time to plan your birthday party," he'd said.

She'd laughed.

In reality, Derek was glad Marlene was home in time for Holly's birthday. All Derek could offer her was cake, presents, Grandpa Hank and Fred, the dirty old basset hound. Her mother could give her the one thing she needed more. A party with friends her own age.

This morning, the sky was overcast, which nixed a trip to the beach, so he decided to go to the office for a few hours before meeting Hank and Holly for lunch at the Diner. He finished up early and decided to stop by the library to see if Gabrielle wanted to join them.

Along the way, he noticed all the new election signs posted along the town line and sporadically in well-traveled places in Perkins.

Bold signs with a bolder message, urging voters to listen to their conscience, to ignore curses and vote for change. In both towns there were fliers announcing a town meeting where people could meet Richard Stern and discover what he stood for. As promised, Richard had stepped up his campaign, putting pressure on his opponent.

The Perkins family's power in town was now, unofficially, in jeopardy. Derek couldn't imagine that Mayor Perkins appreciated the fact.

Derek parked and entered the air-conditioned library. Because it was a nice summer day, the place was empty. He found Sharon alone in her back office.

He knocked on the door to announce his presence and she jumped up, obviously on edge.

"Sorry. I didn't mean to startle you." Derek placed a hand on the doorknob.

Sharon nodded. "It's not you, it's everything else going on," she said.

He inclined his head in understanding.

"So what brings you by?" she asked.

He narrowed his gaze. "Gabrielle, what else? I didn't see her. I even checked the microfilm area. Is she around or did she step out to get lunch?"

Bracing her hands on the desk, Sharon rose to her feet. "Gabrielle isn't here."

"Isn't she working on her book here?" he asked.

"I haven't seen her." She bit her lower lip.

"Not today, but yesterday? Or the day before?" he asked, a bad feeling gnawing at his gut.

She shook her head. "But I'm sure she has a good reason for telling you she was here…." Sharon trailed off.

"I'm sure she just didn't want me to worry." Or get angry with her, he thought. "She probably wanted you out of the loop, too. You have enough on your mind without worrying about whatever she's up to."

Sharon exhaled a deep breath. Wasn't that just like Gabrielle? "Well, the least she could do was let me know she'd need a cover," Sharon muttered.

She glanced at Derek, but he'd already turned and headed out the door. Sharon grabbed the phone to warn Gabrielle—wherever she was—but the ring went straight to voice mail.

Sharon had no doubt Derek would find her. She called one more time and this time she left a message. But it looked as if Gabrielle was on her own.

GABRIELLE SAT AT HER adopted table at the Wave where she'd been working for the past three days. When she'd stopped by to talk to Curious George, Gabrielle had learned that the Wave was more than a nightclub. It was a place where people congregated at lunch hour, too. So Gabrielle had made it her mission to set up shop at a table in the corner, where she worked on her book, while at the same time, interviewed George, his staff and many of his customers.

At first people were wary about talking to her. But it was obvious George trusted her, so by the third day, the barriers had come down and people were sharing stories. She learned more about the Corwin Curse and its effect on the people of both towns; she heard tales of older women who'd been afraid to date the males of Hank Corwin's generation; and she began to renew friendships with people she used to know.

More important than incoming information was the fact that people in town left talking about Gabrielle and her book. People hoped they'd get their names mentioned in print. And because of their piqued interest, they were discussing Gabrielle publicly. She hoped word would make its way to Mary

Perkins that Gabrielle Donovan's newest book would reveal—and dispel—all the towns' secrets.

Gabrielle wanted Mary to be nervous. On edge.

She wanted the mayor to feel cornered and act on impulse. She wanted to catch the mayor in wrongdoing and put an end to her reign of terror once and for all.

Her plan was going well, too. Until Derek stormed in, all his frustration aimed her way.

He walked in and braced both hands on her table, looming over her and her laptop. "Please tell me there's a reason you're here, making a public spectacle of yourself, that won't have me wanting to throttle you," he said.

"I like the food?" She gestured to the plate of sliders George had made especially for her.

He shook his head. "Try again."

"I enjoy the company?" She pointed to George, who waved at Derek from behind the bar.

"Gabrielle," he said, drawing out her name through clenched teeth.

"You know exactly what I'm doing here. If I'd told you what I was planning, you'd have tried to talk me out of it."

"You're damn right I would have—"

She stood up to face him. "And I'd have come here, anyway. Then you'd be upset, and we wouldn't have had such fantastic, amazing sex the past few nights," she said, her voice dropping to a husky purr.

Her body reacted to her own words; the memory of his lips on her—all of her—flooded her mind.

She cleared her throat.

His gaze darkened with sexual desire. But his scowl remained. "You lied to me to protect our sex life?" he asked, folding his arms across his chest.

"I did not lie. I told you I was going to work. I just didn't say where."

He curled his hands tighter around the table. His knuckles turned white. "You said you were going to the library."

She shook her head. "As I recall, you said, 'You'll be at the library with Sharon?' And I didn't answer."

"You led me to believe it, dammit."

Gabrielle nodded slowly. "Well, yes. But... wait. You went to the library to find me? Is Sharon still in one piece?"

He rolled his eyes. "She's in better shape than you're going to be in when I'm finished with you," he muttered. "Let's go. We're meeting my father and Holly for lunch."

Gabrielle knew when to retreat. With a curt nod, she closed her laptop and gathered her things.

His cell phone rang and he grabbed it. "Hello?" he barked into the phone.

He listened.

His frown deepened, the lines in his forehead growing more pronounced. Clearly this wasn't his day.

"What's wrong?" she asked when he'd hung up.

"What isn't?" he asked. "That was Hank. Seems Marlene decided to come today instead of tomorrow. She's waiting for me at the house." He turned and started for the exit.

With a shiver caused more by the idea of meeting Derek's ex than by his current mood, Gabrielle followed him out the door.

CHAPTER SIXTEEN

DEREK PAUSED OUTSIDE his front door, not quite ready to face his ex or to give up his daughter.

Gabrielle placed a comforting hand on his shoulder, her touch conveying more than mere words.

I understand.

She'd always known him best, and even now, when his fear for her safety had caused him to lash out at her in anger and frustration, she was still by his side, still here for him when he needed her.

"Whenever you're ready," she said at last.

He inclined his head, drew a breath and opened the door. Holly's voice drifted out to him, her rush of words conveying both her excitement to see her mother and the desire to catch Marlene up on her life as quickly as possible.

"And then Dad took me shopping for new flip-flops 'cause Fred chewed mine, but we had to stop at the library first 'cause you know how school's running that program where if you read a certain number of books you get a free pan pizza at Pizza Hut?"

"Yes, I remember that program," Marlene said, her familiar voice reaching Derek as he quietly opened the front door. "Have you been reading a lot?"

"Sort of. Anyway, so I dropped off my books and picked up some new ones and then we went for new flip-flops and that's when I met Gabrielle Donovan. She's really cool, Mom. You'll like her a lot. She dresses pretty and she speaks French. Oh, and she was dad's girlfriend back in high school, way before he ever met you, though."

Derek decided Holly had definitely rambled enough. "Hello?" he called out, as if he'd just walked in.

"Dad!" Holly said as both she and Marlene turned toward the front door. He stepped inside, Gabrielle behind him. "Look who's here!"

"I see. Grandpa called to tell me your mom was here a day early." He deliberately held Marlene's gaze a minute too long, hoping to convey that he didn't appreciate the surprise. "How was Europe?" he asked her.

"Truly amazing." Her cheeks were flushed pink and her happiness showed on her face. She'd cut her long brown hair in a short pixie style that suited her.

She looked well. And happy, he thought. He wanted that for her.

Marlene rose from her seat and gestured toward Gabrielle. "Aren't you going to introduce us?" Her question came out sounding as if she was chastising a child with bad manners.

"That's Gabrielle, Dad's old high-school girlfriend. I was just telling you about her," Holly chimed in with all the tact of an unaware eleven-year-old.

Derek held back a groan. "Of course I was going to introduce you." He'd just been being polite first by asking Marlene about her trip. He should have realized she'd feel threatened, so he tried to smooth things over first.

Derek made perfunctory introductions and Gabrielle stepped forward to say hello.

"I've heard so much about you from Holly and Derek," Gabrielle said with a smile.

Only he would know that smile was filled with discomfort.

"I wish I could say the same," Marlene said. "Derek never mentioned you."

Which was true. When they'd met, Derek had been trying to forget losing Gabrielle. He'd never discussed her with Marlene except to say he was coming off a long relationship that had recently ended. His pain was too fresh and his feelings for Gabrielle too private to share with anyone. Same with the curse. He'd hoped to forget the damn thing ever existed.

But Marlene did know about Gabrielle. Once Marlene had become pregnant, Derek had brought her home to meet his family. Hank had filled her in on Derek's past with colorful detail, and whatever he'd left out, she'd learned during a trip to town. Gabrielle was no longer a part of Derek's life then, nor would she ever be, but gossip and history had placed her between him and his new wife.

Before her honeymoon, Marlene had softened. Falling in love had eased her resentment, but she had her guard up today. Her bitchy side had returned, and he wanted this moment over quickly, for everyone involved.

"I thought you were coming tomorrow?" Derek asked his ex.

"I wanted to surprise Holly." She wrapped her arm around their daughter's shoulder.

Derek's stomach lurched. These were the tactics she'd used to separate them at her whim. Derek needed to let her know he wouldn't tolerate it anymore. "Holly, honey, why don't you take Gabrielle and get your things together? I want a few minutes alone with your mom."

"Okay." Holly bounced toward Gabrielle, grabbed her hand and headed for the door.

"She isn't staying *here* with you?" Marlene asked warily.

Gabrielle clearly winced. Derek gestured with

a tilt of his head that she should just take Holly and go. He'd handle Marlene.

He waited until they'd walked out and shut the door behind them before turning to Marlene. "It's complicated. Holly was sleeping here until just a few days ago." He went on to explain the situation in as little detail as possible, ending with how keeping Holly safe was his paramount concern.

"Safe would be with you," Marlene said. "Alone with you. Instead you put your girlfriend's safety before our daughter's."

He shook his head, but he knew better than to argue with Marlene when she'd made up her mind. And if Marlene was resentful of Gabrielle, which she definitely seemed to be, nothing Derek said or did would change her feelings.

He decided to switch subjects. "Let's sit. We need to talk about surprises like these and your sudden scheduling changes in my visitation."

Marlene raised an eyebrow but didn't take him up on his suggestion they sit. She remained standing, rigid and obviously upset.

"What's bothering you?" she asked. "That I missed my daughter and came home to see her?"

He exhaled slowly. "No, that much I understand. But I thought we'd made some progress in our relationship. And if this is a onetime thing because you miss her, that's fine. I just want you to understand how much I value my time with Holly.

I don't get her as much as I'd like, so I'd appreciate it if you'd stick to whatever time frames we set and not cut my visits short or cancel them at the last minute from now on." He tried to sound reasonable and not accusing.

Marlene folded her arms over her chest and met his gaze. "Right now, Derek, I don't think you're in a position to be asking anything of me when it comes to visitation. Obviously there's danger surrounding your girlfriend, and by letting her move in here, you've brought it right to our daughter."

The slap hurt, mostly because of the element of truth to her statement. Marlene wouldn't care or understand that Derek felt the need to protect both Gabrielle and Holly without choosing one over the other.

He decided to remain logical, not emotional in his point of view. "That's not fair. She's next door at night, and during the day she's with me or her grandfather, so we can keep an eye on her at all times."

"Whatever." Marlene waved a hand, dismissing him. "I'm taking her home where she's safe. Right now, you're lucky I don't file for sole custody based on the fact that you've exposed Holly to danger and will continue to do as long as you're with *her*."

Panic and fury filled Derek at her easily tossed-out words. He'd suffered enough loss in his life with his mother's abandonment and the family around him falling apart. He'd lost Holly once by letting his guilt over working too hard and not loving Marlene enough rule his choices. He'd allowed Marlene to manipulate him into having no relationship with his only child.

Never again. "Nothing is more important to me than my daughter. Do not push this," he warned her. But just because he remained firm didn't mean he wasn't choking on the fear of losing Holly.

"We're back!" Holly said, barreling in just in time to stop the argument from escalating further.

Derek kissed and hugged Holly tight. "I promise I'll drive to New York to pick you up next weekend. Or I can meet your mom halfway in Connecticut, if that works for her." Over Holly's head, he met Marlene's gaze, daring her to contradict him in front of his daughter.

Gabrielle remained silent in the background.

"I'll meet you in the car," Marlene said stiffly to Holly. She picked up the large duffel bag with all of Holly's things and strode outside.

"When am I old enough to fly here on an airplane?" Holly asked. "It's so much faster."

Derek laughed. "That's something your mother and I will have to discuss. You have the cell phone I bought you. Call whenever you want. My numbers are programmed."

"Your cell phone is number two, your home is number three and Grandpa Hank's house is number four," she said, parroting what he'd been reminding her of for two days.

He ruffled her hair and grinned. "I loved having you here. You know that, right?"

She nodded, her eyes filling with tears. "I wish—"

"I know." He didn't want her to finish her sentence. Whether it involved him still being married to his mother just so they could live together or whether she wished he lived closer, right now he couldn't bear to hear it.

"Give Fred another hug from me? Don't let him forget me," Holly said.

Derek merely nodded.

By the time he walked her to the car and sent her on her way, he was drained, in no mood to discuss the events of the night, including Gabrielle's blatant flaunting of her book and research in Mary Perkins's face.

He sure as hell wasn't up to revealing Marlene's custody threats to Gabrielle. All he could think about was the emptiness in his heart with Holly gone and his fear that her mother was taking her away for good.

GABRIELLE WOKE UP, HOPING Derek was in a better mood than when he'd gone to bed. She'd given him time and space, knowing it hadn't been easy for him to hand Holly over to his ex-wife. She'd hoped he would turn to her for comfort—sex or even just to be held, she didn't care which—but he'd climbed in beside her, rolled over and gone to sleep.

She could say she wasn't hurt, but that would be a lie.

Making her way downstairs, she approached the kitchen with cautious optimism.

He sat at the table, drinking coffee and reading the paper.

"Good morning," she said with forced cheer.

"'Morning."

She made herself coffee from the coffeemaker, adding milk and Equal before joining him at the table. "Sleep okay?" she asked.

He shrugged. "Fine."

She took a long, hot sip for courage. "Derek, we need to talk about a few things." Reaching out, she pushed the newspaper down so she could see his face. "Please."

He folded the business section and faced her, waiting for her to speak first.

She cleared her throat. Although she'd rather discuss Holly's departure, she knew she had to deal with the more immediate issues between them.

Since he was obviously still upset with her from last night, she decided to tackle the problems head-on. "I'm sorry I didn't tell you I was working and interviewing at the Wave. I knew you wouldn't like it and it was easier not to argue with you."

He raised an eyebrow, obviously surprised by her apology. "Thank you," he said.

"You're welcome." She'd lain awake last night tossing and turning, wondering how she was going to repair things between herself and Derek.

And they'd need repairing. With Holly gone, there was no chatty buffer between them. Nobody to keep them laughing. Nobody to force their minds off what drew them apart—that damn curse—and Gabrielle's work. And Derek, she knew, would keep the walls standing between them because he still feared their love more than he trusted in it.

"And I promise I won't do something like that again. If something comes up that you should know, I will keep you in the loop," she said, adding it sincerely.

"I appreciate that." He reached for the newspaper, but she smacked her hand down on top of it.

She had one more thing he needed to hear from her before he found out on the streets of Stewart or Perkins.

"I'm not finished," Gabrielle said.

He pinched the bridge of his nose. "What is it?"

She wanted to yell at his stubborn silence. She wanted to tell him that she knew he was using his anger at her as a shield, to not deal with the feelings between them. She wanted to tell him she loved him and she wasn't about to let him go, but he obviously wasn't in a receptive mood. And if that wasn't the understatement of the year, she didn't know what was.

Gabrielle drew a deep breath. "A television crew is coming to town today so they can tape a segment on 'A Day in the Life of a Local Author.'"

His scowl deepened. "You being the local author."

She nodded. "Any other local authors you know around here?" she asked cheerfully. She smiled.

He didn't. "Why now?"

She swallowed hard. "Why not now? Who knows why TV and newspapers decide to write and publish when they do?" She glanced down at her intertwined hands.

"Gabrielle?"

"Hmm?"

He leaned over and placed his hand beneath her chin, forcing her to meet his gaze. "Did you set this television interview up now as a way to piss off Mary Perkins? To scare her into showing her hand?"

She bit the inside of her cheek. "Maybe."

"Dammit," he exploded, slamming his hand onto the table. "Have you no respect for your own safety?"

She narrowed her gaze. "I have plenty, thank you very much. I'm not safe as long as that crazy woman is sitting in her big old Victorian house, hiding behind her family power and the fear she's instilled in people over the years. I'm not safe as long as she has the time to plan and to make sure she's not caught trying to hurt me or the people I love!" Gabrielle's voice rose with her temper.

"Then let's go to the police. Let them handle it," he said, his voice low, calmer than hers. His tone imploring.

"Like they'll believe us? That the pillar of her own community is pulling strings to keep herself in power as mayor? That she wants to rule by fear? It sounds crazy."

Derek shook his head. "We'll give them enough information to investigate."

"Richard already tried sending someone to talk to Stan Mancusi, the guy on the waterfront that Sharon's ex-fiancé told them about. He denied calling Tony. He denied knowing about the photos, and he claimed that while he was in prison, all Tony talked about was revenge on Sharon for putting him away."

Frustrated, Derek ran a hand through his hair. "Could it be true?"

"Doubtful. Richard did some investigating into Stan's history. It seems he has a daughter with autism. That's how Stan got into the petty thefts and things he was sent away for—trying to raise money for special schools. Guess where Stan's daughter is now?"

Derek rolled his shoulders back and groaned.

"Some expensive school that nobody knows how he's paying for?" he said, obviously hazarding a guess.

"Bingo. Something else nobody can trace back to Mary Perkins, but I'd lay odds that that's how she got him to get those photographs. We just can't prove it."

Derek rose and spilled his coffee into the sink, then ran water to rinse it away.

She stood and walked quietly to his side, placing her hand on his shoulder. "Do you really expect me to sit back and do nothing while she tries to stop me from doing the thing in life that gives me peace? She's not going to take my writing away any more than she's going to take my life. And she sure as hell isn't going to dictate what my subjects are!"

"So you'll write your book, my feelings be damned? Even at the expense of my daughter?"

Gabrielle stepped back, shocked by his words. "What are you talking about?"

"Marlene wasn't pleased that her daughter was displaced so I could protect you. She wasn't happy that I knowingly brought danger to her daughter's doorstep, and you know what?" He ran a hand through his hair. "She's right. But I'll be damned if I'm going to let her sue me for sole custody on the grounds of the danger that's surrounding you."

Gabrielle's stomach cramped and she eased herself into the nearest seat. "She threatened to do that?"

Derek treated her to a curt nod.

"I had no idea."

"And now that you do?"

Gabrielle swallowed hard. "I'll cancel the television crew, of course." With shaking hands, she fished for her cell phone, and a few minutes later, she was speaking to Kayla Lawson, a friend she'd met from a prior interview for an older book.

Gabrielle made her request and listened to her friend's reply. "I understand, but—"

A few minutes later, she hung up and faced Derek. "It's too late. Kayla's producer thinks this is a solid story. The money's allocated, the time's booked, nobody will pull the plug now." She stepped forward. "I'm sorry."

"I'm out of here."

Nausea rushed over her. "Where are you going?"

"To see a lawyer in case Marlene goes through with her threat," he muttered, storming past her.

Alone, Gabrielle settled back into her seat and exhaled a long breath. She'd have done anything to keep Derek with his daughter, even sacrifice her book. Now that retreat was no longer an option, the logical part of Gabrielle was glad. Because Mary Perkins had to be stopped.

But the emotional side of Gabrielle was torn in two. She'd unintentionally hurt the one person she loved most in the world and she'd do anything to make it right.

If only she knew how.

SHARON'S EYES GLAZED OVER the library budget. Each time she tried to focus enough on cutting back where appropriate, she ended up lost in thought, someplace else.

Gabrielle snapped her fingers in front of Sharon's face as she'd done at least half a dozen times in the past few minutes.

"Okay, so I see Richard's campaign has kicked into high gear," Gabrielle said.

Sharon glanced up, paying attention this time. "He's consumed by it." And not by me, Sharon thought.

"And not by you?"

Sharon put down her pen and laughed.

"What's so funny?"

"You read my mind."

"Isn't that what friends are for?"

Sharon nodded. "They are and I'm so glad I have you."

"You know it'll all be fine once this Mary Perkins thing is over. It's really stressful," Gabrielle said, her voice tight.

Sharon met her friend's gaze. "For everyone,

not just me, right?" No matter how overwhelmed she was by her own problems, Sharon couldn't forget Gabrielle was equally affected.

"Well, yes, I have my share of problems, but that isn't what I meant. We're focused on you right now. You're worried Richard coddles you and thinks you're too fragile? I say you show your fiancé the real you."

Sharon raised her gaze. "You mean…?"

"Buy a teddy, strip for him, show him you aren't as fragile as he thinks." Gabrielle shimmied her top half and laughed.

"He might keel over," Sharon said, imagining the look on Richard's face.

Gabrielle shrugged. "Or he might be relieved. One way or another, you'll know. Then you'll be able to focus again on your relationship and not your differences."

"Or the past?" Sharon asked. The photograph and the incident that still hovered between her and her fiancé.

Gabrielle waved a hand through the air. "It'll stay where it belongs—"

"Once this Mary Perkins thing is over," they said at the same time, and laughed.

"What do you say we forget the budget, forget the writing, and let's go shopping." Gabrielle jumped up from her seat, decision made.

Sharon gathered her papers. "Now, that sounds

like a plan. Victoria's Secret?" she asked, knowing that was Gabrielle's favorite store.

Gabrielle nodded.

"You have this determined look on your face. Why is it I think this trip has less to do with me than with you?" Sharon asked her friend.

Gabrielle let out a long sigh. "I think I've brought more aggravation to Derek's life than joy." She wiped her hands over her eyes.

Was she crying? Gabrielle was an emotional person, but she rarely fell apart.

"What's going on?" Sharon asked.

"Derek's ex-wife is threatening to file for sole custody because he exposed Holly to danger. Because of me. And with the film crew coming, the situation is only going to get worse, not better. I know a stupid negligee isn't going to make any of that go away, but it's the only apology I can think of at the moment."

Sharon sucked in a sharp breath. "I told you I shouldn't be worried only about myself." She pulled her friend into a hug. "Derek knows it isn't your fault. Isn't that what you keep telling me to believe about Richard?"

"There's one difference. I knowingly invited that film crew here. I escalated the danger. For a man who believes bad things are destined to happen when he falls in love." Gabrielle cleared her throat. "Now I'm going to have to live with the consequences."

There was nothing Sharon could say to help her friend or herself because Gabrielle was right. They'd both just have to let things play out and see what the future held.

DEREK HAD LIED TO Gabrielle. His divorce lawyer was in Manhattan, where he'd been living at the time, not in Stewart. But he'd needed some time and space to cool off, away from Gabrielle and his feelings for her, which were so tangled up they didn't let him breathe, let alone make a rational decision.

While driving around letting off steam, he had called his attorney, a friend of his who assured him that Marlene didn't have a leg to stand on if she took this to court. Leaving his child for three nights at his father's house didn't make Derek a bad parent, just a cautious one. He could counter Marlene's accusation with the fact that she left the country and her daughter for a selfish month-long honeymoon. That wouldn't win him sole custody, either but he at least could threaten Marlene back. His lawyer had also assured him they could legally force Marlene to stick to the agreed-upon visitation schedule if she tried to make his time with Holly more difficult to come by.

Derek groaned. He *hated* the thought of being one of those parents who fought and made their children's lives hell. He hoped Marlene would get over her snit quickly and let things go back to what they were.

Though his lawyer had reassured him that he wasn't going to lose his daughter, Derek couldn't shake the nagging discomfort Marlene's threats had caused. History hadn't been kind to Derek, and he wasn't about to trust in the attorney's platitudes.

He'd spent the day out, picking up tools he needed to do work around the house and clearing his head. Hours later, he arrived home to see Gabrielle's car in the driveway. Was she there? He didn't know, as he hadn't touched base with her all day.

Though he was still irritated, he had calmed down since their last conversation. He wasn't fine with her choices, but they were hers to make.

He let himself inside. It was dark downstairs, but a small light glowed from above in the loft. He dropped his keys on the counter in the front hall and headed upstairs.

He found Gabrielle watching television in his bed. "Hey there."

"Hi." She lifted her hand in a halfhearted wave.

Obviously she wasn't any happier than he was at the moment.

He walked over and sat beside her. "What did you do today?"

"I went shopping with Sharon." She gestured to a pink Victoria's Secret shopping bag sitting across the floor.

"I'm glad to see the day wasn't a lost cause." He tried to keep things light.

"Wasn't it?" She glanced down at her fingers as she toyed with the comforter. "I was stupid enough to think buying something sexy would solve all our problems. That I could apologize for risking everything you love with sex. But life doesn't work that way."

"It could." He brushed his thumb over her cheek, loving the feel of her soft skin. "An apology is just that. An apology and I accept it, if you'll accept mine." He owed her one for blowing up at her earlier.

They'd both helped make the mess they were in.

"Do you mean that?" she asked.

He took her hand. "I'm not doing a tap dance that you're antagonizing Mary Perkins, but you wouldn't be you if you didn't handle things out in the open. It isn't your fault I have an ex-wife who will use any excuse to pull my daughter away from me. I'm upset with a lot of things and I took it all out on you. I'm sorry."

She smiled a little. "It's okay. What if Marlene does sue for custody?"

His stomach churned at the thought. "I'll just have to deal with it. My lawyer said Marlene doesn't have a leg to stand on." He spread his hands out in front of him. "I can't say I'm trusting that at face value, though."

She nodded slowly. "I understand."

"I'm actually glad Holly's with her mother right now, though. That means I can focus on keeping you safe without worrying about her. If this television crew is going to be around, you're going to need me to make sure Mary Perkins isn't."

He rose and started to walk across the room.

"Where are you going?"

"To get this." He picked up the shopping bag and pulled out something wrapped in pink tissue paper, which he easily discarded. A red lace garment hung from his fingertips, looking skimpier than ever thanks to his large hands. "Think you can put this on for me?" He barely recognized his own rough voice.

His desire and need for this woman only seemed to grow rather than diminish. For as long as she was in his house, she was his.

And when the threat was over?

He refused to think about it now, burying his face in the warm skin of her neck, just as he'd soon bury himself in her willing body.

CHAPTER SEVENTEEN

THE DAY OF FILMING arrived. Gabrielle and Derek stopped for breakfast in town. They'd just finished eating and were going to meet her friend Kayla and the camera crew at the Wave, the chosen place to begin "The Day in the Life" segment.

Derek paid at the register while Gabrielle waited.

Her cell phone rang and she picked it up on the first ring. "Hello?"

"Darling, guess where I am."

"Maman!"

"Of course it's me. Turn around."

Gabrielle pivoted toward the window facing the street and saw her mother waving at her from the sidewalk. Gabrielle flipped her phone closed at the same time she ran outside.

"What are you doing here?" she asked, surprised to see her mother in town.

"Is that any way to greet me?" Her mother cupped Gabrielle's face in her hands and leaned in to kiss first one cheek, then the next before pulling her into a warm hug.

It didn't matter if Gabrielle saw her mother a week ago or a few hours, her mother always greeted her the same exuberant way.

"Your friend Kayla called to tell me about your television segment and she asked if she could interview me and your papa. He has summer classes, but I was free, so *voilà!* Here I am."

Derek walked out of the restaurant and joined them on the street. "Hello, ladies."

Gabrielle smiled. "Derek, do you remember my mother, Juliette Donovan?"

"Of course I do." He extended his hand. "May I say you haven't changed a bit?" He kissed the back of her hand in the French manner.

Gabrielle bit the inside of her cheek and wondered where he'd come up with that bit of chivalry and whether it was enough to soften her mother's feelings about—"

"Derek Corwin, the man who broke my daughter's heart," Juliette said bluntly.

"Maman!" Gabrielle said, appalled that her mother would go directly for the jugular.

Derek smiled grimly. "That's okay. I understand how your mother feels. I'd feel the same way about any man who Holly got involved with…" As he spoke, his eyes darkened and his expression closed.

As if he'd just gotten a new, enlightening perspective on his relationship with Gabrielle.

Merde.

"I think we have to be at the Wave," Gabrielle said, pulling on Derek's arm. "Kayla, the interviewer, called my mother and asked her to participate in the segment," she explained quickly, hoping to split the two people she loved apart before her mother gave Derek more motivation to pull away from her.

Since Holly's departure, Derek hadn't been the same. Although he'd apologized, Gabrielle sensed he was holding himself back from her, and she didn't think it was only because she'd jeopardized his custody. In her heart, Gabrielle believed that with his renewed fear of losing Holly, came the reminder of the curse and all the loss he and his family had suffered. He wasn't about to let himself love—and lose—Gabrielle, too. He didn't have to spell out his feelings for her to understand them. They were too deeply ingrained for her not to comprehend.

"We'll leave in a moment," her mother said. "Derek, I'm so glad you can be honest with me and with yourself. It's the mark of an honorable man. So can you assure me you won't hurt my daughter again?"

Gabrielle shook her head, her heart pounding hard in her chest as Derek faced Juliette.

"I can assure you Gabrielle is well aware of my feelings and the situation we're in," he said, his explanation vague to her mother.

But crystal clear to Gabrielle.

THE GOOD PEOPLE OF STEWART and Perkins heard that a film crew was in town and turned out in droves for their chance to be on television, even if it was simply local TV and the only people who might see the segment were other locals. Gabrielle was a celebrity and everyone wanted their fifteen minutes of fame, too.

Even Derek's father showed up for his opportunity.

"Think we should remind him he was one of the people who wanted me gone?" Gabrielle asked, laughing.

Derek shook his head. "It won't do any good. My father has a shorter memory than his old dog's."

Gabrielle chuckled. "At least Kayla won't have a difficult time weeding out who she can use in the documentary. I gave her a list of people who knew me, in the past and in the present."

"So Hank just might be in luck after all."

Gabrielle was certain Derek was right. His father was a prime candidate to talk about Gabrielle's past in Stewart and the curse as it pertained to her book. Ironically, *she* was the one who wasn't in the mood to discuss the damn curse. Her mother, in asking Derek to promise he wouldn't hurt Gabrielle again, had brought up Gabrielle's greatest fear. And Derek's answer—or rather his nonanswer—said it all.

As soon as Gabrielle was safe from Mary Perkins, Derek planned to walk away.

Again.

Unless she could convince him that by eliminating Mary Perkins as a threat, the curse, or rather the perception of the curse, would disappear with her.

One way or another, Gabrielle would know whether she was successful soon enough.

"Okay, folks, here's the story." Kayla's voice interrupted Gabrielle's thoughts.

For the past half hour, Kayla had walked around the Wave, surveying the bar and the people. She was all business, and she struck a commanding presence just as she intended. With her straightened strawberry-blond hair and white pantsuit, she stood out in the crowd.

When she barked orders, people listened. Most of the crowd stood in silence, waiting for her to continue. "As far as the camera crew is concerned, we're concentrating on scenery for today. I want you to shoot footage of local hangouts, this place included. While you're at it, get Gabrielle interacting with the locals. Tomorrow when we're all fresh, we'll move onto specific interviews. I want to work on the local flavor first."

Billy, her head cameraman, nodded and began directing his crew.

Kayla was a pro at handling people. Gabrielle wasn't bad herself, but she'd always admired her friend's ability to deal with a situation by reading the people involved. Watching her work was a treat.

"Gabrielle, you go about your day, business as usual. Juliette, we won't get to you today, but we can shoot you first thing tomorrow if that works. Otherwise you name the time and I'll work around you. I'm sorry I made you come out here for no reason today. I never know what I'm going to want to do first until I get the lay of the land."

Gabrielle's mother, who'd taken a seat at the bar and was chatting with George, didn't seem to mind that she'd driven out here for nothing. A people person, Juliette was enjoying herself immensely.

"How the hell are you going to go about your business with camera crews everywhere?" Derek asked.

Gabrielle shrugged. "Good question. I guess I'll just do the best I can. I've seen Kayla work miracles with harder subjects than me. I'll just try to ignore them." She pulled out her laptop and was about to flip it open when she caught sight of the woman she'd come to think of as public enemy number one. "Look. Mary Perkins just walked in," Gabrielle whispered to Derek.

He stiffened. Gabrielle knew he was still unhappy with the idea of antagonizing Mary Perkins, tempting Fate and the damn curse, but they had no choice.

"I have to admit that was faster than I thought

it would be," Gabrielle said. "I figured she'd lay low and see what the TV people intended before showing up."

As they watched, the mayor, dressed immaculately in a summer linen suit with a flower pinned to her lapel, headed directly for Kayla, the head interviewer and lead on this project.

"Are you sure Kayla can handle her?" Derek asked.

"Yes. She's been well versed on all the issues. Kayla might have come here to do a story on a local author, but she also knows the reason I asked. I've informed Kayla about our suspicions regarding the mayor, and told her to expect Mary to want to get herself featured prominently in the story. Since the subject is 'A Day in the Life of an Author,' Mary is going to have to be creative. I assume that she'll want to give her opinion on my latest book and offer herself up as the resident expert on the curse—which is my current work in progress," Gabrielle whispered, explaining to Derek what she'd told Kayla when pitching the project.

"So at a minimum, Kayla is getting herself a local-interest piece on a bestselling author. At best, she's going to get a scoop on abuse of power at a local level?" Derek asked.

"Yep. Complete with bribery, blackmail, sabotage and much, much more. Everything hinges on how far Mary Perkins can be pushed. The plan is

CARLY PHILLIPS   329

to keep her out of the spotlight and ignore her so-called power and authority."

As they spoke, Gabrielle and Derek kept an eye on Mary Perkins. As if scripted, the mayor had already approached Kayla and introduced herself. As planned, Kayla shook her hand and excused herself, walking away from the mayor.

Kayla headed straight to Gabrielle's table, where she paused, leaned over as if she had something important to discuss, and winked at Gabrielle before zeroing in on someone else.

The mayor tried once more to talk to Kayla, but found herself brushed aside for Gabrielle's mother. Kayla continued to make notes and book interview times—with everyone but the town's long-standing mayor.

Derek placed his hand on the back of Gabrielle's chair protectively. "She doesn't look happy," he said, sneaking a glance at Mary Perkins, who'd turned her attention to the sole cameraman at the Wave.

As per instructions, he was to keep the long-distance camera angle on Gabrielle at work, not on the mayor or anyone else.

"It's going to get worse," Gabrielle said. "There's one more part of this plan." What she found fascinating was that Mary Perkins was so predictable that they were able to play this out exactly as they'd hoped.

Gabrielle picked up her phone and dialed.

"Richard?" she whispered to her best friend's fiancé. "It's time," Gabrielle said softly, and flipped her phone shut.

A few minutes later, the telephone behind the bar rang. George answered, then called out to the crowd. "Ms. Lawson?" the bartender called out to Kayla.

She turned. "Yes?"

"Phone call for you."

Kayla shook her head. "Take a message, please?"

George spoke to the person on the other end of the phone, then called out, "It's Mr. Richard Stern. He says he's a personal friend of Gabrielle's and he'd be happy to add his insights to your project. His fiancée, Sharon Merchant, is Gabrielle's best friend. Isn't that right, Gabrielle?" George asked her.

"It is. Sharon and I went to high school together, so you'll want to interview them," Gabrielle said to Kayla. "Besides, Richard is running for mayor. People will be interested in hearing from him, too."

Beside her, Derek groaned. "Boy, when you plan, you plan big."

Gabrielle didn't meet his gaze.

Kayla glanced at her appointment book. "Tell him he can have 10:00 a.m. tomorrow morning," she called to George.

The older man gave her a thumbs-up and re-layed the message.

Mary Perkins's face turned beet red at the conversation shooting around the bar.

"I wasn't keeping the plan from you." Gabrielle pretended to work as she spoke to Derek. She lifted her laptop open and hit the power button. "If you'd been around yesterday, I'd have filled you in. And I would have done it last night, but you insisted I try on my newest purchase, and after that, you couldn't keep your hands off me," she said, deliberately reminding him of how good things had been between them.

The thought turned her insides soft, and despite the crowd and the intense scene playing around them, desire thrummed low in her belly. With Derek behind her, his body heat surrounding her, the yearning only grew.

"I can't keep my hands off you now," he said, his voice low in her ear.

Meanwhile, obviously feeling impotent, Mary glared first at Kayla, then unmistakably at the source of all the media attention—Gabrielle— before storming out of the Wave, extremely unhappy at being ignored.

Gabrielle shivered. "I think she left frost in her wake," she murmured.

Derek's hand moved from the chair to Gabrielle's back in a warm, protective gesture. "I'm more worried about what she's going to do to get even."

DONALD WATSON, EDITOR-IN-chief of the *Journal,* the leading newspaper in both Perkins and Stewart, stared at the photograph in front of him in disbelief. Even if he hadn't been forewarned and asked not to run this picture, there was no way he could print it, anyway. He was in charge of a *newspaper,* not a porn magazine.

When Richard Stern had approached him off the record and asked to be notified if any photographs of his future wife passed Donald's desk, he'd agreed. Hell, he'd have endorsed Stern if he wasn't afraid of Mary Perkins's wrath.

The favor might be off the record, but Donald was a newspaperman and unable to contain his curiosity. He'd done his research. Donald glanced at the photo and shook his head. Poor woman. To be so violated at such a young age. At least she'd had the guts to send the guy who'd drugged and photographed her to jail.

But, then, who'd sent the photograph in an unmarked envelope to the newspaper? And how had they gotten their hands on police evidence?

Donald had earned the editor-in-chief position the old-fashioned way. He'd started sweeping floors during high school and worked his way up, earning the trust of the editor-in-chief before him. Along the way, he'd built up some good friends in important places. Even small-town papers had to get their scoops.

Another glance at the photograph, and he decided to call his "friend" who worked the evidence room at the police station. "Hey, Rob, I'm calling in that favor." Two months ago, he'd covered for Rob with his wife, claiming Rob had been at their weekly poker game when, in fact, he'd been with his mistress.

He asked Rob if anything was missing from the Evidence Room and Rob began to stutter before saying no. Since that was his poker tell, Donald knew the man was lying.

"What kind of trouble are you in, buddy?" Rob wasn't just a cheater, he was a gambler, and he often owed more than he had on hand.

Five minutes later, Donald had his answer. He also had, thanks to Rob, the evidence Richard Stern needed to take down his mayoral opponent.

AFTER JULIETTE'S INTERVIEW, Hank Corwin was granted his turn. Kayla sat across from him at the Wave and waited as they did a sound check on Derek's father.

Derek couldn't help but laugh. Hank's tune about discussing the curse in public had certainly changed. Not his views on the curse, those he expressed in detail, reminding the world—and Derek—how tragedy had befallen every Corwin man who fell in love.

How tragedy always would follow.

Derek couldn't shake the foreboding that settled over him. Without Holly and her cheerful voice bouncing around him, Derek felt the loss keenly. He could live with the temporary custody arrangement because he could look forward to the next time he could be with his daughter.

But what if there wasn't a next time?

What if Marlene's threat became reality?

He shivered and forced his attention back to his father's interview, trying without success not to internalize the older man's words.

As he listened to Hank, his gaze was drawn over and over to Gabrielle. His beautiful Gabrielle, perched on a bar stool in her emerald sundress that offset her hair, watching the crew work. He couldn't let himself think about his feelings or anything else about her, for fear his father's prophetic words would kick in at any time.

Kayla wrapped up Hank's interview and Hank headed outside, preening and proud of himself and his time in front of the camera.

"Derek, do you have a minute?"

Derek turned to see Richard Stern. "Hey, Richard." Derek shook the other man's hand. "What's up?"

"I think I have the information we've been waiting for," he said quietly.

"Hello, boys." Gabrielle joined them. "Why are

your two heads together?" she asked, clearly not intending to be left out.

"Richard was just saying he had information for us."

Richard leaned in closer. "The photograph of Sharon was stolen from the Evidence Room at the police precinct. The guy who works the day shift has skeletons in his closet, which left him vulnerable to blackmail. But he wasn't stupid. He refused to deal with a middleman. He wanted to know who he was stealing for."

Derek had no doubt what was coming next. "Mary Perkins?"

Richard nodded.

"Why in the world would she have told him? She could have just used whatever leverage she had against the cop to make him cooperate," Derek said. "It doesn't make sense that she'd leave herself open and vulnerable after years of being so careful."

"Richard is the first viable candidate running against her in years. She got scared," Gabrielle mused.

"And scared people get sloppy," Richard confirmed. "According to my source who spoke directly with the cop in question, she wanted that photograph desperately."

"Enough to show up herself to get the information?" Derek asked.

"Apparently, she was beyond reason," Richard

said. "She wanted insurance and that photograph was it."

Gabrielle let out a low whistle. "Wow. What do you plan to do with the information?" she asked Richard.

Suddenly, people came screaming toward the front of the bar.

"Fire!" someone yelled, barreling past them and rushing out the front door.

Chaos ensued.

Derek thought only to grab Gabrielle's hand as he jerked his head toward the back of the restaurant and saw flames licking around the curtains and traveling toward them.

"Oh, my God!" Gabrielle screamed.

"Let's go," Derek said.

"Follow me." Richard headed out first.

Derek pulled Gabrielle, and along with the rest of the crowd, they bolted outside. The Wave had been more crowded than Derek had realized and someone pushed between him and Gabrielle, breaking their hands apart. He turned to call her, but the people behind him shoved him forward in their rush to escape.

Once they were outside, the firemen had already arrived and began directing people far from the burning building. Derek turned to look for Gabrielle, but he didn't see her in the crush of the crowd directly behind him.

He was forced onto the far grass by a fireman.

Others began cordoning off the area and prohibiting people getting anywhere near the Wave.

"Derek!"

He heard his name being called and he whipped around at the sound of his father's voice. "Dad! Over here!" Derek waved so his father could see him.

"Thank God!" Hank said, hugging him until he couldn't breathe.

"You weren't inside, were you?" Derek asked. He'd thought his father had left once his interview ended.

Hank shook his head. "I was outside when I heard someone screaming about the fire. I looked up and saw the flames. I just wanted to find you." Hank wiped the sweat from his brow. "I couldn't bear to lose my son," he said, his voice cracking.

"I'm fine," Derek assured him, emotion and so much more clogging his throat. "Have you seen Gabrielle? We got separated trying to get out of the building."

Hank shook his head.

Derek glanced back again, but there were too many people crowding around to see everyone.

It had been too long since he'd made it out and he still hadn't seen her. Panic nearly suffocated him. "I've got to find her."

He started for the building, only to be stopped by his one-hundred-ninety-pound father jumping onto his back.

"You aren't going near that fire," Hank said in Derek's ear.

"At least let me tell the fireman she's missing."

Hank released himself and rushed with Derek toward the nearest firefighter. His father never released his grip on Derek's collar. Derek was choking on the material pulling against his neck but figured it was his father's way of keeping him safe.

"I'm looking for a woman. Reddish hair, about five foot five. Last time I saw her was inside the building," Derek said to the fireman.

"I'll relay the information," the man in uniform promised.

As he waited, Derek clenched his hands into fists, his nails digging into his skin.

"She'll be fine," Hank said, placing an arm around Derek's shoulders.

"Because our good luck says so?" Derek asked his father.

The older man looked at him with wise eyes but said nothing. How could he, Derek thought, when he'd lived through his share of pain and tragedy, too?

"Don't hold it against me for not letting you run back into that building, son. You wouldn't want Holly to be fatherless, now, would you?"

Derek shook his head, unable to speak as he waited for news on Gabrielle.

CHAPTER EIGHTEEN

DEREK COULD BARELY BREATHE as he watched the burning building. Finally, he caught sight of Gabrielle along with Kayla being helped out of the bar by a fireman.

Coughing, she made her way toward him, throwing her arms around his neck. "Oh, my God! You're okay, too."

He shut his eyes and squeezed her to him, all the while, thanking God that she was safe. Everyone he loved was safe. Now he just had to keep them that way.

"What happened?" he asked.

She dropped to the ground, sitting cross-legged on the grass.

He and Hank knelt beside her.

"After we got separated, I was heading out when I heard Kayla scream. I turned and saw a beam had hit her. The fire wasn't surrounding her, so I ran to get her. It just got harder to get out." She shook her head, obviously still overwhelmed. "I have to check on Kayla."

Derek glanced over at the waiting ambulance. "She's with the paramedics. She's awake and talking, so you can relax here for a few minutes first." He stroked her hair as she breathed in and out, pulling herself together.

"My bar!"

They turned at the sound.

George was pacing right beside them, clearly distraught.

Gabrielle eased herself to her feet, her legs trembling as she stood. Derek kept his arm around her shoulder as she walked up to the older man.

"George? It'll be okay." She offered lame words of support. There was nothing else she could do for him.

He turned to her, looking older than he had just half an hour before as his beloved bar burned behind him.

"You mean, my *family* bar." Elizabeth Perkins appeared, as if out of the blue. She had a dazed look in her eyes and a red gasoline can in her hands.

Gabrielle blinked, certain she was imagining the image, but the woman and the red can in her hands remained.

George narrowed his gaze. "What are you talking about?" he asked, staring at the mayor's granddaughter in disbelief.

"You mean, Seth never told you he couldn't get the financing to turn your old bar into a nightclub?" Elizabeth asked.

George shook his head.

"He told me. In bed. I knew Seth would come in handy one day. He knows everyone and everything that's going on. I didn't think his pillow talk would be so helpful, but it was. Of course, I suggested to my grandmother that we lend him the money. Owning this bar was an important step in cementing power in this town."

Elizabeth's tone indicated her plan had been long-standing and well-thought-out even if the blank expression in her eyes showed everyone that something inside her had snapped.

"My son wouldn't touch your family's dirty money," George spat.

"Why not? He touched me." Elizabeth laughed. She'd obviously intended her words to be sultry, but the sound came out high-pitched and deranged.

Gabrielle winced while George glanced around, desperately looking for his son. Gabrielle caught sight of Seth beneath a tree, staring at the burning building with utter shock and pain on his face.

Gabrielle had no doubt Elizabeth was telling the truth.

George turned back to face her. "Let's say he did borrow money from you. That would explain all the times he defended your grandmother and let her hold her holiday party at the Wave. That doesn't make it your bar."

A satisfied expression eased her lips upward in

a nasty smile. Gone were all vestiges of amiability covering her true personality. Gone was any trace of sanity. "It does if the payments haven't been made. And they haven't."

"He wouldn't let me see the books." Tears filled George's eyes.

Gabrielle couldn't watch his pain. She strode closer to George, intending to walk him away.

Derek, meanwhile, walked up to Elizabeth. "What is that in your hands?" he asked, although with the woman reeking of gasoline and waving the can around as she spoke, the answer was obvious.

"It's her new perfume. Eau de Gasoline," Hank said in disgust.

Elizabeth shook her head. "Do you people think you can stop me?" She gestured wildly, poking herself in the chest. "My family founded this town. My grandmother owns you all. I'm her successor. My name gives me power. Just look at all the generations of Mary Perkins there have been, and the things that they have done. I dare you to defy me."

"That's enough!" The mayor stepped through the crowd and approached her granddaughter. "Not another word," she said to the young woman, obviously looking to protect her from her own insanity.

But it was equally obvious it was too late.

The police edged closer. "Elizabeth Perkins?"

"Mary Elizabeth," she shrieked back at them.

A uniformed officer stepped forward. "Mary Elizabeth Perkins, you are under arrest for arson," he said, and then read the woman her rights.

"That's okay, darling, Grandma's right here. I'll take care of everything."

Roger, the only officer Gabrielle knew, wedged himself between Elizabeth and the mayor. "I'm sorry, ma'am, but you're under arrest, as well," he said, gently grasping the mayor's arm.

"For what?" Mary asked, assuming a haughty "I own you" tone Gabrielle hadn't heard from her before now.

"Bribery. Theft from the police Evidence Room. And whatever else the district attorney comes up with," he said, then read the mayor her rights, as well.

"Nonsense," Mary spat. "I'm the mayor!"

"Which doesn't make you exempt from the law," Derek said, facing the woman who had been the bane of his family's existence, at least in this generation. "Apparently you feared Richard Stern so much you must have panicked." And Richard had managed to inform the police.

"We have proof you paid someone to steal evidence. We have an eyewitness," Richard said.

As people surrounded her, the other woman began to shrivel into the old, frail woman she really was. "There was no bribery involved. I had no intention of exposing the photograph," Mary said.

"I only wanted to scare Richard into not running in order to protect his fiancée, but I never got the chance."

"Then who sent me the note asking for money?" Sharon asked, stepping out of the shadows.

Gabrielle wanted to applaud her friend's bravery. She didn't have to. Richard was beaming enough for them both.

"Did you really think I was going to let the fact that age was softening you prevent you from winning, Grandmother?" Elizabeth tried to shrug off the police, but they held on tight. "I found the photo. I discovered the history behind it. I put the blackmail into motion. I thought the mousy librarian would go crying to her fiancé and beg him to drop out of the race. When she didn't make the first drop, I realized maybe she was cockier than I thought and I stepped up the game. This is my town," she said, hysterically. "Mine!"

"Grandma, Beth, come on." Lauren Perkins, Mary's other granddaughter whom Gabrielle had met in the mayor's office, stepped forward and put a hand on her grandmother's shoulder. "Let's just go with the police. We'll sort things out when we're alone." Her voice shook as she spoke, but she took control, instructing the police to take her family to the station and end the public spectacle.

The officers complied, but before they reached the police cars, George came running forward.

"Why?" he asked. "Why burn down my building? I have to know."

"You're as foolish as your son!" Elizabeth, her hands cuffed behind her back, said. "Isn't it obvious? I burned down the building for the money. I'll call in the loan for lack of payment and it'll be mine."

"You're pathetic," George spat.

"You all thought you could ignore my grandmother. Making that documentary and treating her as if she didn't exist. But that film needs to include my grandmother, the mayor. Mary Perkins. That name means everything in this town. Instead you interviewed that sniveling man who thought he could take the job that belongs to my family. Mine." Her eyes were wide, bulging, her insanity clear.

"Take her away," Lauren insisted, her eyes filled with tears.

"Not yet. I have one more thing to say," Elizabeth said. "You!" She turned her glare on Gabrielle.

The blood drained from Gabrielle's head as she met the other woman's icy stare. Maintaining her composure, Gabrielle wrapped her hands around her arms to stop the shivering and refused to show fear. Derek stepped up from behind and eased her against him, supporting her with his strength.

"Do not think you can undo the curse with one of your pathetic books. Everyone in this town knows the curse exists. And you'll know it again when your life falls apart." Elizabeth laughed again, the sound slicing through Gabrielle's heart.

Derek squeezed her tighter.

"Not a chance." Gabrielle stood up to the other woman. "Your family's days of spreading fear are over. Whatever you wanted in life, you destroyed other people to get it. *That's* your power, not some old, unproven curse. It's over now. You've been exposed."

Elizabeth shrieked, but before she could act, the police pushed her into the car. Her grandmother had already been taken away.

Lauren shot Gabrielle and the rest of the crowd an apologetic, sick look before following the police into the last remaining vehicle.

Gabrielle squeezed Derek's hand. She couldn't help feeling sorry for the young woman who, until now, had no idea what her own sister and grandmother were capable of.

As things calmed down, Gabrielle tried to remind herself both Mary Perkins and her granddaughter were insane, yet Elizabeth's words chilled Gabrielle despite the summer heat. Elizabeth obviously meant to scare Gabrielle into not writing her book, but her words, if dissected, could go much deeper, to include her relationship with Derek. Her entire future was at stake.

She looked back at the Wave. The firemen had finally begun to get the blaze under control. The bar was basically destroyed. The ownership and insurance issues would have to be sorted out later. But the harm done by Mary Perkins and her granddaughter would be much harder to contain.

Gabrielle glanced at Derek, the man she loved, and prayed they wouldn't become part of the other woman's collateral damage.

"HELLUVA DAY," GABRIELLE said as they walked into Derek's house at last.

Exhaustion pummeled at Derek, settling in his bones.

They'd dropped Hank off at his house after stopping by to assure Uncle Thomas everyone was in one piece. The fire and Elizabeth Perkins's breakdown and the mayor's arrest was the talk of the town.

For Derek, coming off the argument with Marlene, and the idea of losing Holly fresh in his mind, today had been draining in ways he still couldn't come to terms with.

"Who could have guessed that Elizabeth Perkins was determined to carry on her grandmother's evil legacy?" he said.

"More like family insanity." Gabrielle shivered. "Although Lauren seemed refreshingly normal. I hope she's okay."

Derek nodded. "I hope so, too. Thank God nobody was badly hurt in the fire."

"The paramedics said Kayla didn't have a concussion, just a nasty bruise."

Derek was still struck by how close he'd come to losing Gabrielle. The minutes he'd waited for her to come out of that building had been the longest of his life.

She tossed her bag onto the couch.

The couch, Derek thought, where they'd made love. He didn't think he'd ever forget. The memory would live with him forever.

Even if she couldn't.

"Derek?"

"Hmm?"

Gabrielle walked over to him. She had no makeup on, her hair was a mess and her face was streaked from tears. She was the most beautiful woman he'd ever laid eyes on.

"We need to talk," she said.

Everything inside him rebelled at the notion. As long as things between them remained unspoken, they could go on as they were. But the moment they *talked,* this life they'd created, the illusion, came to an end.

But she was right.

It was time.

"Mary Perkins's reign of terror is over. The police will sort through what she caused and what damage Elizabeth did, but it's over. She can no longer claim her family's curse over the Corwins

gives her power. She's been exposed as a fraud."
Gabrielle's eyes flashed with the fire he so admired.

Despite the day she'd had, she maintained the
spunk and determination that was a part of her.

"Hopefully people will feel freed," he said, because he did agree with her. People who'd been
blackmailed, bribed and hurt in Mary Perkins's
quest for power would feel vindicated.

"Do you?" She perched her hands on her hips,
clearly challenging him. "Do you feel freed?"

He exhaled long and hard. "I feel relieved." He
chose his words carefully. "I'm relieved you're
not in danger anymore. I'm glad your plan to push
Mary Perkins out into the open worked. But do I
feel freed from the curse? Not really, no."

A muscle worked in her jaw. "Why am I not surprised?" she asked sarcastically, her anger simmering just below the surface.

He understood. He did. He was angry at Fate,
too. But he hadn't lied to her. He'd never once
made her a promise for more than *today,* and he'd
never denied the fact that his family's history
played a role in the choices he made.

"Mary Perkins tormented people by preying on
their weakness. Those people are freed. But me?
The men in my family? Nothing that happened today changes the fact that for generations, every
male who has fallen in love loses in unfathomable
ways." He drew a deep breath. "And, as an added

bonus, not one of the women who've been involved with a Corwin man has escaped unscathed. Look at what nearly happened to you today. Because you were writing about my family. We are cursed," he said clearly.

"That is such bull. How has the curse kicked in for you? It's not as if you've said you love me, Derek. I doubt you'd even let yourself think it. So how does what happened today fit into the curse?" she asked, obviously frustrated.

He groaned, unable to argue with her logic. But logic wasn't ruling his decisions. Fear and past evidence was. "Even if it doesn't, I can't take the constant fear that something awful is going to happen to you because of me. I'm not going to let you be hurt."

She cupped his face in her hands, refusing to let him pull away. "Then don't walk away from me."

He swallowed hard, fighting not to respond to her plea, to keep his distance when everything in him rebelled against it. "I have to."

"Make no mistake, Derek. If I leave this house today, it's you walking away from me. Not the other way around. I don't believe in curses, but if there is one, I believe our love is much more powerful."

Her heart was in her voice and her eyes.

His heart filled every time he looked at her. "I've seen the history. Hell, I've lived it. I'm not tempting Fate." He couldn't.

Like his daughter, Gabrielle was too precious.

"That's your final decision? Despite the fact that I love you with everything inside me?" she asked.

He shook his head. "Not despite the fact that you love me, Gabby. *Because* you love me."

FOR THE FIRST FEW DAYS after the fire, Gabrielle kept herself busy with work. She had lost her man, but she was determined to write her book. Even if she'd failed to prove to Derek that circumstances, not curses, dictated the course of one's life, she still believed it herself.

Like Gabrielle, Kayla wasn't about to let the fire prevent her from continuing her story, which had grown in scope since Mayor Perkins's arrest. Kayla wanted to continue working in Stewart and Perkins, so instead of moving home, she returned to Mrs. Rhodes's inn for the duration of filming.

It wasn't easy to stay in town and no longer be with Derek, but Gabrielle powered through. She'd be back at her big, lonely apartment in Boston soon enough. After five days, Kayla declared she had enough interviews and footage to go forward. She packed up her crew and returned to Boston.

Freed up from the constant camera presence, Gabrielle headed for Sharon's house with a bottle of wine. Though she'd spoken with Sharon since the fire, they'd agreed not to hang out until they could have a girls' night—no men and more important, no camera crew tagging along.

Sharon's parents were at the movies and they had the family room to themselves. Sharon put the DVD of *Ocean's Eleven* on television, satisfying Gabrielle's George Clooney fix while giving Sharon her fill of Brad Pitt.

Half a bottle of chardonnay later, Sharon raised her glass in a toast. "To handsome men."

Gabrielle grinned. "To handsome men who know how to treat women." She clinked her glass against Sharon's.

"To fictional men," Sharon said with a wistful sigh.

"What's going on? I thought with the threat to Richard's campaign over, things between the two of you would be back on track." Gabrielle took a sip of her wine.

Sharon stretched her legs out in front of her and wiggled her toes. "I think my toes are numb," she said, laughing.

"Quit avoiding the question."

Sharon shrugged. "You're assuming things were ever normal. I told you, I don't think he really knows me. I felt so lucky a good man would want to marry me, I let him think I'd become this docile, fragile female."

Gabrielle frowned. "I thought that's why you bought the lingerie at Victoria's Secret. To show him the real you." She nudged Sharon's feet with hers. "What happened?"

"He's been working nonstop. Or he's been avoiding having the big discussion. I'm not sure which."

Gabrielle raised an eyebrow. "Don't you think it's time you found out?"

Sharon downed the last of her glass. "You know what? I think you're right. I'll be right back." She stood and ran upstairs.

Sharon was gone for a while. Whatever she had planned, Gabrielle figured the wine had put her up to it. But Sharon did need to face Richard once and for all.

Sharon came back down the stairs wearing the teddy she'd purchased on their shopping trip and a pair of high-heeled sandals.

Gabrielle's eyes opened wide. She jumped up from her seat on the floor. "Where are you going dressed like that?"

Sharon opened the hall closet and pulled out a light trench coat and pulled it on, wrapping the belt tight around her waist. Then she grabbed her car keys. "To show Richard the real me."

Gabrielle reached out and snagged the keys from her hand. Neither one of them were in any shape to drive. "I'll call a cab to drive me home and we can drop you off along the way."

She hoped her friend had better luck during her upcoming conversation with Richard than she'd had with Derek.

THE EFFECTS OF THE WINE had started to wear off in the cab. Now, standing on the doorstep, Sharon shivered and pulled the trench coat tighter as she rang the doorbell once more, waiting for Richard to answer. The light in the upstairs room told her he was home. She couldn't, wouldn't back out now. Richard would love and accept her or he wouldn't. At least she would know.

Finally, he opened the door, startled when he realized she was waiting on the other side. "Sharon!"

"Hi." One hand gripped the top of her coat collar. With her free hand, she waved.

"What are you doing here at this hour?" he asked, concerned.

"Can I come in?"

"You don't need to ask. It's your house, too." He pushed open the door and let her inside. "Which begs the question, why didn't you use your key?"

"I didn't want to scare you half to death. You weren't expecting me."

He nodded. "Can I take your coat?"

"Not yet." She clutched it closer.

He had on an old pair of gray sweats and nothing else. His chest and his feet were bare.

"I got you out of bed, didn't I?"

He narrowed his gaze. "Honey, you're acting really odd. Is everything okay?"

She nodded. "You've been acting odd, too," she said, taking his opening. "With Mary out of the race, you're running unopposed. You should be freer than ever and yet you're not available." She swallowed hard. "At least not to me, and I want to know why."

He strode across the room, placing distance between them. "For the same reasons you've been uptight around me, I guess."

"The picture? It turned you off? Showed you things you didn't want to ever imagine?"

He shook his head. "It showed me things I couldn't bear to face. I hate what that bastard did to you. It just reinforced what I've felt all along. That you're special and precious and you need to be treated gently and with care."

"That's not what I want. Not what I need. It's not even who I am," Sharon said, pulling at the ties that held her coat together. Her hands were trembling as she worked to free the buttons next. "You seemed to want a politician's wife, a perfect china doll. I was so grateful you wanted me after everything that had happened, I would have become whatever you expected."

Tears fell from her eyes as she admitted the most painful thing of all. "But that's not me. *This* is me." She finally shrugged off the coat and displayed the sexy lingerie she'd bought just for a reveal like this one.

He sucked in a startled breath.

Silence greeted her.

"This is me, Richard. I don't want to be treated as if I'm made of fine bone china. I want to know what it's like for you to want me. I need you to be so turned on that you can barely think."

He exhaled. A low groan escaped from the back of his throat. She took it as a good sign and stepped forward, trying to ignore the fact that her legs shook and her body trembled.

"I thought you were avoiding me. Then I worried that you wouldn't want me if you knew I wanted, needed more than you've given me so far."

His eyes darkened. She hoped it was desire she saw in those depths. "Not want you?" he asked in a gruff voice she barely recognized. "I go to sleep wanting you. I wake up missing you. And when I'm with you, I'm so afraid you'll shatter, I can't do anything right." His body was tense.

But she wasn't ready to touch him yet. "And now that you know I let you believe I was some fragile flower? Now that you know I'm not…I'm over the past, over what Tony did to me. I'm just a woman who wants you. What happens to us now?" she asked him.

He slid his finger beneath the strap on her silk

teddy, then suddenly yanked hard, tearing the soft fabric. The garment slipped, exposing one breast.

Her nipple puckered beneath the cool air, but she didn't rush to cover up.

"You don't realize it, but before those pictures resurfaced, I saw glimpses of the real you. I knew you were still getting over your past and I was happy to give you the time you needed. Then, suddenly, you reverted." He ran a hand through his hair. "I didn't know you were being blackmailed, but I knew something had changed. So I backed off even more. I was giving you time."

She swallowed hard. "I don't want time. I just want you."

"Thank God. I want to know the real you and I want you to know the real me," he said in a husky tone. Then, slowly, tantalizingly, he lowered his head until just his breath hovered over one tight nipple.

"And then?" she asked on barely a whisper.

"Then we get married as planned," he said, enclosing his mouth around her.

And that was just the beginning….

CHAPTER NINETEEN

DEREK NEEDED A CHANGE of scenery, so he drove to
New York to pick up Holly instead of meeting
Marlene and John halfway. The newlyweds had
bought a house a half hour outside of the city, in a
place called Larchmont. Holly wanted Derek to
see where she'd be living in a few weeks, so he
agreed to pick her up there. His daughter was
actually looking forward to living in a house
instead of an apartment and starting a new school.
Derek was sure her nerves would kick in closer to
the first day, but for now when he spoke to her on
the phone, Holly seemed like her easygoing self.

He rang the doorbell of the colonial-style house
and was greeted by Holly, who'd come to a skidding
halt in her socks as she opened the front door.

"Hey, kiddo!" He greeted her with a wave.

She hugged him tight. "Dad! Come check out
my new room. It's so much bigger than my room
in the city. And Mom even said I can use the sheets
and comforter you got for me."

"She did?" he asked, unable to contain his surprise.

"I did." Marlene came up behind Holly. "Honey, why don't you go get your bags packed to go to your dad's?"

"I'm packed."

"Then double-check you didn't forget anything," Marlene said pointedly.

Holly rolled her eyes. "The grown-ups want to talk," she said, stomping back toward the stairs with added force on each step.

Marlene shook her head and laughed. "I swear, sometimes I think I'm already living with a hormonal teenager."

"Soon enough," he said, shuddering at the thought.

"Come on in," she said, holding the door open. "I thought we could talk."

He followed her into the house, which was still empty of furniture. "We're having the place painted next week," she said.

"It's a beautiful house. Great place for Holly to grow up."

Marlene nodded. "John wanted to be here to say hello, but I explained to him that we needed to talk alone."

"Okay," Derek said warily.

She led him into the kitchen where a bridge table and chairs had been set up. "Have a seat. It's the best I can offer," she said, waving at the folding chairs.

Since she wanted to talk, he remained silent until she broached whatever she needed to say. He wasn't about to give her an opening, or heaven forbid, more ammunition to use against him. Although he had to admit that ever since he'd called to confirm this weekend, she'd been more than accommodating with him. But that was Marlene, at least where he was concerned. He never knew what to expect.

"I told John what went on when I picked up Holly from you last week."

Derek inclined his head. "I'm not sure exactly which thing you're referring to."

Marlene's cheeks flushed pink. "Well, he wasn't thrilled that I picked Holly up a day early," she said without meeting his gaze. "John didn't think that was fair to you. Especially with us coming home early. And then, when I told him I'd threatened to sue you for full custody and accused you of putting Gabrielle before Holly…" She twisted her hands together nervously. "John was furious," she said, the admission obviously not an easy one for her to make.

Derek leaned forward in his seat. "Why was John upset with you?"

She laughed nervously. "He just knows me so well. And I'd promised him and myself I'd stop using Holly as a weapon against you. As you said, we'd gotten past a lot of old baggage. But last week…John accused me of being spiteful and jealous of Gabrielle. He said if knowing you were with Gabrielle bothered me, then obviously you and I have unresolved issues," she said, gesturing between them.

Derek cocked his head to one side. "And you agree with him?"

"Yes, I do." She let out a sigh. "This isn't easy for me. Meeting *her* wasn't easy for me. She's always been between us, you know."

He shook his head, denying it. "I never wanted you to feel that way."

She shrugged. "In the beginning, I had no idea, but after my first trip to Stewart with you, I learned more about her than I ever wanted to know. It put her between us. And the harder you worked and the less time you spent at home, I felt sure it was because you wished you'd never gotten me pregnant. Never had to marry me. I always thought you wished I was Gabrielle," Marlene admitted.

Derek was stunned. In all their years together, they'd never talked about Gabrielle. They'd never talked like this.

He met Marlene's gaze. "I'm sorry. That was never my intention. If I could have been with Gabrielle, I would have been. I chose to marry you."

She waved her hand through the air. "That's all

old news. But she's in your life now and I have to come to terms with it. Just like you've had to come to terms with John in mine and in Holly's."

Derek shook his head. "She's not in my life. I was giving her a place to stay while she was in trouble and making sure she was safe, but we're not… We aren't together anymore."

Marlene narrowed her gaze. "Why the hell not?" she asked him.

He blinked at the vehemence in her tone. "Because…" He struggled for a way to explain himself that wouldn't hurt Marlene's feelings. He'd cared about her in a special way, and if he confessed that he couldn't be with Gabrielle because he loved her, it would be the same as admitting he'd never been in love with Marlene.

He loved Gabrielle.

Holy—

"Derek, did you hear what I said?"

He shook his head, wishing he hadn't heard his own thoughts.

"I said that the curse is bullshit," Marlene said.

He raised his gaze, focusing on his usually polite ex-wife. She rarely cursed. "Excuse me?"

"You heard me. You might never have explained the curse or your feelings for Gabrielle to me, but other people have. And I've spent enough time with your father to understand the way of things with you Corwin men. You were madly in love with Gabrielle but you broke up with her rather than admit it, to spare yourself the pain involved in the curse."

Derek opened his mouth, but when she raised her hand to stop him, he shut it again.

"Let me finish," Marlene demanded.

"Go on." He gestured for her to do just that.

"You married me because I was pregnant, but most important you married me because you weren't *in love with me.*"

"I never said that."

"You didn't have to. You never told me you loved me, either." She spoke evenly, indicating she was long over the fact he hadn't loved her and long over him.

Which didn't alleviate his sense of guilt or shame. "Marlene—"

She shook her head. "Let it go. I have. Or at least I thought I had until I had to face Gabrielle in the flesh. But I'm past that now. You and I have a great little girl. We did something good together."

"That we did." He smiled at the thought of Holly.

"But now you have a second chance to make things right with Gabrielle. Why aren't you two together? Because you're afraid to admit you love her and let some crazy curse kick in?" She stared at him as if he were mad.

The way he was feeling lately, she might just be right.

"Things happen in life. Divorce statistics are high. People die every day for no reason. They might get hit by a bus or a car. Others have affairs and ruin their lives. People make choices, but bad things do not happen because of a curse!" she said, her voice rising. "Sorry. But think about it."

He rubbed his hand over his burning eyes. "It's all I have thought about. Don't you think Gabrielle's said the same things to me?"

Marlene smiled. "I'm sure she has. But you obviously aren't listening to her, so I'm asking you to listen to me. This woman has been a part of you for the past fourteen or fifteen years. She will continue to be a part of you whether or not you deny her a place in your life. So you have a choice. You can be lonely, stubborn and stupid like your father and his brothers or you can reach out and grab what you've always wanted." She rose to her feet.

Derek stood, too. "I can't stand by and lose her in some awful way." The fire came to mind. The waiting desperately to see if Gabrielle had lived or died…only to push her out of his life hours later.

His head began to pound. So did his heart, with possibilities he'd never allowed himself to imagine. Could Gabrielle and Marlene be right?

Was it worth it to live like a shell of himself in case the curse kicked in? Or was he better off diving into those deep waters and at least enjoying whatever life gave him?

Gave *them,* here and now?

"Come on, Derek. Loss is a part of life. Are you any less miserable now than if you two were together and something happened later? Like I said, she's a part of you and always has been. She always will be. The question is, what are you willing to do about it?"

He nodded, finally getting it. Finally hearing what Gabrielle had been trying to tell him for so long. "Thank you," he said to his ex-wife.

"Thank your daughter. She's the one who told me what a great person Gabrielle is, how happy she makes you and how she makes Holly feel as important as John does." Marlene shrugged. "An eleven-year-old reminded me that I don't need to feel threatened because she doesn't. Go figure." Marlene laughed.

Thinking of his precocious daughter, Derek grinned.

He still had more to mull over. He couldn't just dump years of ingrained beliefs in ten minutes, but Marlene had given him a lot to digest. Gabrielle had always been a part of him. She always would be. What *was* he accomplishing by keeping them apart?

The answer was simple. He wasn't accomplishing a damn thing. But did he have the courage to defy the old family curse?

GABRIELLE LOOKED AT THE invitation to Holly's birthday party in disbelief. A smiling picture of

Holly and Fred stared back at her. She was certain Derek had to know Holly had invited her to his house for a party. Certain he'd know how difficult it would be for her to attend. But knowing Holly, she'd probably bounced up and down until he'd agreed, and Derek wouldn't have wanted to disappoint his daughter. The grown-ups would have to—well—grow up in order to make Holly happy on her twelfth birthday.

The invitation had a phone number and an e-mail for RSVPs. Gabrielle chose the easy way, shooting off an e-mail letting them know she'd be there.

One week later, she drove her freshly painted convertible back to Stewart. She pulled around behind Derek's place and parked, then made her way out back where music floated in the hot summer air.

Since this wasn't Holly's main home, Gabrielle didn't expect to find a large amount of people and she was right. Holly was hanging out with a group of girls, while a handful of adults mingled in the yard. She saw Hank and Thomas standing together, and to her surprise, Holly's mother and a nice-looking man whom Gabrielle assumed was her husband sat at the old picnic table. Gabrielle had assumed Derek's ex wouldn't be here. She was wrong. Obviously.

Her discomfort level increased, but she pushed herself forward. For Holly's sake.

Something cold nudged her leg and Gabrielle glanced down to see Fred, wearing a party hat, pressing his nose into her calf.

"Hey, old man. You really are a sport, aren't you?" she asked him, bending down to scratch beneath his ears.

"Gabrielle!" Holly shouted her name and came running toward her, a happy bundle of energy.

Gabrielle rose to greet her. "Hey there! Happy birthday." She held out the gift that she'd spent a long time choosing. "I hope you like it."

"I'll love it." She accepted the gift and placed it beside the others on a table beside her. "I'm just glad you're here. Once you said you'd come to my party, I knew you weren't holding the fact that my dad's such a dork against me."

Gabrielle chuckled.

"Who are you calling a dork, dork?" Derek strode over, looking handsome as ever. He was tanned and relaxed and the light green of his T-shirt brought out the hue in his eyes. She'd missed him like crazy and her heart pounded hard in her chest.

"Holly!" Marlene called. "I need to talk to you."

The young girl glanced at her mother and stepfather. "Coming!" She turned back to Gabrielle. "I'll be back in a second," she said, then ran to the picnic table, leaving Derek and Gabrielle alone.

She drew a deep breath and met Derek's gaze. "Hi," Gabrielle said to him.

"Hi, yourself." His gaze traveled over her, head to toe. "You're looking good," he murmured, nodding in appreciation.

She glanced down at the strappy dress she'd never admit she'd bought just for seeing him today and smiled. "Thank you."

"It was nice of you to come for Holly. I know she was worried you'd change your mind."

Gabrielle shook her head. "I wouldn't do that to her."

"I know you wouldn't," he said, his voice deep and husky. Warm and inviting. Understanding.

She shivered beneath the sun.

"Derek, the barbecue won't light!" Hank called out to him.

"I have to help him if we're going to eat. Make yourself at home."

Make yourself at home.

She wondered if he knew how deep his words sliced. She'd done that once. And though he hadn't promised her anything, she hadn't realized until she'd had to pack up and leave immediately after the fire, how much she'd counted on changing his mind about them.

She swallowed past the lump in her throat and headed to a cooler that held cans of soda. She filled a cup with ice, then poured herself a cold drink before settling into a chair overlooking the back of the old barn.

"Mind if I join you?"

Gabrielle glanced up at Marlene, who'd walked up to her. "Of course not," she said warily.

Their last meeting hadn't exactly been warm and friendly. And considering the other woman had threatened to use Gabrielle as a means to pry Holly away from her father, Gabrielle worried about what the other woman wanted now. But it couldn't hurt to find out.

"I owe you an apology," Marlene said, taking Gabrielle off guard. "I wasn't all that pleasant the first time we met."

"It's okay." Gabrielle shrugged casually. "I'm really not one to hold a grudge."

Marlene smiled. "I'm glad. Because my daughter adores you and I'd like it if you'd give me another chance."

Gabrielle wasn't sure where this sudden peace offering was coming from, but she owed it to Holly to be civil with her mother. Besides, after today they wouldn't be seeing each other all that often.

Gabrielle swerved in her seat so she could face Marlene. "You have a wonderful child, so I have to assume you're a good person, too."

"Thank you. I think she's special."

Their gazes drifted to Holly, holding court among a circle of her friends.

"I didn't think she knew that many people in town," Gabrielle said.

"She doesn't. John and I brought her closest friends with us for the weekend to celebrate Holly's birthday."

Gabrielle nodded. "Aah, that explains the big group."

An awkward silence followed, punctuated by occasional giggles and girlish screams across the way.

"I wanted to hate you," Marlene said at last.

Gabrielle raised an eyebrow, startled by the other woman's blunt words. "Excuse me?"

Marlene tucked her short hair behind one ear. "I wanted to hate you. Maybe I needed to, because for all the years I was married, you still had the one thing I wanted."

Gabrielle shook her head, confused. "I really don't understand."

"You had his heart. His love. The one thing I desperately wanted, belonged to you."

Gabrielle opened her mouth, then closed it again, struggling to find the right words. "I was alone, trying to find a life and a world that could make me happy. But…you had *him*. And you had his child. All the things I wanted but could never have," Gabrielle said, admitting the painful truth out loud.

"I guess neither one of us had the whole package," Marlene murmured.

Gabrielle nodded in agreement. Her throat grew thick and her eyes damp. She turned away to compose herself before glancing back at Marlene. "But you have that now?" she asked.

The other woman nodded. Her fingers went to the diamond ring and matching wedding band. "I'm very lucky. I think I forgot that for a minute. The night you walked into the house beside Derek, all the wonderful things in my life flew out the window and I went back in time." She shook her head, her cheeks pink. "Anyway, I just wanted to apologize. I appreciate you letting me explain."

"Thanks. I wish you all the best." Gabrielle rose from her seat. She suddenly needed to be alone for a few minutes to pull herself together.

Marlene's words had brought up emotions Gabrielle wasn't ready to handle. She might have had Derek's love, but it didn't mean anything. It never had. He wasn't hers. He never would be.

She headed for the street, hoping Holly wouldn't notice. She'd just take a short ride, blast some music, open the top of the convertible and clear her mind. Once she could breathe without wanting to cry, she'd come back and celebrate.

She reached the car when she heard Derek calling her name. God, not now, she thought, yanking open the door.

"Gabrielle, wait."

He caught up to her before she could shut herself inside. "Where are you going? You just got

372   LUCKY CHARM

here and we haven't even had a chance to light the candles yet."

She leaned against the open door for support. "I'll be back. I just need a few minutes alone."

"Why? What did Marlene say to upset you?" he asked, his voice dark. "I saw you two talking. If she said anything—"

"She didn't upset me. She apologized for how she acted the first time we met. She's lovely. Now, can I just go get some fresh air? I'll come back for Holly's cake, I promise."

He put his hand on the top of the window. "Not until you tell me what's wrong."

Gabrielle exploded. "You're wrong. Inviting me here was wrong. Hearing Marlene tell me how much she resented me because I had your heart— that's wrong." All the frustration she'd never vented at him came pouring out now. Frustration that he'd made her leave him again when they had so much to fight for. "Because really, Derek, what good has me having your heart ever done?" she asked, half yelling at him, half crying.

She turned to duck inside her car, but he pulled her back, turning her around and sealing her lips with his.

She fought him at first, not wanting to succumb, not wanting to feel the love he aroused so easily, only to have him take it away from her again. But he was relentless, kissing her until her lips softened, until she melted against him and kissed him back.

Only once she'd completely relaxed, did he step back. "Better?" he asked.

She drew a deep breath. "That's playing dirty," she said, her lips stinging wonderfully from the assault.

"Its only playing dirty if I'm not playing for keeps." His gaze never left hers.

Her heart skipped a beat. She was sure she'd heard him wrong or she was misunderstanding him somehow. "Derek?"

He grasped both her hands in his. "I'm not telling you I don't believe in curses. I'm not saying my family hasn't been proof of the Corwin Curse for the past who knows how many generations."

Her heart beat fast in her chest. "Then what *are* you telling me?"

"That I can't go on living without you anymore. Not one more day. Not even another minute." His eyes were as dark and as serious as she'd ever seen them. "Whether it's a curse or Fate, we'll just have to fight it together, because without you, I'm lost."

Her head spun with the impact of his words. It was everything she'd ever wanted, everything she'd ever dreamed of. Everything he'd sworn he couldn't give her.

"How? Why?"

She needed to hear what had finally changed his mind before she could let herself believe.

"Would you believe it was my ex-wife who convinced me?"

"At this point, I'd believe anything." She covered her eyes from the glare of the sun as she glanced up at him. "What did she say?"

"Nothing that you hadn't already told me, except for one thing. The same thing she apparently told you. That you've always been a part of me and you always will be. Then she asked me what I was willing to do about it." He shrugged, but Gabrielle knew nothing about this was easy for him.

He'd been fighting the curse for a lifetime. His family had been fighting it even longer.

"What are you willing to do about it?" she asked softly.

He cupped her face in his hands and her heart felt like bursting. "I love you, Gabrielle Donovan. I loved you when I was eighteen, I loved you in between and I love you now."

Tears flowed unchecked from her eyes at the words she'd longed to hear for so long. "Aren't you afraid of what will happen now?"

They both knew she meant the curse.

He shook his head. "No. Well, maybe a little," he said, laughing. "Old habits die hard. But I feel pretty sure we can overcome anything life throws at us together."

She grinned and Derek swore to himself he'd make it his mission to keep her smiling for the rest of their lives, the curse be damned.

He loved her. He'd told her. And the earth hadn't opened up and swallowed him whole.

"You really believe our love can overcome anything?" she asked.

He nodded. "I do. Want to know why? Because I have you by my side."

The look on her face filled him with everything he needed.

"I love you, too," she said, her gaze never leaving his.

"So what do you say we go give Holly her birthday present?" Derek suggested, taking Gabrielle's hand.

She tipped her head to one side. "Which present is that?"

"News of our engagement…if you'll marry me," he said, pulling a ring from his front pocket.

He'd purchased it the day Holly had asked him to invite Gabrielle for her birthday. Derek had asked his daughter how she'd feel to have Gabrielle as her stepmother. Lucky for him, Holly had loved Gabrielle as much as he did.

"I'm stunned."

He grinned. "I do think we've waited long enough, don't you? Gabrielle, will you marry me?" he asked.

"Yes!" She wrapped her arms around his neck.

He knew, together, they'd make it. After all, he had his very own lucky charm.

* * * * *

Wait! It's not over yet! Derek's luck might have changed, but what about the rest of the Corwins? Mike Corwin is going to find himself on a
LUCKY STREAK, *in June 2009.*
And Jason Corwin's LUCKY BREAK *comes the following October.*
Don't miss them!

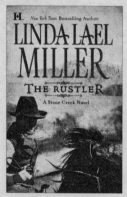

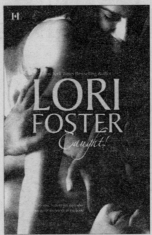

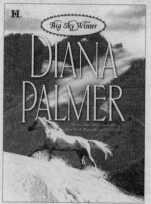

REQUEST YOUR FREE BOOKS!

2 FREE NOVELS
FROM THE ROMANCE/SUSPENSE
COLLECTION PLUS 2 FREE GIFTS!

YES! Please send me 2 FREE novels from the Romance/Suspense Collection and my 2 FREE gifts (gifts are worth about $10). After receiving them, if I don't wish to receive any more books, I can return the shipping statement marked "cancel." If I don't cancel, I will receive 4 brand-new novels every month and be billed just $5.49 per book in the U.S. or $5.99 per book in Canada, plus 25¢ shipping and handling per book plus applicable taxes, if any*. That's a savings of at least 20% off the cover price! I understand that accepting the 2 free books and gifts places me under no obligation to buy anything. I can always return a shipment and cancel at any time. Even if I never buy another book from the Reader Service, the two free books and gifts are mine to keep forever.

185 MDN EF5Y   385 MDN EF6C

Name _____ (PLEASE PRINT) _____

Address _____ Apt. # _____

City _____ State/Prov. _____ Zip/Postal Code _____

Signature (if under 18, a parent or guardian must sign)

Mail to **The Reader Service:**
IN U.S.A.: P.O. Box 1867, Buffalo, NY 14240-1867
IN CANADA: P.O. Box 609, Fort Erie, Ontario L2A 5X3

Not valid to current subscribers to the Romance Collection,
the Suspense Collection or the Romance/Suspense Collection.

Want to try two free books from another line?
Call 1-800-873-8635 or visit www.morefreebooks.com.

* Terms and prices subject to change without notice. N.Y. residents add applicable sales tax. Canadian residents will be charged applicable provincial taxes and GST. Offer not valid in Quebec. This offer is limited to one order per household. All orders subject to approval. Credit or debit balances in a customer's account(s) may be offset by any other outstanding balance owed by or to the customer. Please allow 4 to 6 weeks for delivery. Offer available while quantities last.

Your Privacy: Harlequin is committed to protecting your privacy. Our Privacy Policy is available online at www.eHarlequin.com or upon request from the Reader Service. From time to time we make our lists of customers available to reputable third parties who may have a product or service of interest to you. If you would prefer we not share your name and address, please check here. ☐

BOB08R

carly phillips

77333	HOT PROPERTY	___ $7.99 U.S.	___ $7.99 CAN.
77326	SEDUCE ME	___ $7.99 U.S.	___ $9.50 CAN.
77239	SEALED WITH A KISS	___ $7.99 U.S.	___ $9.50 CAN.
77208	CROSS MY HEART	___ $7.99 U.S.	___ $9.50 CAN.
77284	SIMPLY SEXY	___ $6.99 U.S.	___ $8.50 CAN.
77110	SUMMER LOVIN'	___ $7.99 U.S.	___ $9.50 CAN.
77122	HOT ITEM	___ $7.99 U.S.	___ $9.50 CAN.
77055	HOT NUMBER	___ $7.50 U.S.	___ $8.99 CAN.
77001	HOT STUFF	___ $6.99 U.S.	___ $8.50 CAN.

(limited quantities available)

TOTAL AMOUNT	$ _____
POSTAGE & HANDLING	$ _____
($1.00 FOR 1 BOOK, 50¢ for each additional)	
APPLICABLE TAXES*	$ _____
TOTAL PAYABLE	$ _____

(check or money order—please do not send cash)

To order, complete this form and send it, along with a check or money order for the total above, payable to HQN Books, to: **In the U.S.:** 3010 Walden Avenue, P.O. Box 9077, Buffalo, NY 14269-9077; **In Canada:** P.O. Box 636, Fort Erie, Ontario, L2A 5X3.

Name: _____
Address: _____ City: _____
State/Prov.: _____ Zip/Postal Code: _____
Account Number (if applicable): _____

075 CSAS

*New York residents remit applicable sales taxes.
*Canadian residents remit applicable GST and provincial taxes.

HQN™

We *are* romance™

www.HQNBooks.com

PHCP1008BL